Grits and Greed

Jenna Ross Thriller Book 4

Judith A. Barrett

Wobbly Creek

Wobbly Creek, LLC

GRITS AND GREED

JENNA ROSS THRILLER BOOK 4

Published in the United States of America by Wobbly Creek, LLC

2025 Georgia

wobblycreek.com

Cover by Wobbly Creek, LLC

ISBN 978-1-967288-25-0 eBook

ISBN 978-1-967288-26-7 Paperback

Dedication

Grits and Greed is dedicated to the colors peach and purple and to wind chimes.

Previously

I'm Jenna Ross. My sweet Golden Retriever, Katy, has been my constant companion and confidante since my husband was killed in action overseas five years ago.

When I inherited a failing bed-and-breakfast from my husband's side of the family over a year ago, I didn't hesitate to leave my high stress corporate accounting career in the city for the small town of Paisley, Georgia. Katy and I enjoy having room to roam and spending our days together.

I threw all my energy into reviving the inn, hoping I would find a renewed purpose to heal my grief.

Surprisingly, the bed-and-breakfast soon flourished beyond what one person could manage alone. At the insistent nudging of my chef, Darlene, I hired an operations manager, Morgan Farley, who was a former hotel manager and is my best friend. I also hired a fulltime housekeeper, Wendy, who is transitioning into a sous chef role.

Ethan Bentley, a general contractor and landscaper, and Shane Lawson, an architect who is now engaged to

Morgan, updated the Peach Blossom Barn to be an event center. We held our first event in the barn, and despite the unexpected issues that popped up, including a serial killer in our midst, the group will return next year.

I probably should explain I have always had a gift of feeling someone's joy, sorrow, or anger as if it were my own. My gift however, has an intense side of intuition so sharp that it manifests as visions or overwhelming sensations when I touch certain objects or people. Because of my gift and my natural tendency to be an introvert, I shy away from touch like shaking hands or handling other people's personal items.

My gift occasionally weighs on me like a burden that could have been unbearable except for the support and help of Nettie Wyndham's portrait. Nettie was the owner of the Wyndham estate in the 1920s, and her portrait has a quiet presence that inspires me.

Ethan and I had a rocky start when I first came to the Peach Blossom Retreat, but his rough exterior has softened, and maybe my prickly side has too. You caught that maybe, right? But I trust him, and we've grown closer.

Chapter One

Jenna burst into the kitchen from the office, her blue eyes blazing, with strands of her long blond hair falling from her messy bun.

"Qué pasa, Boss Lady?" Darlene asked. "You look like somebody set your registration book on fire."

"That's an excellent description of my day, Darlene."

Jenna narrowed her eyes. "Morgan, we have a problem; we need to talk in my office."

Morgan and Katy followed Jenna. "Last I heard it was our office, but okay."

When they were inside the office, Jenna pointed at the old wooden table that served double-duty as a conference and work table. "We might as well sit because I need answers."

Morgan slipped Katy a treat, and Katy flopped down on the cool wooden floor.

After Morgan sat at the table, Jenna glared at her and then sat across from her. "You told me the innkeeper association was all online."

Morgan furrowed her brow. "Oh no, is there something missing from their website? Is it a topic the event coordinator association might address? I'd be happy to ask them. Has something new come up? Do we have another new event to schedule? What is it?"

"The innkeeper association has a three-day annual meeting in Savannah, Georgia, this year."

Morgan tilted her head. "That's great news, isn't it? Don't most conferences usually meet in Las Vegas? When will their speakers' presentations be online?"

"The speakers' presentations will be online one week after the meeting in Savannah, and the conference is next week, from Monday through Wednesday."

Morgan nodded and then raised an eyebrow. "I haven't heard what the problem is yet."

Jenna drummed her fingers on the table. "The problem is they've offered me a scholarship to the conference. According to the email, they select one of the new members every year to receive a scholarship based on the one-page essay that each new member included with their application for membership." Jenna crossed her arms. "What essay did I submit? And why did they assume I would be attending the conference?"

Morgan shrugged. "You were busy with everything that was going on, so Layla and I wrote a little something. You proofread it."

"I've only proofread ad copy." Jenna narrowed her eyes. "And my biography for the website, which was one page. What a coincidence."

Morgan beamed. "Your corrections were great too. You really are an excellent editor."

Jenna waved her hand as she rose. "Whatever. It won't take me long to write a polite decline."

"Why don't you wait until tomorrow and think about it? Did they send an agenda? Do you know who the speakers are? Do they have any panels?"

Jenna growled, "I didn't bother to look at the agenda. You know I can't leave the inn for a three-day conference on such short notice."

Morgan's eyes widened. "Oh."

Jenna continued, "Being stuck in a conference with a roomful of strangers is my idea of torture. I would literally walk out the first time someone said the word, icebreaker."

Morgan narrowed her eyes. "Explain to me why you can't leave the inn for three days."

"You know I can't. I haven't left the inn for one day since I came here. I would feel like I was abandoning it."

"Abandoning?"

"Yes."

Morgan stared at Jenna, then cleared her throat. "So, if there isn't anything else, I have things to do."

Jenna glared at the door to the kitchen after Morgan left. "Morgan knows how I feel about the inn, Katy. What was wrong with her? Besides that, it's not fair. Morgan always looks so professional and pulled together. She's wearing her sage green silk shirt that goes so well with her dark skin and her gray pressed-pleat slacks, and to top it off, she's tall."

Jenna glanced down at her jeans and her red and gray flannel shirt she wore over her pink peach blossom long-sleeved T-shirt. Even though she had anchored her hair with a clip, strands of fine hair fell across her face. "I look like I'm ready to go out to the barn to milk goats, but only the short ones." Jenna exhaled.

Jenna's phone buzzed with a text from Ethan. "Would you like to have dinner with me tonight?"

She glared at her phone. "Ethan has terrible timing, Katy. The last thing I would like is to go to a crowded restaurant with all the noise while I stumble through meaningless small talk that neither one of us can hear without shouting like everybody else."

She exhaled. *Maybe Morgan will release me from my promise not to be mean to Ethan just this one time.*

When she opened the door to the kitchen, only Darlene was in the kitchen. She had covered her salt and pepper hair with an oversized pink paisley bandana she had tied in the back and was wearing her favorite pale pink Peach Blossom Retreat apron.

She hummed while she poured batter into a large cake pan.

After Katy dashed ahead of Jenna and flopped down at her favorite spot in front of the oven, Darlene reached down and scratched Katy's ears then glanced up at Jenna.

"Where's Morgan?" Jenna asked.

"She said she had a call about an event reservation and wanted to check something at the barn," Darlene said. "She always rides with Shane to work these days, so I asked her if she wanted to take my car since it's so cold, but she said she needed the exercise. You need help with something?"

"No, I just had a question for her. What are you baking?"

"This is an apple spice sheet cake, and next I'll bake a chocolate sheet cake. Wendy and I decided that baking cakes today would get us ahead for this week. We'll freeze and then frost them later. Since we don't have any guests until tomorrow, Wendy is doing her deep cleaning. Today is my solo baking day." Darlene pulled out another baking pan.

"I could use a walk myself. I'll check in with Wendy, then I'll be at the barn with Morgan if you need me."

Darlene nodded. "Morgan needs to see you; she told me you were mad at her, but I think you hurt her feelings. For somebody who is supposed to be so sensitive, you blew it, Boss Lady. I hope your question is an apology. She must have been terribly upset to walk to the barn in this cold weather."

Darlene turned away and opened the pantry. Jenna bit her lip as she left the kitchen. *Maybe I overreacted.*

When she was in the hall, Jenna heard the vacuum running on the second floor.

As she passed the living room, Jenna's phone buzzed with another text from Ethan. "I know a quiet place that is very relaxing."

She grumbled, "You're pushing it, Ethan."

Come talk.

Jenna strolled into the living room and sat in her yellow chair, which gave her the perfect view of Nettie's portrait.

After she sat down, Jenna felt the tension disappear, and she relaxed as she gazed at Nettie's portrait.

A sunbeam brightened Nettie's face. *Go.*

Jenna grumbled, "I really don't want to go. I can't be gone from the Peach Blossom Retreat for that long."

Ouch.

Jenna glanced at Nettie, then furrowed her brow. "I hurt Morgan's feelings when I said that, didn't I?"

The wind blew the tree branches, and they scraped against the living room windows.

Jenna whispered even though she still heard the vacuum cleaner upstairs. "I'll be too far away."

Jenna bit her lip as she stared at the floor. "I won't have any help."

Take me with you.

Jenna blinked in confusion and cocked her head as she gazed at Nettie. "How can I do that? I can't take your portrait."

A gust of wind rounded the corner of the inn, and the chimes on the front porch jingled.

Jenna smiled. *I'll bet that's exactly what Nettie's laugh sounded like.*

The safe in the office.

"What safe? The safe in my office? The safe in my old office?"

You'll know.

Jenna stared at Nettie's portrait and waited for more.

Jenna examined the portrait for a long while, then sighed. "You have more confidence in me than I do."

She narrowed her eyes at the guest rooms that were on her way to the stairs. *Shane would know where there might have been a safe in the original office.*

She dashed up the stairs, hanging onto the smooth, curved wooden banister, and found Wendy in room five. Wendy glanced up and turned off the vacuum.

"Do we have an unexpected reservation?" Wendy asked.

"Nothing like that." Jenna smiled. "Morgan went to the barn, so Katy and I are going to join her. I just wanted you to know it's just you and Darlene here for a bit."

Wendy returned her smile. "Thanks for letting me know."

As Jenna left, Wendy turned the vacuum back on.

When Jenna went into the kitchen, Katy was waiting next to the door.

Darlene said, "She's been waiting for you. Wear a hat, and you have gloves, don't you? You're such a lightweight, those gusts will carry you away."

After Jenna put on her warm navy blue wool coat, she buttoned up and pulled the hood over her head before they stepped outside. "We should take the car, Katy; this wind is wicked."

When an icy blast of wind took away her breath, Jenna pulled up the neck of her coat to cover her mouth as she and Katy raced to the cottage.

After they went inside, Jenna grabbed her keys. "Just getting out of the wind made a difference, didn't it?"

She sent a text to Morgan. "Stay at the barn. Katy and I will pick you up."

Jenna and Katy dashed to her car. After she opened the back door for Katy, she slid into the driver's seat.

Morgan replied, "Thanks."

Before she reached the end of the driveway, her phone rang. *Ethan.*

When she answered, he asked, "My place or yours?"

"What?"

"I'm cooking tonight, so I'm wondering if I'm cooking at your cottage or my house."

Suit yourself was on the tip of her tongue, but Jenna said, "Come to the cottage, and we can cook together. I'd like to talk to Shane today. Do you mind if I invite Morgan and Shane to have dinner with us?"

"Brilliant as always. I'll bring enough for all of us." He hung up.

Jenna headed toward the barn. "I suppose I should have asked what he's cooking, but Ethan's an excellent cook. Whatever he plans will be delicious."

Katy yipped.

"You're right; that is something I should tell him."

Jenna's car was buffeted on the way to the barn. "We've got a front coming in. Do you think we might have to cancel dinner at the cottage?"

Jenna parked close to the front door.

When they dashed inside, Morgan was sitting on the floor in front of the open, empty cabinets with cleaning rags and a spray bottle of Wendy's favorite commercial cleanser in front of her. Behind her were two clothesbaskets and a pile of tablecloths.

Morgan glanced up. "I saw some mouse droppings near the back door. I checked the cabinets and didn't see anything, but then I got sidetracked inspecting the tablecloths for stains or damage. I wanted to check the linens before we take them to the inn. Meanwhile, I should probably clean the cabinets while I have them empty."

Jenna and Katy strolled to Morgan. Katy gave Morgan a quick nudge on her cheek. Morgan stroked Katy's neck, then Katy trotted to the back door and laid down.

Morgan peered at the window in front of her. "The wind came up fast, didn't it? When I checked the weather earlier, the forecast said it's going to be stormy around five o'clock. I already asked Shane to pick me up earlier than usual."

"Makes sense. What can I do to help?"

"Nothing. I'm fine."

"Are you sure? I could help clean or organize the tablecloths."

No, thank you. I've got it. You're busy."

Morgan sprayed the cleanser and scrubbed inside the cabinet.

"It was a good idea to store the tablecloths here for convenience, but it's not working out as well as we hoped because they're not getting good air circulation. They smell a little musty even though we washed them right after we used them. I think we should rewash all of them. I'll talk to Wendy about rearranging the items on the storage shelves in the laundry room so we can store them where they'll get better circulation, but still be in an accessible spot so we can pull what we need for an event."

"That should work."

Morgan snorted.

Jenna picked up a tablecloth, then sat on the floor near Morgan. "I want to apologize for being so rude earlier. I could claim I was caught off-guard, but that's no excuse for what I said. I have full confidence in your ability to manage the inn for the time I'd be at the convention if I were going or even longer."

"Thanks." Morgan exhaled and turned to face Jenna. "I didn't really think it through. I could claim I was just completing your application, but that wouldn't be entirely true. I was being a little sneaky because I thought you'd decide not to apply at all for the membership if I said anything." Morgan rolled her eyes. "I was hoping you would be selected for the scholarship, but dreading what you'd say if you were."

Jenna smiled. "I hope I didn't disappoint you."

Morgan chuckled. "You exceeded my expectations."

Jenna frowned at the tablecloth in her lap. "This has a ballpoint pen ink stain."

Morgan nodded. "I noticed that on several other tablecloths. I'm tossing those with stains into the small clothesbasket."

After Jenna handed Morgan the tablecloth, Morgan dropped it into the small clothes basket behind her then continued, "I'll ask Wendy if she has any tricks on how to get the stains out. I didn't notice them before I washed them, so I'm afraid they might be baked in by the dryer."

Jenna examined the next tablecloth. "I glanced over the agenda and the descriptions of the speakers and panels. The keynote speaker is a tour mogul who specializes in haunted houses and old buildings. She expanded her business model and bought several inns and touts them as haunted. The topic of her talk is 'Find Your Niche and Make it Bigger.'"

Morgan furrowed her brow as she unfolded the next tablecloth. "What's our niche? A historic inn? Being rural?"

"Do we have to have a niche?"

"We should at least investigate the benefits of having a niche," Morgan said.

"True. We could claim historic unofficially, but I don't want to go through the official process to declare the inn a historical site. Maybe our niche is the barn and hosting events. What do you think?"

Morgan nodded. "That would help us in so many ways in branding and marketing."

"I hadn't thought about the marketing benefits of having a niche."

Morgan's dark eyes twinkled. "It would help target the marketing I'm doing. What about panels? I seem to remember a panel on caterers and other service partners and how to integrate a service partner into your business model. If you were going to be on a panel, what would it be?"

Jenna snorted. "I could be the expert on how to do everything wrong from start to finish."

"I think we do just fine overall." Morgan peered into the cabinet. "I have everything out, and I don't see any signs of bugs or mice. Is there any free time to do any sightseeing during the conference?"

"It looks like there is, but I'm sure most people would take advantage of the spare time and hide in their rooms and work. I know I would, but it doesn't matter because I'm not going."

Morgan rose and picked up the larger basket. "I'm ready to go back to the inn."

Jenna picked up the smaller basket, and Katy raced to the front door.

Jenna smiled. "Katy's ready too."

Morgan pushed hard to open the door against the wind as it whipped around the corner; she held the door open so it wouldn't slam shut while Jenna came out of the barn.

After they were in the car, Morgan exhaled in relief. "I couldn't have walked back in this wind. It wasn't like this when I left."

The wind continued its assault on Jenna's car as she headed toward the inn. She slowed down and gripped the steering wheel while she fought the wind blasts that threatened to push her car off the road and onto the shoulder.

Jenna exhaled in relief when she turned at the driveway. "I have another obstacle as far as leaving the inn and going to the conference is concerned."

Morgan nodded. "Nettie. Your sensitivity is a remarkable gift, but she has always had your back. You've already talked to her, haven't you? What did she say?"

She said I should go. Jenna exhaled. "We agreed I couldn't take her portrait with me, but she told me to check the safe in the office, which means I have to talk to Shane. I think she meant my old office, which would have been her office."

"What are we looking for?"

"I have no clue, but she said I'd know when I found it."

"That's so Nettie, isn't it?" Morgan chuckled.

Jenna parked close to the inn's back door instead of her usual spot next to her cottage. After Jenna held her back car door open for Katy, Katy raced to the back door and barked while Jenna and Morgan grabbed the clothesbaskets.

Darlene opened the door for Katy and waited for Jenna and Morgan as they carried in the clothesbaskets.

Jenna followed Morgan into the laundry room. After she dropped her basket, Jenna pushed back her hair, which had completely covered her face, and re-anchored her hair with her clip.

Morgan giggled. "I was wondering why you were practically walking on the backs of my shoes."

Jenna smoothed back the strays with her fingers. "I couldn't see a thing but the ground; I had to stay close enough to see your feet, or I would have walked into the wall."

Morgan pulled out her phone to check the weather. "The storm is moving faster, and the time for it to hit here has shifted to four o'clock. I'll have to let Shane know."

Jenna put the small clothesbasket on top of the large one and slid them to the laundry room before she sent Ethan a text. "Rainstorm at four."

Ethan replied, "Just saw that. We're wrapping up early to have everything secured by three."

"Just you, me, and Katy tonight."

"Not surprised. Thanks."

Jenna stared at the clothesbaskets. *This is Wendy's turf. I've already stepped on Morgan's toes today; I'd rather not have to apologize to Wendy too.*

Before she reached the kitchen, Morgan and Wendy came out. "Shane will be here in half an hour; Wendy and I are going to the laundry room," Morgan said.

"Thank you."

When Jenna went into the kitchen on her way to the office, Darlene asked, "What are the dates for the innkeepers' conference?"

"It doesn't matter; I'm not going." Jenna continued to her office.

"Come sit at the counter. I didn't hear what you said."

"I'm not going to the conference. I can't leave the Peach Blossom Retreat for four days."

Darlene glared at Jenna and crossed her arms. "Did you say that to Morgan?"

"Yes, but I apologized."

Darlene growled, "You apologized, but you still aren't going? How sincere was that apology?"

Jenna glared at Darlene. "I meant it."

Darlene snorted. "Oh, did you now?"

Darlene turned her back on Jenna and opened the empty oven. "Oh, look. I forgot to turn on the oven, and it's as cold as an apology with no action to back it up."

Jenna stormed to her office and slammed the door behind her.

Why is everybody so fired up about this conference?

She sat at her computer and read over the agenda again. *It really is perfect for innkeepers.*

Jenna checked to see how long it would take to go from Paisley to Savannah. *Four hours. I can leave after lunch on Sunday.*

Jenna typed her response and wrinkled her nose as she sent her email. *Done.*

After Jenna checked the registrations, she went into the kitchen.

Darlene was putting away the sheet cake pans while Wendy and Morgan sat at the counter. The three of them smiled at her.

Jenna narrowed her eyes. "What is going on?"

"Nothing." Morgan avoided Jenna's gaze.

"Right, nothing. For your information, I'm going to the innkeepers' conference in Savannah next week. I'll leave on Sunday after lunch and be back on Thursday in time for lunch," Jenna said.

Morgan spoke loudly so Darlene could hear her. "Darlene, would you like to do the honors?"

Darlene nodded and opened the pantry door. She removed a gift box with a peach colored bow on the top and handed it to Jenna.

Jenna stared at the box.

"I want to go home," Darlene growled. "Open it."

Jenna lifted the lid and giggled. "It's a baseball cap with a peach blossom."

"We had a variety of choices for the color of the cap, but the rustic rose was our unanimous favorite," Wendy said.

"We thought the single peach blossom was perfect for a logo," Morgan added.

"I love it." Jenna put it on and then posed with her cap. "What do you think?"

Darlene opened a drawer and handed Jenna a hand mirror. "See for yourself."

"I think it's perfect," Morgan said.

Jenna admired her hat in the mirror. "I do too."

After Jenna returned the mirror to Darlene, she peered at Morgan. "When did you order this?"

Morgan shrugged.

"I'm done for the day, Boss Lady, unless you have anything for me," Darlene said.

Jenna sighed. "I don't have anything else. My cap is beautiful; thank you."

Darlene nodded. "Good. I'll see you in the morning."

After Darlene left, Morgan said, "Wendy and I need you to go into the laundry room."

Now what? Jenna followed Wendy and Morgan to the laundry room. "It's not another surprise, is it?"

Wendy giggled. "No, but wouldn't that have been a great idea? Maybe a matching rustic rose T-shirt or something."

When Jenna was in the room, Morgan pointed to a tablecloth on the shelf that was two levels below the top shelf. "Move the tablecloth to the shelf above it."

Jenna grabbed the tablecloth and narrowed her eyes at the target shelf. When she tossed it, the tablecloth landed squarely on the shelf.

"Good pitch, Boss Lady." Morgan chuckled.

"The ball cap made a difference, didn't it?" Wendy giggled.

Morgan nodded. "You win, Wendy. I misjudged how high that shelf was."

Wendy smiled. "Jenna, we didn't want to make it hard for you to reach the tablecloths, so we'll stack our first choice of tablecloths on the lower shelf and the overflow on the shelf above it."

Morgan added, "The overflow will be the tablecloths with ink or stains."

Jenna sighed. "We could use a step stool."

"Morgan bought one last week because I can't reach the top shelf, and we wanted to use it," Wendy said. "I installed some hooks and hung it on the wall behind the door."

"Have you heard about this afternoon's weather, Wendy?" Jenna asked.

"Morgan told me. I'll see you in the morning."

After Wendy left, Jenna said, "I could use a cup of hot tea."

On their way to the kitchen, Morgan said, "Darlene made a Greek feta dip for us to have with crackers. She said we might need a snack as a fortification before the storm."

While they waited for their tea to steep, Morgan pulled out the dip while Jenna found an open box of the rosemary and olive oil crackers that she and Morgan loved.

"Table or counter?" Morgan asked.

"Let's be fancy and sit at the kitchen table."

"Fancy is right; we usually grab a quick bite and rush to the office." Morgan put the dip and their cups of tea on the table.

After she tasted the dip and took a sip of her tea, Jenna said, "Is the innkeepers' association going to be one of those things I'll regret in the morning?"

Morgan snorted. "You're not allowed to regret it until after you get back, so you'll have stories to tell. So, what are you going to wear to the banquet?"

Jenna stared at her. "I don't know; I guess I'll wear a shirt and jeans. Why?"

Morgan smiled. "Wendy and I found the perfect blouse for you, and Darlene approved it."

Morgan opened the pantry and pulled out a sack. "See what you think."

Jenna held up the long-sleeved, pale peach, cotton blouse that buttoned down the front. "It looks a little low-cut."

"Try it on."

Jenna grumbled as she carried the blouse to the restroom. When she came out, she modeled it for Morgan.

"It's perfect. What do you think?" Morgan asked.

"Tell Darlene and Wendy I grumbled so they don't get too big for their britches, but I love it."

Morgan snickered. "I knew you would."

Katy whined.

Morgan rose from her seat. "Shane must be here. I didn't hear his car over the noise of the wind."

While Morgan and Katy went to the back door, Jenna quickly changed back into her shirt before they returned with Shane.

Shane lifted his glasses as he peered at the dip and crackers. "Darlene has struck again."

He wore his favorite dark blue shirt and bright yellow tie with his khakis. His sharp, professional architect look was softened by his blond flyaway hair with its out-of-control cowlick.

"How about a glass of sweet tea?" Morgan asked as she put ice into a glass, then poured the tea.

"Thanks, honey." Shane joined Jenna at the table. "I like your ball cap. Is that our new logo?"

Morgan nodded. "It's a proof of concept."

"Is that for the convention?" Shane asked.

Morgan glared at him.

"What?" Shane scooped up another spoonful of dip and smeared it on two crackers.

Jenna rolled her eyes. "Did everybody know I was going to the association convention except me?"

Morgan's eyes twinkled. "Why do you think Darlene won't let you do the grocery shopping?"

Shane laughed. "Sorry, Jenna, but can't you hear a cashier announcing, 'Attention, shoppers. Jenna is going to the conference.'"

Jenna narrowed her eyes. "No, I can't."

Morgan crossed her arms.

Jenna sighed. "Maybe it was kind of funny the way you said it. Shane, there's a safe in my old office; could you help me find it?" Jenna asked.

He furrowed his brow. "There's no wall safe because we took down all the walls when we remodeled your old office into the two en suite guest rooms. Wait, is this from Nettie?"

Jenna nodded.

Shane gulped down half his tea and spooned up a heaping helping of dip and scraped it onto a cracker.

"Has to be a floor safe, then. We should be able to find it. I need a broom."

"We can grab one on our way," Morgan said.

When they were in the bedroom that had been the office, Shane said, "We didn't pull up the original floor because it was still in great shape. I'll go back and forth like mowing a yard or vacuuming a carpet and tap the floor. We're listening for a tap that sounds more like a thud."

Jenna and Morgan watched and listened as Shane started at one corner and went back and forth across the room, tapping with the broom handle as he went.

When he was close to the middle of the room, he slowed his pace.

Jenna said, "If I had a floor safe, I'd want it under my desk or on one side of my desk chair."

One board is different.

Jenna smiled. *Thanks, Nettie.*

Jenna peered at the floor, then she saw it. "Tap here." She pointed at the board that was different.

"I already tapped there," Shane said.

Jenna cocked her head. "Tap again."

When Shane's tap yielded a dull thump close to the foot of the bed, he narrowed his eyes. "How did you know?"

"The board is different."

Shane inspected the board. "I can't see any difference; I don't suppose you have any chalk I could use, do you?"

"No, but I can give you some duct tape if you want to mark the boundaries." Morgan dashed out of the room and returned with pink duct tape.

"Pink?" Shane asked.

"According to Darlene, it was on sale," Jenna smiled.

Shane examined the tape. "This might leave residue on the floor. Do you have something else?"

Morgan took the roll of tape from him and pulled a strip close to ten inches long then pointed at the tape that was close to the rest of the roll. "Cut here."

After Shane pulled out his pocket knife, he cut the strip where Morgan had indicated. Morgan folded the strip down the middle with the sticky sides together.

"This won't stick to the floor and ruin it, but we can mark the edges," Morgan said.

"Let's cut three more pieces of tape, then we need Ethan."

"What do we need Ethan for?" Ethan's lanky frame filled the doorway.

Ethan wore his usual flannel shirt, jeans, and work boots. His icy blue eyes twinkled as he gazed at Jenna, and she returned his gaze. She pressed her lips together to stop her mouth from tingling when she shifted her gaze to his mustache she'd grown so fond of.

"We think we've found a floor safe, and you're the only one I know who can lift these boards without ruining the floor," Shane said.

Ethan tilted his head. "Nettie had a floor safe?"

"Yes, and there's something in a safe in her old office she wants me to have," Jenna said.

Ethan nodded. "Show me where it is."

Shane tapped the floor in front of him, then tapped next to the pink tape.

"I hear it. I need my toolbox." Ethan strode out of the room.

"We have plenty of important things to do besides hover over a working man," Morgan said.

Jenna snickered. "You go right ahead and do your important things; I'm going to hover."

"I'm your backup, so I have to stay."

"Just stay out of the way," Shane said.

"They won't," Ethan said. "I'll need your help, Shane."

Morgan whispered, "I think we were just insulted."

"We can hear you, and I deny everything," Shane said.

Jenna strolled out to the foyer, and Morgan followed her.

"What are we doing out here?" Morgan asked.

"I wanted to look at the sky to see if any clouds were rolling in."

"Look at the trees; it's still blowing as hard as ever," Morgan said.

Jenna examined the sky. "Have we killed enough time yet? Can we see what's going on?"

"Let's go," Morgan said.

Before they stepped away from the front door, Ethan called out, "Hey Jenna, we found the safe under the floorboards; what's the combination?"

Morgan snorted. "Did you hear that? He just assumed you would know the combination for a safe from the 1920s."

As Jenna and Morgan hurried back to the guest room, a fleeting thought occurred to Jenna. *The year Henry was born.*

"One eight nine two," Jenna said.

"How did you know that?" Morgan asked.

Katy stared at Morgan.

Morgan shrugged. "You're right, Katy; silly question."

When Jenna reached his side, Ethan gave her a pale blue silk-covered box. Jenna opened it and immediately pulled out a necklace with a gold chain and a pale pink pendant.

Morgan peered over Jenna's shoulder. "There's more jewelry in the box."

Jenna handed the box to Morgan. "Put it in the office safe; I'll look at it later. This is what I'll wear."

Morgan examined the necklace. "I've never seen a stone like that. What is it?"

Shane narrowed his eyes as he studied it. "It's a pink opal. It's a symbol of peace and healing."

"How do you know that?" Morgan asked.

"My mother is a jewelry guru. Dad calls her the queen of rocks, but only behind her back."

"There's nothing else in the safe. I'm going to close it up," Ethan said.

Jenna put on the necklace and hurried to the living room.

"Thank you, Nettie. I'm going to wear it all the time."

Shane called out, "Pink opal soaks up water. You don't want to wear it in the shower."

Jenna rolled her eyes. "I stand corrected."

The wind howled.

Jenna crossed her arms. "I can't hear the chimes because the wind is so loud, Nettie, but I still know you're laughing."

Morgan joined her in the living room. "We're leaving now, Jenna. I think the storm is moving in sooner than they expected. See you in the morning."

Ethan came out of the guestroom with his toolbox.

"Are you ready to go?" he asked. "I can drop off my toolbox and pick up the groceries from my truck."

Jenna stared at Nettie's portrait. "Are you sure this is right for me to do?"

The wind died down for a moment, and the chimes jingled.

"Thanks." Jenna smiled.

"I'll help carry groceries, Ethan."

"There's not that much; you and Katy could hold the door open for me so I can dash right in."

Before they reached the back door, a loud clap of thunder rattled the inn's windows.

Ethan opened the door. "Run, Jenna. I can smell the rain; it's close."

As Jenna and Katy raced to the cottage, a light shower turned into fat raindrops. Jenna opened the door for Katy, then turned to wait for Ethan.

The rain became a downpour as he hurried to the cottage with his head down while he carried six grocery sacks and a gallon jug of sweet tea with a bottle of wine under one arm.

After he was inside, he exhaled as he set the sacks and wine on the kitchen table. "It's going to get rough out there."

Before Jenna closed the door, pea-sized hail slammed the porch.

While Ethan unloaded the sacks and put groceries in the refrigerator or on the counter, Jenna said, "I could have unloaded the truck all by myself in only four trips, except for that hail thing."

He stared at her and then burst out laughing. "Are you making fun of me for bringing in everything at once?"

She held back a giggle as she shrugged. "If the man-carry stereotype fits..."

"My mom has a picture of my dad and me when I was five. The two of us were carrying in loads of firewood. I couldn't see over the top of my stack, and neither could he."

Jenna laughed. "Genetics."

"Mom would agree with you."

Ethan pointed to the bottle of wine. "I bought a bottle of wine when I thought Morgan and Shane were joining us. You aren't likely to get into a shootout tonight, so I thought you would enjoy a glass of wine with your dinner."

"What are we having for dinner?"

Ethan smiled. "Spaghetti and toasted baguette with lemon gelato for dessert. It's my mom's spaghetti sauce. She makes it in batches and freezes it. I'll skillfully warm it up while the spaghetti cooks."

Jenna returned his smile. "Shall I toast the baguette?"

"That would be great."

While they worked side by side, Jenna told Ethan about the conference.

"It sounds like there will be quite a few opportunities to learn from experienced innkeepers."

"I hope so because I'm definitely going under protest."

Ethan smiled as they sat down to eat. "The good news is that you have six days to remind Morgan of how miserable you'll be."

Jenna giggled. "Since when are you the expert at seeing the bright side?"

During dinner, Jenna and Ethan ignored the raging thunderstorm while they talked more about the conference, the inn, and Ethan's new project.

"I have to show you something." Jenna pulled her hat out of her backpack. "I think Morgan ordered this when she signed me up for the conference."

"That's a great cap for you. The peach blossom would be great in a logo, wouldn't it?"

"I'm sure that's what Morgan had in mind."

When they heard a crack then a loud thud over the howling wind, Ethan strode to the front window and peered out. "We have a large limb down between the cottage and the inn. You might have an overnight visitor."

"Mr. Moore told me a second bedroom is always handy for guests, and Wendy insisted it had to always be ready. She dusts it once a week."

"Do I have to sign the guest register?" Ethan's eyes twinkled.

Jenna giggled. "Only if you ask Wendy or Morgan."

Ethan's tone became serious. "Does Nettie think something will happen at the conference? Is that why you have to take the necklace? For protection?"

"No, I needed the reassurance that she'd be close while I was in Savannah because I was so nervous about going, so she told me about the safe."

While Jenna loaded the dishwasher and Ethan put away the leftovers, Ethan paused. "Hear that?"

Jenna cocked her head. "The wind has died down."

"Yep. It was a fast-moving storm."

When they sat together on the sofa, Ethan pulled Jenna close.

"Tell me more about your new project," Jenna said.

While Ethan talked, she leaned against him and relaxed. She closed her eyes and slowly drifted off to the sound of his comforting voice.

When it was close to nine o'clock, Katy yipped, and Jenna jerked awake.

"I'm so sorry; I fell asleep." She yawned.

"Katy and I don't need an apology; we decided you'd had a long day," Ethan said. "The wind has stopped, and Katy's ready to call it a night."

Ethan rose and put on his brown canvas jacket with the tan and green plaid flannel lining. "I'll take Katy for a walk. I want to see if there are any more branches down."

When they returned, Ethan said, "You have several branches down, but the cottage and the inn are fine. I'll have a crew clean up the area tomorrow. Katy and I walked to the road, and the driveway was clear."

He put his arms around her, and she sighed as she rested her head on his chest.

"I have a friend of a friend who is going to Savannah next week. I might ask if he needs someone to ride shotgun with him."

"It's only three days. You don't have to do that."

He nodded. "You're right."

When she gazed up at him, he cupped her chin with his hand, then smiled as he returned her gaze and leaned down. Jenna met his warm lips with hers as she gently stroked the smooth skin on the back of his neck.

His breath was lemony and tart from the gelato, and his mustache tickled her upper lip and made her shiver. Ethan groaned as their lips parted and he released her.

"Thank you for dinner," she whispered.

"Anytime; thank you for the kiss." He brushed back her hair with his fingertips while he studied her face.

She giggled. "Anytime."

With one last lingering kiss, Ethan smiled, then left.

Jenna peered out the window as he strode to his truck and sighed. "I do love to watch his cute bum."

Chapter Two

Sunday, Six Days Later

After Jenna parked in the nearby multi-level parking garage, she slipped on the straps of her backpack, which doubled as a computer bag, and pulled her roller bag to the entrance of the Glenwood Hotel in the historic district of Savannah.

Her eyes widened when she went into the coolness of the lobby. The hotel electrical and other systems had obviously been updated, but the elegant handcrafted glass chandelier, the rich dark wood of the intricately carved reception desk, and the plush deep hues of upholstered chairs with button backs honored the style and Southern charm of a grand establishment in the late 1800s when the hotel was rebuilt.

Jenna's nose twitched at the lingering aroma of old money and opulence; she listened as the voices from the registration desk were muffled by the faint whispers of long-gone conversations in the lobby. Her breathing was shallow, and her heart pounded.

I didn't think about what it might be like for me in a historic hotel.

Jenna wheeled around and rushed outside. She stepped away from the door and breathed in the cold air and listened to the traffic noises. *Should I walk back to my car and go back to the inn?*

She pressed her hand against her pink opal pendant. *I'm here, sweet pea.*

Jenna whispered, "Thanks."

After she exhaled, she strolled inside, and her eyes widened as she surveyed the old hotel with its typical period furnishings that had faded with age. Jenna snapped a photo and sent a text to Morgan. "Late-1800s atmosphere. Less intense after I adjusted to it."

Morgan replied, "Well done."

She strode to the registration desk and stood in line behind a young woman four inches taller and at least five years younger than she was. Her short, spiked hair was dyed a bright purple, and she had a snake tattoo on her neck. She was dressed in jeans and a deep red, long-sleeved flannel shirt.

Jenna glanced down at her own jeans and plaid flannel shirt over her pale yellow T-shirt. *I was afraid I'd be underdressed.*

The young woman turned slightly and cocked her head. "Are you here for the innkeepers' convention?"

"Yes, I am; are you?"

"Sure am. I'm Calliope. My mother and I own a bed-and-breakfast. She kind of inherited my grandparents' old, Victorian-style house; we updated the plumbing and electrical, and here I am. This is my third year of coming to the convention."

"That's interesting because I inherited a bed-and-breakfast too. I'm Jenna; this is my first convention. Nice to meet you."

Calliope nodded. "You too. If you don't have any plans for dinner, several of us are going to a nearby restaurant that has Southern country food. I plan to order their specialty, shrimp and grits. We'll meet in the lobby and then leave at six. It's within walking distance."

"Thanks; I'll be there."

"I like your ball cap. Is that the logo for your inn?"

"It might be. I think we're doing a proof-of-concept thing."

"Peach Blossom, what? Inn?" Calliope asked.

"Peach Blossom Retreat."

Calliope nodded. "Retreat. I like the idea."

A man joined the line behind Jenna.

"Hey, Gary. It's good to see you," Calliope said. "This is Jenna; she's here for the conference too."

Jenna turned to greet the man. He was a few years older than her. His broad shoulders and muscular frame suggested a history of high school football. His head was cleanly shaved, and his thick, crimson mustache highlighted his ruddy skin.

He smiled. "I'm Gary."

"I'm Jenna."

"Are you going to dinner with us, Gary?"

"I'm planning on it. Do we know where we're going?"

"It's my favorite place for shrimp and grits."

Gary smiled. "That place gets packed. I could never convince Kendra to go there because the noise would bother her."

Jenna grimaced.

"Do loud noises bother you too, Jenna?" Gary asked.

"Yes, but I do have insertable earplugs for hearing protection. Should I take them?"

"If my wife were along, she'd say yes," he said.

The man at the counter picked up his suitcase and strode away.

Calliope replaced him at the counter. "Calliope Nikitas."

"Is this your first time coming to the association conference?" Gary asked.

"Yes, and I'm not exactly sure what to expect."

Gary nodded. "I understand, but the presentations have always been helpful."

Jenna relaxed as Gary told her about some tips he'd picked up over the years.

This may not be so bad after all.

After she checked in and received her key, Calliope said, "See you guys later."

Calliope headed for the elevator, and Jenna moved to the counter.

After she had her key, Jenna strolled to the elevator and pushed the button. The elevator creaked and rattled as it slowly descended. A muffled ding announced the elevator had arrived on the second floor. When it resumed its downward travel, the creaks and rattles became louder.

Jenna shuddered. *I'll take the stairs to the third floor. I need the exercise after my five-hour drive, anyway.*

When she opened the door to the stairs, she cringed. *They're so narrow. It would be hard to pass anyone going down while going up without turning sideways.* She craned her neck to peer up the stairs. *It isn't very well lit.*

The elevator dinged behind her. She glanced back and shook her head. *I'll stick to the stairs.*

Jenna slipped her arms through the backpack straps and picked up her roller bag then exhaled as she went through the door to the main floor landing to take the stairs. The door slammed shut behind her, and she jumped.

Jenna stroked her pink opal pendant for encouragement, then began her climb to the third floor as she counted the number of steps.

She stopped midway between the first and second floors and listened to the creaks and groans of the old building. *I'm standing on step number seven.* She glanced up. *Six more to go. It's going to be a really long three days, except it's four because of today.*

After she reached the second floor, she frowned. *Maybe I miscounted the number of steps, and it really wasn't thirteen.* Jenna carefully counted as she went from the second to the third floor. *Thirteen.*

She opened the door and entered a dimly lit hallway. She turned right and found her room two doors from the stairwell.

When she unlocked the door and went into her room, she flipped on the light and her eyes widened. "Wow, talk about a step back in time."

Jenna examined the sconce that lit the small entryway. It was an electric light fixture with a decorative gas cock, a gently curved pipestem arm, and an open-top etched glass shade.

The room was half the size of the Peach Blossom Retreat guest rooms, and the faded floral wallpaper made it appear even smaller than it was. There was room to walk on both sides of the bed, and its white eyelet coverlet and two fluffy pillows gave the room a welcoming feel. The marred small writing desk near the window with its mismatched desk chair blended in so well with the wallpaper, they seemed to disappear into the wall. The wide window was covered by lacy curtains over the typical light-blocking hotel drapes that ended at the bottom of the sill.

The deep blue and cream striped upholstered chair and its three-legged footstool were in the corner of the room near the head of the bed along with a floor lamp that extended a warm invitation to relax and read. The multi-colored braided rug that was at the foot of the bed hinted that the guest was only a step away from a portal into the past.

Next to the bathroom was a tiny alcove that reminded Jenna of a broom closet with no door. Half of the alcove was shelves, and the other half had a bar with hangers. *My roller bag might fit there.* Jenna peered into the bathroom and exhaled in relief at the updated walk-in tile shower.

She snapped photos of the guest room and the bathroom and sent them to Morgan.

After she hung up her shirts and pants and placed her pajamas and underwear on the shelves, Jenna slipped her laptop out of the backpack.

Before she set up her computer, her phone rang.

"Your room is beautiful," Morgan said. "I wonder if they have rooms with queen or king beds. The double is fine for you, isn't it? I'd have to sleep on the diagonal. Does the hotel have a creepy vibe?"

"It did at first. The lobby had odd acoustics that muffled and distorted sounds, but I could have just been tired from the long drive. I'm on the third floor and planned to take the elevator, but it creaked so much that I took the stairs. There are thirteen steps from one floor to the next."

"Nobody but you would count the stairs, but I think thirteen steps are creepy."

While they talked, the sconce briefly flickered. Jenna furrowed her brow. *I wonder if the bulb is loose.*

Jenna giggled. "I didn't think about that. I met someone who is younger than I am. Her name is Calliope, and she's here for the convention. I'm going to meet her and some other people in the lobby, then we'll walk to a nearby restaurant for dinner."

"Calliope's an unusual name."

"It fits her. I expected all the association members to be at least twice my age."

Katy barked.

Morgan giggled. "Katy says hi; I'm holding the phone so she can hear you."

"Good girl, Katy. I'll be home soon."

"Check in when you can tomorrow. Shane's here; we're going for a long walk before we go home." Morgan hung up.

I miss Katy. Jenna sighed.

She sent a text to Ethan with the photo of her room. "I'm here; my room is small but cute."

She frowned as the sconce on the wall near the door flickered again, then jumped at the loud hum that suddenly roared from below the window curtains. She strode to the window and stared at the heating and air conditioning unit. After she flipped open the control door, Jenna groaned at the control dial with a triangular indicator pointing halfway between the labels of high on the left and low on the right. *What does that even mean?*

When her phone rang, she smiled as she answered.

"Hi, Ethan."

"I miss you," Ethan said. "What are your plans for this evening?"

"I met two other innkeepers at check-in. I'm meeting them and a few others in the lobby at six, and we're going to dinner together at a nearby restaurant. We'll be walking."

"Take your carry piece. Do you trust these people?" Ethan exhaled. "I guess I'm hovering."

"You are, but just so you won't worry, I have it."

"That does ease my mind a little, but why do you have to leave the hotel for dinner? Doesn't the hotel have a restaurant?" Ethan asked.

"It's more of a coffee shop, but there are a lot of great restaurants nearby according to the pamphlet the desk clerk gave me when I checked in. I'll be an expert in the best places to eat by the time the conference is over."

"You win, just be careful. I'm glad you met some people so you can go out to dinner with a group. You would have skipped dinner otherwise, wouldn't you?"

Jenna chuckled. "You know me only too well."

He exhaled. "It's almost six, babe. Call me when you get back."

After they hung up, Jenna smiled. *He called me babe.*

Jenna grunted. *No reason to get all mushy. This room is a bad influence.*

She grabbed her coat and her backpack and left her room.

As she went down the narrow staircase, she held onto the handrail. When she reached the landing on the second floor, a middle-aged woman opened the fire door and jumped when she saw Jenna.

Jenna flinched, then a wave of rose perfume washed over her, and she sneezed at the potent scent. "Excuse me."

The woman wore black patent leather heels, a slim black skirt with a hem just below the knee, a cream-colored blouse with ruffles at the neck and a gold chain necklace with an open circle pendant with a gold 3-D sandpiper in the middle.

She cleared her throat. "Pardon me; I'm running late."

Jenna held her breath as the woman rushed to the stairs, then clutched the handrail and slowly descended.

Jenna stayed on the landing until the woman was halfway down so she wouldn't cough from the heavy perfume and cause the woman to fall. *It's scary enough to watch her.*

The woman slowly maneuvered each step. "You startled me. I didn't expect to see anyone else using the stairs. I rode the elevator up to my room, and that was enough. When I came to the landing, I thought I was on the main floor, so I've been wandering around the second floor for the past twenty minutes. I'd be asking for a room on the first floor if my room were any higher than the third floor. I'm Delilah; you might have heard of me. Are you here for the convention?"

"Yes, I am. I'm Jenna. This is my first convention, so I'm not sure what to expect, but the agenda looks interesting."

"That's encouraging; I'm the keynote speaker, and I'm on several panels." Delilah stopped two steps from the main floor and looked back at Jenna. "That's a cute little necklace you have. It's amazing what they can do with acrylic these days, isn't it?"

Delilah patted her necklace, then pushed her hair behind one ear to show off a matching earring. "A dear friend of mine, who was a talented artist, hand-crafted the sandpipers in my necklace and earrings with 14-karat yellow gold years ago. I have to be careful with the earrings because they have a tendency to slip off because the gold is so heavy."

She peered down and then took another step before she glanced at Jenna and raised an eyebrow. "Are you going to dinner? There's a small group of us who always go to dinner together. Safety in numbers, you know. We'd love for you to join us, or did someone in the group already invite you? Our group tries to watch for new people, but my assistant probably already invited you, didn't she?"

Jenna had stopped on the stairs to wait for Delilah to take the last two steps. "Calliope was in the registration line with me and invited me."

"Calliope?" Delilah snorted. "She's nice enough, I suppose, but I'd be careful around her. Sara's such an average person; makes you wonder what Calliope's father was like. She's a bit wild, which I'm sure you probably noticed."

Jenna shrugged. "Not really."

Delilah's eyes briefly twinkled, and then she narrowed her eyes and sneered. "You young people stick together, don't you?"

Delilah stepped down to the main floor and let go of the handrail to open the door to the hall.

Jenna's mouth broke into a slight smile. *She just put me in the same age group as Calliope. Wait until I tell Morgan.*

When they stepped into the lobby, Delilah glanced toward the right and growled, "What's he doing here?"

Jenna quickly strode away toward the middle of the lobby where a small group had gathered.

Calliope met her before she reached the group. "I told Mom about your cap, and she agreed we need to come up with a new logo that was a little less cookie-cutter. You were smart to bring a coat. I brought mine too."

She nodded toward her lined leather jacket on her arm. "It's only a little chilly now, but the wind will come up later, so it will be downright nippy when we return."

Calliope wrinkled her nose. "You ran into Ms. Delilah Drake, didn't you? You have a cloud of roses clinging to you."

"I met her on the landing on the second floor. Thank goodness we're going outside."

"I don't like the elevator either. I'm on the second floor, so I ran up the steps for a little exercise. The stairs are too steep for me to run down even one flight."

Jenna nodded. "Steep, narrow, and thirteen steps."

Calliope narrowed her eyes. "You counted them too?"

Jenna shrugged. "Doesn't everybody? While the stairs spooked me, the elevator was far too creaky for me. It sounded like the cable was ready to snap any minute."

"I think I'd have a heart attack if I got stuck in it."

As they headed toward the group, Calliope said, "Everybody might tell you their name, but you aren't required to remember them. We'll all have name tags tomorrow so you can put names to faces then."

"Thanks for the heads up; I would have been trying to take notes and asking people to spell their names. It wouldn't take long for everyone to avoid me, would it?"

Calliope chuckled. "I love it. Can I steal your idea? I love talking to people, but I'm not a fan of small talk. Our dinner group is just the right size. It's large enough that no one can put you on the spot, but it's small enough that you can chat with the people sitting next to you. It's safer, too, because no one will have to go to dinner or walk on the streets alone after dark."

"There you are, Jenna," Delilah said. "Come walk with me, and we can chat."

She reached for Jenna's arm, but Jenna motioned toward the door. "Oh look. The group is leaving, but it looks like they aren't sure which way to go."

Before Jenna finished speaking, Delilah called out as she bustled to the front of the group. "To the left, everyone. I'll be right there. What would you do without me? Has anyone seen my assistant? She should have been at the front of the line. I swear that girl gets more unreliable...." The door closed behind Delilah.

"Slick," Calliope said. "Are you still okay with going to dinner with the group?"

"Of course. Didn't you say the restaurant's specialty was shrimp and grits?"

After they caught up with the slow-moving group, Calliope said, "Delilah gets under my skin because she acts like she knows everything, but she's been extremely successful in developing a franchise-like model of bed-and-breakfasts, which I wouldn't have considered possible." Calliope shrugged. "Maybe she does know everything. Anyway, I'm looking forward to her talk."

"I am too. The topic of her talk, 'Find Your Niche and Make it Bigger,' really intrigued me."

"She has been on panels in the past. She likes to be the center of attention, but she knows her stuff and knows how to convey her ideas."

"Tell me about your bed-and-breakfast," Jenna said.

"We're here." Calliope pointed to the overhead neon sign. "We're about to enter the chaos zone. We can talk after we order or tomorrow on break. We'll probably get separated on our way to our table, but I'll save you a seat. Just find me; I'm the one with the purple hair."

Jenna laughed, and Calliope grinned.

When they were inside, they were herded through the crowded restaurant by a host who wore a white sleeveless T-shirt that was a startling contrast to his ebony skin and showed off his rippling pecs and his bulging biceps. He had a pink scar that ran from his drooping left eye to his jawline.

"Stay close." The host's low, booming voice cut through the clamor in the restaurant.

Jenna gaped as he nimbly threaded his way through the crush of people with the grace and agility of a leopard on the prowl. The group rushed to stay behind him before the open path he left in his wake closed.

Calliope hissed, "Don't get separated from the group, or you'll never find us."

Calliope disappeared in the crowd, but a man behind Jenna said, "Slight left then straight ahead and into the side room on the right."

When she went into the side room, Jenna saw Calliope sitting at the end of a table with empty chairs on both sides of her.

Jenna sat on Calliope's right, and Gary sat across from Jenna.

"I thought your voice sounded familiar," Jenna smiled as she turned to Calliope. "Gary was the voice behind me that kept me on track. I would have gotten turned around if he hadn't been there."

"Thanks, Gary," Calliope said. "You're the best."

Gary grinned. "You probably say that to all the bald, sexy men."

Calliope laughed. "Nope, just you."

A server appeared between Calliope and Jenna. "Are you ready to order, or do you want menus?"

"Shrimp and grits and sweet tea," Calliope said.

Jenna nodded. "Same for me."

"I can't break rank," Gary said. "Make it three."

After their server left, Gary asked, "What brought you here, Jenna?"

Jenna rolled her eyes. "My best friend signed me up."

Gary chuckled. "My wife's sneaky like that too. We've been members of the association for five years. We agreed we'd take turns coming to the association meetings, but her turn's always next year."

Jenna asked, "What about you, Calliope?"

"Mom came the first year after we joined, but she says she realized she can't sleep anywhere except in her own bed, so I'm here every year."

"What did you think of the agenda?" Gary asked.

While they discussed the agenda items, a young, curvy woman with heavy eye makeup and beautifully manicured fingernails pushed her way to the table. Her fine blonde hair framed her face, creating a shimmering halo. "Sorry. Excuse me. Sorry, I'm late. Did anybody order for me?"

She rushed to the end of the table as people scooted their chairs to make room for her. The host carried in a chair and put it in the spot the others had cleared for her.

"Nice of you to join us, Mia," a man sneered.

The young woman beamed. "Thanks."

Jenna snickered. *I love how she handled that sarcastic remark.*

When their food arrived, Jenna's eyes widened at the giant-sized bowl of grits with grilled shrimp on top. "There's no way I could eat all this in one sitting."

Calliope smiled. "I've never finished a bowl yet, but I do somehow manage to eat all my shrimp."

"I'll make that a priority." Jenna returned her smile.

While the three of them were eating, Delilah's voice carried from the other end of the long table and caught Jenna's attention.

"I thought I saw you at the hotel. What are you doing here? You're not on the agenda until Wednesday."

Jenna leaned forward as she glanced toward the other end of the table. Delilah sat at the end, and a gray-haired man who wore rectangular half-frame eyeglasses, a black suit with a black shirt and a white tie pulled up a chair from the table whose customers had just left and sat next to her. The man smiled, but his eyes were hard.

Jenna strained to hear his response, but he kept his hand near his mouth.

Delilah hissed, "Just stay out of my way."

A roar of laughter from a nearby table drowned out the rest of the conversation.

"Who is the man sitting next to Delilah at the other end of the table?" Jenna asked.

Calliope glanced up. "That's Victor Grimes. He's a big shot too; he owns the attraction, Ghost Realms, Theatrical Paranormal Events. He's actually a big shot in the world of illusions."

"There's bad blood between those two. I might have known why at one time, but I've forgotten most likely because I didn't care," Gary said.

Calliope pulled out her phone. "Now you've piqued my curiosity. I'll ask Mom." Calliope sent a text.

When Calliope's phone chimed, she said, "Mom said she wasn't sure, but she'll get the straight scoop."

"We didn't mean to cause her extra work," Jenna said.

"Extra work? We just gave Mom a reason to call an old friend of hers." Calliope smiled.

Gary glanced at the other end of the table. "Victor's face is red, and he's leaving. He barely touched his food. I wonder if he's sticking Delilah with his bill."

Jenna watched as Victor Grimes headed toward the exit but was stopped by the host. After a few words, Victor gave the host money, then stormed out.

"I think Victor paid for his meal because he just gave the host some money," Jenna said.

Gary snorted. "Smart decision on Victor's part."

"People who know Harrison say he's a kindhearted guy, but he doesn't put up with any nonsense," Calliope said.

"Why is he a host and not a bouncer?"

"Maybe the pay and hours are better," Gary said. "Which would you rather be? A bouncer or a host?"

"If I had to choose, I'd rather be a bouncer; I'd love to see Mom in action as a bouncer. She'd take away their cell phones and give them a time out," Calliope said.

Jenna and Gary laughed.

After they paid their tabs, the three of them walked together back to the hotel.

A brisk wind rounded a corner, and Jenna buttoned her jacket up to her neck. "Brr. You were right, Calliope; it's definitely colder."

Jenna reached into her pockets for her gloves, but her pockets were empty.

She moaned, "I always have my gloves in my pocket. They must have fallen out."

"Let me know if you want to go shopping tomorrow," Calliope said.

"I'm not much for shopping, but I'll go along too," Gary said. "I wouldn't mind surprising Kendra with a gift, and gloves sound perfect."

"Thanks. We can see what our time looks like tomorrow," Jenna said.

"If either of you gets bored, just say the word," Calliope said. "I know the hotel is old, but I see signs of deferred maintenance. What do you think about it?"

Jenna shrugged. "The light sconce on the wall near my door flickers occasionally. Does the hotel have a brownout problem?"

Gary frowned. "Talk to the desk clerk when we get back. The hotel should have an electrician check your light fixture; you might have a short."

"I'll do that. I didn't think about a short. I'll talk to the desk clerk before I go to my room tonight."

"Did you notice the hotel has a library?" Calliope asked.

"No, I didn't," Jenna said. "That's great. I was surprised there was no television in my room, but we don't have televisions in the rooms at the inn, either."

"I heard some rooms have TVs, and others don't," Gary said. "It doesn't matter to me because I've got work to do, but I did hear some grumbling over dinner this evening."

"I have a TV, but maybe I should keep quiet about it unless somebody irritates me." Calliope smirked.

"As thin as the walls are, I hope the rooms next to me don't have TVs," Gary said.

Jenna groaned. "So do I; I don't know if I could take a loud TV late at night on top of the roar of the heating unit under the window."

"You have one of those too?" Calliope asked. "When I first arrived, a guest was complaining about theirs at the desk. Supposedly, the hotel is full, so there are no other options except asking for a refund and finding somewhere else to stay."

Gary moaned. "First impressions have a tremendous impact on any business, don't they? I'd be scrambling if we had complaints like these at our inn, but I'm going to talk to Kendra. Are we missing something that's annoying to our guests, but we're used to it?"

"Mom checks the reviews for other bed-and-breakfast inns to see if she can spot a common theme in the complaints to be sure we aren't doing the same thing."

"That's genius," Jenna said. "We talk to our guests regularly during their stay, and our reviews are excellent, so I thought we were doing fine, but your mom is more proactive."

After they reached the hotel, Gary said, "If there are any breakout sessions, how do you feel about being rule busters and being our own group?"

"I'm all for it," Calliope said.

"So am I," Jenna said.

When Calliope and Gary turned toward the hallway that led to the elevator and stairs, Jenna said, "I'm going to talk to the desk clerk."

"Do you want me to stick around for moral support?" Calliope asked.

"No, I'll be fine."

"See you in the morning."

When Jenna strolled up to the desk, a different desk clerk was there.

The new desk clerk smiled, but there was a hint of no-nonsense in her eyes. She wore jeans and a salmon-colored T-shirt under a dark blue blazer with the hotel logo embroidered on the pocket. Muscles showed beneath her rounded figure, the kind built from lifting real things like boxes and equipment and not from hanging around a gym. She had pulled her hair back into a tight bun; her nametag pinned on the pocket above the logo said 'Lucy'.

Lucy asked, "Flickering lights, noisy heating unit, or no TV?"

Jenna chuckled. "Lights and heating unit. I don't care about the TV. How did you know?"

"I haven't been here long, but I feel like an old hand. I'm the housekeeper half the time and desk clerk the other half, so I see everything. If they fire me, I'll move back home, and my mother would love it. She says I work too hard, but I'm saving up to finish my last year of school next fall."

Jenna furrowed her brow. *None of this is true. What is she hiding?*

Lucy continued, "First, the lights, because that's easy. They shouldn't be flickering. It's been an ongoing problem that is being reported more frequently. The electrician will be here in the morning to check out the electrical system. How's your hearing?"

"Excellent," Jenna said.

"Congratulations, but that's actually too bad. Unfortunately, the heating units are loud. Most people don't notice because their hearing has declined. I can offer you earplugs, a white noise machine, or both. I can give you a full refund if you want to find another nearby hotel to stay, but I recommend you wait until tomorrow to leave."

"I don't want to go anywhere else. The conference is here."

"I understand, and I'm sorry," Lucy said.

"I'll take you up on the earplugs and a white noise machine though," Jenna said.

Lucy handed her a sealed packet with earplugs and a new white noise machine that still had the manufacturer's twist ties on the electrical cord.

Jenna examined the machine. "This is new."

"Yes, the hotel got them for free by offering to test and rate them."

"That's smart."

"Thank you."

Jenna smiled. "Your idea, right?"

The desk clerk grinned. "My manager's focus is elsewhere. Anything else I can do for you, Mrs. Ross?"

"No, thank you." Jenna tilted her head. "How did you know my name?"

"Process of elimination. There are only two young women attending the conference, and you don't fit the description of the other one."

Jenna smiled as she headed toward the hallway. *At least the noise machine isn't too heavy and has a handle.*

She glanced up the stairs and groaned. As she trudged up the steps, she grumbled, "People pay a lot of money to join a gym and heft weights. They should try hauling their puny weights up two flights of stairs."

When Jenna arrived at her room, she unlocked the door and went inside and sighed. *The heating unit must cycle, but it stays on more than off.*

She put her backpack on the chair next to the desk and frowned at her open laptop. *I thought I'd closed it.*

Jenna shrugged as she checked it. *Screen's locked.*

After she closed her computer, she set the white noise machine on a corner of the desk, then plugged it in. She fiddled with the settings and listened to the selections of sounds, including the whirring sound of a fan, then left it on soft music.

She turned up the volume of the music before she texted Ethan, then Morgan with the same message. "Back at the hotel."

Morgan replied, "Thanks. We can talk tomorrow."

After she kicked off her boots and changed into soft pants, her phone rang. She smiled and answered Ethan's call.

"Katy went to work with me, and then I dropped her off at Shane's house. So, that was my day. How was yours?"

Jenna propped up the pillows on the bed and leaned back with her feet up.

"It's been a day." She told him about her room, Calliope, Gary, dinner, and Lucy.

"Wow. I'm surprised at how much you've learned already. Have you already jotted down your notes for today?"

"No, I thought I'd talk to you first. I miss you, but you would hate it here. My feet almost go off the bed as it is."

Ethan chuckled. "If I were there, we'd be at a decent hotel where the heater didn't roar and the bed was long enough to keep either of us from getting cold feet."

Was that a double entendre? Jenna felt her face warm. *Did I imply the wrong thing when I mentioned the bed?*

She shook her head. *No, Ethan just took the opportunity to tease me and make me blush.*

Ethan continued, "I'm glad you found people you can sit with at the sessions. I was worried you'd be alone, not that you'd care, but I should have remembered you always find your people. I noticed that when the genealogy group was at the inn."

Isn't that what everybody does? Jenna shrugged. "I'll type my notes and send them to Morgan so we can brainstorm as soon as I get back."

"Text me in the morning. After you get back, we'll have to continue that conversation about warming up cold feet."

Jenna's eyes widened. *Definitely a double entendre.*

"Ethan, are you trying to make me blush?"

"Maybe." He chuckled. "Good night, babe. I'll talk to you in the morning."

I was right; he was teasing me. Jenna smiled. *No one else has ever called me babe. I like it.*

After she changed into her pajamas, Jenna set the white noise machine on the small table next to her bed. *What about charging my phone?*

She unplugged the desk lamp so she could charge her phone, then frowned at the white noise machine. She changed the setting from music to the sound of the whirring fan, then lowered the volume to be loud enough to hear, but not too loud.

She sighed. *Why am I so fidgety?*

After she climbed into bed, she turned off the bedside lamp and listened to the competition between the whirring machine and the constant roar of the motor of the heating unit.

My feet are icicles.

Jenna snorted. *Should I text Ethan?*

She doubled the coverlet over her feet, but when she rolled to her side, the coverlet flopped open.

When she heard footsteps overhead that sounded like someone stomping grapes, she exhaled. *My room is a battleground for total aggravation, and so far, I'm losing.*

She rested her hand on her pink opal pendant and drifted off to sleep.

Jenna suddenly woke to a sound of scratching behind the wall near the headboard. As she jumped out of bed, she kicked the small footstool with the ball of her foot, then smacked her small toe against the leg of the upholstered chair.

She yelped and hopped on her other foot as she collapsed in the chair while holding onto her injured toe.

While she groaned, the scratching behind the wall lessened, disappeared.

Push the chair.

"Thanks, Nettie."

She pushed the chair almost two inches closer to the wall, then exhaled. "It's heavy; that's the best I can do."

Jenna sat in the upholstered chair and held her small toe while tears rolled down her cheeks.

She sniffled. "My toe hurts, my phone is on the other side of the bed, and everything is frustrating. I hate it here."

Jenna woke an hour later with a jerk of her head. She crawled into bed.

Chapter Three

When her alarm on her phone beeped the next morning, Jenna mumbled, "We'll go out in a minute, Katy. I forgot to set up the coffee."

Jenna struggled to sit up to stretch, and clutched at the mattress as she tumbled out of bed, then screamed when she landed on her hip and bumped her elbow on the bedframe.

Jenna groaned. "What a way to wake up."

She held onto the bedside table as she climbed to her feet and silenced the alarm. *At least the chair was out of the way; I would have hit my head on a leg.*

Jenna limped to the bathroom and turned on the water in the shower. While she waited for the water to be warm enough to step into the shower, she hobbled back to grab her phone. *My necklace.*

She put her necklace on the bedside table and tentatively returned to the bathroom, where the steam had filled the room. After Jenna stepped into the shower, she turned her back to the spray for hot water therapy.

She sighed. "I'll just stay right here until I'm all shriveled."

After her shower, Jenna dressed and put on her necklace then slipped her computer into her backpack and texted Ethan. "The alarm went off, and I rolled out of bed. Literally. How's your day?"

She strolled to the window and turned off the white sound machine. After she opened the blinds, Jenna peered outside. *It's still dark, and the puddles in the street are reflecting the streetlights. It must have rained last night, but I didn't hear it.*

While she was at the window, her phone rang.

When she answered, Ethan said, "Good morning, sweet thing. What did you mean by literally rolling out of bed?"

"When my alarm went off, I thought I was at home and Katy wanted to go out. I must have been on the edge of the bed because when I sat up, I rolled out of the bed and onto the floor."

"Are you okay?"

"If cranky doesn't count, I'm fine. The hotel had plenty of hot water for my shower, so even my attitude is a little better."

"What does your day look like?"

"I think I'll be busy. The program starts after breakfast with the keynote speaker. After a break, we'll have a panel discussion and a breakout session, then lunch. The afternoon is free, but the conference room will be available for informal discussions. The hotel has offered a behind-the-scenes tour of the hotel today in the afternoon."

"What about dinner?"

"I don't know yet. What are you doing today?"

"I'll be at the job site. It will be colder today, so I suspect Katy will stay at the inn with Darlene and Morgan. Shane's working on a proposal for another new client. He'll call me when he's ready for me to review it. I just had a thought; do you have coffee in your room?"

"They have coffee in the lobby, but not in the rooms."

"I'll bet you're ready for coffee after your rough start. I'll talk to you later. Learn lots."

"Thanks."

After Jenna hung up, she stared at her phone and bit her lip.

The pink opal pendant tingled against her skin, and when she touched it, the opal felt warm. "I knew I'd miss Katy but didn't realize how much I'd miss Ethan too. Nettie probably knew." She sighed. "I miss the chimes."

Jenna made her bed and straightened her room out of habit before she picked up her backpack and headed toward the stairs. The elevator stopped at the third floor, and instead of the usual ding, it jingled.

Jenna smiled. "Thanks, Nettie."

When she opened the door to the landing, she squinted at the dim lighting. *I really don't like these stairs.* She exhaled, then held onto the hand railing as she headed toward the first floor.

When she reached the lobby, the café hadn't opened yet, but she spotted three people who stood near a coffee station in front of the café entrance while they chatted and sipped coffee. She recognized Victor Grimes by the black suit with a black shirt and white tie. *His black suit must be his professional uniform.* The two women, one tall and slender and the other petite and round, were a study in contrasts.

As she strolled toward the group, the shorter woman waved at her. "The name tags are outside the conference room."

When Jenna was closer, she recognized the woman who waved. *She's Delilah's assistant, Mia.*

Mia pointed. "The conference room is just down that hall, but if you're like me, you'll want to grab a cup of coffee first."

"You're right. I didn't realize how spoiled I was by my automatic coffee maker at home."

Victor raised his eyebrows and peered at her over his glasses. "Are you a member, or are you here with your parents?"

Jenna blinked. *Am I insulted or flattered. Let's see.*

Jenna casually waved her hand. "Oh, you know."

Mia sputtered and coughed. "Sorry. Coffee went down the wrong way."

Victor sniffed. "The hotel provides the coffee, but you aren't allowed into the conference room."

Jenna nodded.

Mia winked at Jenna. "That's right. You have to wear a name tag to attend the conference."

Victor glared at Jenna, then mumbled as he strode away, "This generation is too coddled and lazy and has no idea what it means to work. Let Mommy Do It is their motto."

Mia giggled as she handed Jenna a cup of coffee. "You have totally made my day."

The other woman said, "You saved Mr. Grimes from a bloody nose because I was about to deck him. In self-defense, of course. I'm Frankie."

Jenna sipped her coffee and then grinned. "I'm Jenna. It absolutely would have been self-defense, and you have at least one unbiased witness right here. Is he always so insufferable, or did I just catch him in a bad mood?"

"You can make that two witnesses. He used to be almost tolerable, but he's gotten worse since he and Delilah got into a territorial feud over the old inns that are supposed to be haunted," Mia said. "I'm Mia."

Frankie chuckled. "Jenna, I still can't get over how cool you were with that old snob. I'll have to practice that hand wave thing you did." Frankie held up her hand, then waved her hand. "No, that's not quite right."

"He caught me before I had any coffee, which was a dangerous move on his part," Jenna said.

Mia's eyes twinkled. "Ooo. If you're that sharp before coffee, you must be lethal after your first cup."

Frankie said, "They're unlocking the café door on time, so I won't starve after all. I understand they have a breakfast menu that isn't very extensive, but it does include eggs, grits, and bacon, which are the three basic food groups as far as I'm concerned."

After they were seated, Jenna ordered a scrambled egg with a small bowl of grits, Frankie ordered a full breakfast of two fried eggs, grits, and bacon, and Mia ordered a fruit cup.

Mia quickly ate and left. Jenna had finished eating but sat with Frankie until two of Frankie's friends joined the table.

Jenna excused herself and was on her way out when she met Calliope and Gary who were entering the coffee shop.

"Have you already eaten?" Gary asked.

"I just finished," Jenna said.

"I peeked into the conference hall, and it's set up with tables that seat six. If you go into the conference room, grab a table close to the exit and put something in front of the three seats that face the podium. We'll be there after we eat," Calliope said. "See you soon."

Jenna hurried to the conference hall.

The name tags were on lanyards on a table in the hall outside of the conference room.

Jenna found hers, put on her lanyard, and then opened the door to the conference room and inhaled the tantalizing aroma of freshly brewed coffee mingled with the faint but distinct chemical odor of new carpeting.

When she went inside, Jenna scanned the room. *This room is larger than I expected.* The new carpeting dominated the room with its oversized circles of bright green, red, and yellow.

Jenna wrinkled her nose. *The floor reminds me of large plastic hoops a child carelessly dropped on the floor.* She caught herself stepping carefully over the rings in the carpet so she wouldn't trip. She glanced around. *Good. No one noticed me doing that strange dance.*

Jenna selected a table that was close to the door she came in and was not far from the emergency exit.

As more people came into the room, they rushed toward the front, and the tables that were close to the podium filled up. Jenna cringed as the energy in the room escalated. She glanced behind her. *I would have had my choice of tables in the back.*

Victor came into the room and scanned the room.

She pulled out her computer and put it on the table. After she draped her jacket across the back of the chair on one side of her, she placed her backpack on the table in front of the chair on the other side.

Victor strolled to her table. "Where did you get the name tag? Does Jenna Ross know you have it?"

Jenna wrinkled her nose. *It would be tempting to run with it.*

"I'm Jenna Ross, and thank you for flattering me earlier."

Victor scratched his head as he peered at her. "You young people fool me every time."

"You are..."

"Victor Grimes. My business is Ghost Realms, Theatrical Paranormal Events. I'll be speaking on a panel later this morning. Ignore anything Delilah Drake says about me. I saw you talking to her. You probably work for her, don't you?"

"No." Jenna narrowed her eyes when Victor raised his voice.

"She'd blackmail me if she could, but she has absolutely no evidence that I'm committing fraud by faking hauntings. My theory is that people blame others for what they themselves are doing."

Victor stormed out of the conference room. Jenna stared at the door after he left. *What did I say that set him off?* She chuckled. *And how do I do it again?*

When she sat down, she inhaled, then slowly exhaled before she opened her laptop and checked the inn registrations. *No guests until Friday, and I forgot to text Morgan.*

She texted Morgan. "Had breakfast. Waiting for the program to start."

Morgan replied, "Darlene wants breakfast details."

Jenna smiled. "Scrambled egg and grits."

"You have Darlene's approval. Katy's a good girl. We all miss you."

Jenna sniffled back a tear. *If today doesn't go well, I'll leave. Correction. If this morning doesn't go well, I'm outta here.*

While Jenna typed up her notes for Morgan, she couldn't block out the conversations as people came into the conference room. *I wish I'd brought my in-ear hearing protection.*

Jenna furrowed her brow when she realized she was keeping a mental tally of people who disliked Victor and people who were definitely not fond of Delilah. She jotted down the numbers. *So far, they're about even.*

"Is this going to be a sales pitch?" a woman sitting at a table in the middle of the room asked.

"Probably, but you should still take notes because she's making lots of money, and her guests love her."

"I hear she's a tyrant and went through five assistants in the six months before Mia joined her three years ago. Mia must be a saint."

When Calliope and Gary joined Jenna, she was thankful they interrupted the wave of conversations around her.

"You picked the perfect table, but what's with this carpet?" Calliope picked up Jenna's coat and handed it to her. Jenna slid her laptop back into the backpack.

"It's geared up for the ugly sweater contest." Gary sat on the other side of Jenna. "We would have been here sooner, Jenna, but we had to linger over finding our name tags because we were busy listening to an argument over who would introduce Delilah."

"Delilah wanted Mia to introduce her, but the president of the association, Twyla, insisted it was her job," Calliope said. "Gary and I were certain Twyla had plans to sabotage Delilah, but decided that was too far-fetched because neither of us could come up with a reason for Twyla to discredit Delilah. I tried to get Gary to find us some popcorn while I grabbed a couple of chairs because it was quite a show."

"Mia is slick," Gary said. "I didn't see her sitting in one of those comfortable lobby chairs until she stood up and joined Twyla and Delilah. It was sad how hoarse she was."

Calliope giggled. "Delilah was completely deflated."

"Any bets on whether the president will slip in a dig during her introduction? This might just be the highlight of the whole conference." Gary rubbed his hands together. "Kendra will be sorry she didn't come along with me."

Twyla strolled to the front of the room with the grace of a cat. Her black, shoulder-length hair was sleek, and her makeup was artfully applied. She wore gray slacks and a fire-engine red silk blouse.

After she picked up the microphone, she glanced toward the hotel's audiovisual expert who sat at a small table against the far wall. "Is this on?"

He nodded and pointed at her.

Mia slipped into the chair next to Calliope. "Is it okay if I join you?"

"We'd enjoy your company. We heard about your terrible affliction." Calliope patted Mia's hand, and the two of them giggled.

"Well done," Gary added.

"Good morning, innkeepers." Twyla paused and raised her eyebrows.

She smiled at the enthusiastic response. "Good morning."

"Welcome to our new members, and I'm delighted to see so many returning members here today. I'm Twyla Hughes, the president of the innkeepers' association and the founder of Hughes Signature Events. I'm an experienced certified event planner. Before I launched my own business, I was Senior Director at a high-end destination event company in Atlanta. My specialties were corporate retreats, luxury weddings, and charity galas. My hobbies include rubbing elbows with the rich and famous."

She smiled and paused for the appreciative chuckles.

"Before we begin our scheduled sessions, I'd like to take a few moments to talk about our board nominations.

"Nominations for open board positions will be due two weeks after the close of this meeting. The election itself will be conducted electronically, and members will have one week to cast their votes after nominations close.

"I encourage each of you to take time over the next few days to meet and talk with potential candidates, and if you know someone who would make a positive, committed, and effective board member, please encourage them to run."

She nodded toward a table. "Would our new members please stand to be recognized?"

Three women and a man rose. Jenna remained seated, and Mia flashed her a thumbs up.

"If any of our new members would like to tell us your name and something about yourself, we'd love to get to know you."

The four new members glanced at each other and sat down so quickly it looked choreographed.

Twyla's cheeks reddened as she mumbled, "Thank you for being here with us."

A brief frown crossed her face as she turned and picked up the agenda from the podium.

Jenna raised an eyebrow. *That didn't go as planned.*

Twyla's voice regained its tone of authority. "Our keynote speaker, Delilah Drake, is a lifelong resident of Savannah. Her parents owned an Italian restaurant, and Delilah began bussing tables at an early age. She has delighted us all with her stories of climbing up onto a chair to reach glasses that were in the middle of the table or chasing down a customer who pocketed their silverware."

Twyla paused and raised her eyebrows at Delilah, and the audience chuckled.

"Delilah is now a tour guide for haunted buildings and will enlighten us today with her presentation she has titled 'Find Your Niche and Make it Bigger.' Please join me in welcoming Delilah Drake."

Twyla feigned a golf clap, and the group applauded.

"Did you catch the tour guide dig?" Calliope whispered.

Jenna narrowed her eyes. "I think the president just turned off the microphone."

Gary shook his head. "Brutal."

Mia's eyes twinkled. "I believe that's pronounced deliciously brutal."

Jenna and Calliope snickered.

Delilah raised an eyebrow at Twyla, then turned on the microphone as she picked it up from the podium.

"Thank you so much. I'm Delilah Drake, the owner of Gravely Gracious Inns and Tours."

Delilah stepped away from the podium, and her stance and body language relaxed into a casual posture, and her voice took on an intimate, conversational tone. "People always ask me if I believe in ghosts. What a question. Believe in them? Honey, they are my bread and butter."

Delilah paused for the chuckles, and then her demeanor became serious, and her voice hinted of a warning.

Jenna shuddered as her skin crawled with an unknown dread. *Does she know there are thirteen steps between floors? She might have intended to be dramatic, but the warning is real.*

"Unfortunately, there are those who fake hauntings to boost their business, but there's more here than meets the eye or in this case, the ear. If you listen closely, you'll know I intend to reveal a truth about misguided funds that will shake the foundations of ghost tourism before the conference is over."

Delilah feigned a slight shudder, and a few people shuddered or rubbed their arms.

"See, in the world of this business we're in, most folks build a business plan, and others look for shortcuts to cheat the ghost story game. I built a business plan after my inspiration walked down the stairs and slammed a door. Her name is Temperance Thorne, and she's one of my most loyal, if not the most temperamental, residents at the Thorne House Inn, just outside of Savannah."

Delilah strolled away from the podium, slightly to her left, and then she stopped as she gazed at her listeners. Her eyes twinkled as though she was reliving a fond memory.

"Temperance lived in that house in the 1890s. She was a spinster piano teacher; southern to the bone and twice as stubborn. She had three rules: no piano on Sundays, no whiskey in the parlor, and no men allowed in the house past dusk unless they wore a collar or carried a Bible."

Delilah shifted her gaze to the other section of the room.

An icy chill ran down Jenna's back, and she shivered. *This is a true story.*

"The entire community was shocked when Temperance found herself a sweetheart. He was a traveling preacher with a slick smile and too much charm, according to the clucking neighbors when they peeked through their lace curtains. He promised her a ring and a future in Charleston, and she promised to write him every day until he returned. But what she got was a telegram saying he had married a sugarcane widow two counties over. Temperence was left alone to sit in her parlor with her piano silent and letters unwritten."

Delilah touched an earring when she paused, and the room remained silent in anticipation.

Jenna narrowed her eyes. *Temperance Thorne lived in the house, but the rest of this story is false.*

Delilah lifted her chin and spoke with conviction. "The river flooded that year in the fall. They say no one could reach her in time."

She lowered her voice. "But the neighbors said she waved them off and slipped under the water."

Jenna laid her hand on her pink opal pendant and frowned. *I need to check, but I think Temperance lived a long life.*

Delilah nodded at the sighs as she strolled back toward the podium.

She stopped and seemed to gaze at each person as she touched her ear, and everyone shifted forward in their seats. "Now, they say her piano echoes her favorite hymn when it rains, and the chandelier trembles."

Her voice became louder. "One man dared to carry a bottle of bourbon into the parlor, and the room turned ice cold. Did you ever feel regret creep up your spine like it was wearing lace gloves? That's Temperance, reminding us some rules don't die easy."

Jenna stared at Delilah, then narrowed her eyes. *There's a dark story behind Delilah's fairytale.*

"I need to check something." Jenna put her computer on the table.

After she connected to the internet, Jenna soon found what she was searching for. "Listen to this. Temperance Thorne died two months before her ninety-seventh birthday."

"So much for Temperance walking into a flood to drown," Calliope said.

Delilah stepped behind the podium and sighed as she lowered her head.

When she raised her head, she smiled.

Her tone shifted to business-savvy as her southern accent deepened. "Now, I didn't set out to run haunted bed-and-breakfasts, y'all. I was in marketing. I understand atmosphere, I understand storytelling, and I understand you don't just sell a room; you have to sell an experience. And in Savannah? Haunted sells."

"She got that much right," Gary whispered.

Jenna searched Delilah's face for answers. *Temperance's story was pivotal to Delilah's business. Why?*

Delilah slammed her hand on the podium. "But here's the truth: it only works if you're authentic. If your brand is strong. If the sheets are crisp, the biscuits are hot, and the ghosts feel like family that show up like clockwork even though you're not quite sure you invited them."

She smiled as heads nodded.

"My business, Gravely Gracious Inns and Tours, runs on three pillars: charm, curiosity, and chill bumps.

That's right; goosebumps have a conversion rate. I know because I've measured it. If you give someone a decent story that they can retell at the dinner table for years, they'll book again before they leave the porch swing." Delilah nodded and winked.

"Temperance Thorne may have lost her man, but thanks to her, I gained a waiting list and a bestselling candle scent called 'Sunday Silence.'"

"Good marketing," Calliope whispered.

Jenna nodded. "She's definitely tapped into the full potential of goosebumps, and I'm sold on her candles. Now, I want candles too."

Delilah continued, "So yes, I believe in ghosts. But more than that, I believe in stories. And I believe in turning grief, grudges, greed, and ghost tales into good business."

Delilah's words sliced into Jenna's heart. *Her motto is whatever it takes.*

A woman in the front raised her hand.

Delilah smiled. "Let's take a few questions, and then I'll wrap up." Delilah held the microphone close to the woman who asked, "Were you ever scared to stay in one of your own inns?"

Delilah chuckled. "Scared? Heavens to Betsy, only when the biscuits burned. The ghosts? They have better manners than most weekend guests, but don't let that get around. I always say if the spirit pays rent in goosebumps, they're welcome to stay."

A man in the middle of the room raised his hand, and Delilah rushed to him with the mic.

"How did you turn ghost stories into a profitable business?"

"By understanding that fear is a thrill, and stories are currency. People don't just want a place to sleep; they want something to talk about. I give them mystery, history, and southern hospitality and charge extra for a monogrammed robe."

The man chuckled. "Got it."

A woman who was sitting behind Delilah raised her hand and cleared her throat.

Delilah turned with the microphone and stood next to the woman.

The woman asked, "What's the most haunted place you own?"

"Oooh, that's like asking a mother which one of her littles is her favorite child, assuming her children regularly slammed doors and rearranged the silverware. But the Thorne House has the most 'activity,' as the ghost hunters like to call it. I just call it lively."

As Delilah returned to the podium, Jenna's stomach churned as she stared at Delilah. *Does Delilah know Temperance is not happy with her lies?*

"I have a question," a man sitting at a table in front of the podium said as Delilah walked past him.

She held the microphone close to him.

He asked, "Have you ever made up a ghost story just to help with bookings?"

That's why. I wonder if it's worth it.

Delilah continued to the podium as she answered, "Never had to. Savannah's got more drama than a

Southern soap opera, and the dead just keep on whispering. My job's not invention; it's curation."

The conference room lights flickered.

Jenna snorted. "I believe Temperance begs to differ."

Gary stared at the lights. "You might be right."

Delilah stood at the podium. "One last question, and I'll ask it. What advice do I have for entrepreneurs, especially women? My answer is don't wait for permission. Own your story, even the messy, weird, or haunted parts because that's where your magic is."

Delilah furrowed her brow. "When I started out, my niche wasn't just narrow, it was downright peculiar. Haunted inns? Ghost tours with etiquette? Selling goosebumps with a side of grits? But here's what I learned: the weirder your niche, the stronger your story. The stronger your story, the bigger your brand."

When Delilah nodded, a majority of her audience nodded with her.

"So if you've found something that makes people pause, lean in, or whisper, 'Wait, what do you do exactly?' You're not too niche. You're just in your early niche. And your job isn't to fit in; it's to stand out, show up, and serve something unforgettable."

She smiled, and her voice was strong. "Find your niche, then make it bigger. Invite people in. Hang up the 'Welcome' sign. Light the chandelier, even if it flickers sometimes." Delilah tentatively glanced up, then quietly exhaled.

Delilah gazed at the audience. "Because whether you're hosting the living or the dead, if you lead with authenticity, hospitality, and a little mischief, your people will find you. And they'll come back with friends. Thank you."

The group jumped to their feet as they applauded.

"This is my cue." Mia dashed out the door.

Twyla joined Delilah at the podium with a genuine smile.

"Thank you so much, Delilah. You have given us much to ponder, and I know I'm not the only one who couldn't take notes fast enough. I also know you have a surprise for us. Why don't you tell everyone what you have brought?"

"Thank you, I would love to. So many people have asked me to write a book for entrepreneurs, and so I did. Y'all are the first to hear about it. It's called Gravely Gracious with the subtitle, Build a Brand That Haunts. My assistant has set up a table outside this room, and we have a limited supply of signed books for you to hold, inhale, and take home. Thank you again for your kind attention. I love you all."

The applause and sharp whistles filled the room. Jenna cringed at the noise, then dashed out of the conference room.

Calliope and Gary followed her out to the lobby.

"Is the noise too much for you?" Gary asked. "Kendra has sensitive hearing."

Jenna leaned against a column to steady herself and nodded.

Calliope handed Jenna her coat and backpack. "The topic for the panel session is Shortcuts to Success, but I think that's what Delilah already covered. Isn't the answer to success finding your own niche?"

"I've kind of had my fill of niche drama. Delilah may have a keen eye for business, but her dramatic story was not as true as she claimed," Jenna said.

"Most people think she's charismatic, but even if she's a phony, she's entertaining," Gary said. "So, what do you want to do instead?"

Jenna exhaled. "Take a quiet coffee break, then go to the panel discussion."

Calliope nodded. "The coffee shop will be deserted because everyone is in line. We can go in there. I need a cinnamon roll."

Jenna glanced at the number of people in line to buy Delilah's book. "Her public personality is definitely charismatic."

Two women who were carrying sacks with the Gravely Gracious Inns and Tours logo on them strolled past them. One whispered, "Did you notice the copyright?"

The other woman said, "I looked at it as soon as I saw the cover."

"I flipped through the book, and I'm not sorry I bought it. Finding your niche does make a lot of sense. Delilah is definitely a talented storyteller, isn't she?"

"Did you hear what they said about the copyright?" Jenna asked.

Gary shook his head. "No, but I think I should get Delilah's book for Kendra. She's a planner. If she likes the idea, she'll run with it."

"I'll wait for the movie," Calliope said. "We'll be in the coffee shop, Gary. Do you really want a cinnamon roll? I'll grab you one before they are all gone."

"That would be great; I'll be there as soon as I can."

After Jenna and Calliope sat at a table away from the door, they ordered coffee and cinnamon rolls, including one for Gary.

"Why did the story about Temperance Thorne bother you?" Calliope asked.

"I'm extra sensitive to things and people especially when I touch them, but I've never been so in tune with just a story. The only thing that rang true about Delilah's story was Temperance Thorne lived in the Thorne House. It bothered me when Delilah said she didn't make up stories about the inns. There was a dark side to Delilah's story that she was hiding, but I don't know what it was." Jenna took a bite of her cinnamon roll.

"A dark side? Temperance's story wasn't true? How do you know?"

"I felt it."

Calliope examined Jenna's face. "You said you're extra sensitive to touch. Is that why you don't shake hands or want people to touch you?"

Jenna raised her eyebrows. "You're really observant."

Calliope shrugged. "I notice things. Like, are you going to eat all of your cinnamon roll?"

Jenna grinned. "Yes. I'm just slow."

Calliope took the last bite of her pastry, then stared into her coffee cup. "I need a refill of my coffee. What about you?"

Jenna drained her cup. "I'm out too."

"I heard that." The server smiled as she breezed to their table and refilled their cups. "Anything else?"

"No, thank you." Jenna smiled.

"I need one more bite of cinnamon roll; what about you, Jenna? Would you like to split one?" Calliope asked.

"I'm not sure I can finish this one, so I'll have to pass."

"Maybe Gary would like another half," Calliope said.

"One cinnamon roll coming up." The server disappeared.

While they waited for Gary, the coffee shop filled up with people carrying Gravely Gracious Inns and Tours sacks.

When Gary joined them, he put three Gravely Gracious Inns and Tours sacks on the table. The server set a cup on their table and filled it, and Calliope slid his cinnamon roll toward him.

He smiled. "Thanks."

After he sat, he said, "It was the darnedest thing. When I reached Mia, she picked up three sacks she had on the floor next to her and told me these were the three books Jenna had paid for. When did you pay for three books, Jenna?"

Jenna giggled. "Never. I think sneaky Mia gifted us the books."

Calliope pulled a book out of a sack. "Look at this. The authors are Amelia Cross and Delilah Drake."

"Could our Mia be Amelia Cross?" Gary stared at the cover.

Calliope frowned. "Mia could be a nickname for Amelia. Do we know her last name?"

"I don't, but who owns the copyright?" Jenna asked.

Calliope opened the book. "You probably already guessed the copyright owner is Amelia Cross."

"Does that mean our business expert is really Mia?" Gary pulled his book out of its sack.

Jenna tapped her index on the tabletop as she stared at the cover. "Maybe we'll be able to tell by the voice of the author. Now, I have to read it."

"Or we could take a shortcut and ask Mia," Gary said.

"What's the fun of that?" Calliope rolled her eyes.

Frankie came into the coffee shop and furrowed her brow as she scanned the crowd for a seat.

"Do you mind if I invite someone to join us?" Jenna asked.

"Not at all. Who's your friend?" Gary asked.

Jenna waved at Frankie to catch her attention. When Frankie saw her, she smiled and began weaving her way toward their table.

"A woman who offered to punch Victor Grimes in the nose on my behalf when he assumed I was here with my mother."

"I like her already." Calliope narrowed her eyes. "Oh wait, I know Frankie."

When Frankie joined them, Jenna introduced her to Calliope and Gary as the server stopped by the table with an empty cup and her bottomless coffee pot.

While she poured coffee into the cup, the server said, "We have cranberry orange scones and commercial bear claws left."

"Cranberry orange scone, please," Frankie said.

"Good choice." The server disappeared.

"What did you think of Delilah Drake's keynote?" Calliope asked.

"I've heard Delilah speak before. She's good at what she does," Frankie said.

Calliope and Jenna exchanged a glance.

Gary rolled his eyes and rose. "I'll see you at the breakout session. I owe Kendra a call. I'll pick up our tab since Jenna so kindly purchased our books."

He chuckled as he headed to the cashier.

Calliope sighed. "I have to call Mom. I promised I'd call her after Delilah's keynote to give her an update. I'll grab a table for the panel discussion if Mom and I aren't on the phone too long."

After Calliope left, Frankie asked, "What did you think about Delilah?"

"I'm not really a fan, but her talk made sense," Jenna said.

Frankie nodded. "She's definitely an impressive speaker. The story she told about the Thorne House and Temperance wasn't true, of course, so I was surprised when she claimed she never made up a story. What's worse is the way she came to own Thorne House."

Jenna stared at Frankie. *Why is Frankie so bitter about the Thorne House?*

Chapter Four

"How did Delilah become the owner of the Thorne house?" Jenna asked.

"The elderly owners weren't well enough to keep up with necessary maintenance and put the Thorne house up for sale, but because of the state of disrepair, buyers were not interested in the house. Unfortunately, both of them died before it sold," Frankie said.

"So they didn't have any heirs?"

"They had had only one child, a boy, who drowned while he was in high school. He was their only relative."

"That's terribly tragic, isn't it? At least they had each other."

Frankie nodded. "The story of the Thorne house turned dark when a rumor spread that the people who had lived in the house died suddenly under horrible circumstances at the hands of a malevolent ghost, Temperance Thorne. The estate didn't have enough funds left to cover the accumulated property taxes, but before it went into foreclosure, Delilah Drake bought it from the estate for a fraction of its worth."

Jenna stared at her. *What is it about the Thorne house that brings out lies?*

"That's quite convenient. Was Delilah the source of the rumors?" Jenna asked.

"A lot of us think she was, but it could have been Victor Grimes because the two of them have always been in competition. She could have slipped in her offer before he had a chance," Frankie said.

The server brought Frankie her coffee and scone, then hovered the pot over Jenna's cup. "More coffee?"

Jenna smiled. "No, thank you."

After the server left, Jenna said, "I hate to abandon you, but I need to check in at home too. Do you mind?"

"Not at all. I appreciate you waving me down, so I'd have a place to sit. This place is still packed."

Jenna glanced around. "Sure is. Are you going to the panel discussion?"

Frankie smiled. "I'm on the panel, so I guess I better be there."

"That's exciting. I will definitely be going then." Jenna returned Frankie's smile.

After she was in the lobby, she furrowed her brow. *I can't call Morgan or Ethan because it's too public here.* She glanced toward the hall to the elevator and stairs then checked the time on the enormous clock on the wall over the registration desk. *I wouldn't have enough time to go to my room even if I didn't hate the stairs.*

She glanced again at the hallway and spotted a young woman in a gray housekeeper's uniform. Her hair was pulled into a ponytail, and she pushed a cart towards the first floor rooms. *There's Lucy.*

While Jenna strode across the lobby toward the hallway, Lucy glanced up and smiled.

When Jenna reached the cart, Lucy said, "I'll show you where the ice machine is, ma'am."

Jenna followed Lucy down the hall and heard the thunk of ice dropping. After they went into a small room with vending machines and the ice machine, Lucy smiled. "Sorry I had to be so weird and impersonal, but the housekeeping manager has a rule against housekeepers chatting with guests. I think he's afraid we might tell some of the hotel's dirtiest secrets."

Jenna giggled. "That was a terrible pun."

"Thank you, ma'am." Lucy curtsied. "So, how's your day so far?"

"Interesting to say the least. When I attended professional accounting conferences, I thought nobody could be as jealous and petty as accountants, but today has proven me wrong."

Lucy chuckled. "That's actually been true of every conference I've seen here. Some people are at their worst when they're away from home, aren't they? Are you going on the hotel tour this afternoon?"

"I'm looking forward to it."

"Good, because I'm going to be assisting with it by making sure no one gets lost. If you hang with me, I'll fill you in on some tidbits that are left out of the official tour."

A door opened, then closed in the hallway.

"You're quite welcome, ma'am. If there's anything, just let us know."

Lucy winked, then hurried back to her cart.

Jenna stared at the vending machine then selected her favorite candy bar as a man and woman argued about their day's plans as they hurried toward the lobby.

She stuck her new emergency snack into her backpack, then strolled to the lobby and continued to the small conference room where the panel discussion was scheduled.

When she strolled into the room, Calliope said, "Mom said to tell you hello, and she can't wait to meet you. She may show up this evening and go to dinner with us, since we won't have any guests at our B&B until the day after tomorrow."

Jenna smiled. "That's great news; it will be fun to meet her."

Calliope rolled her eyes. "I'll have to warn you; she's nothing like me. Mom doesn't even have a tattoo."

"I'm sure we'll be fine." Jenna set her backpack on the table, then scanned the room. The carpet was muddy brown with stains, and the room smelled slightly musty with an undertone of citrus.

"This room hasn't been used in a while," Jenna said.

"When I got here, the maintenance man and his helper were scrambling to get it set up. I wonder if the original plan was to use the large conference room," Calliope said.

While other association members trickled into the room, Jenna said, "Frankie told me she was going to be on the panel."

Calliope's eyes twinkled. "Are we allowed to heckle her?"

Jenna giggled. "It depends on who else is on the panel. She might sit back to enjoy the fireworks and not say a word."

Gary joined them. "Speaking of fireworks, I think there may be a little warm up in the hall. Delilah announced she'd rather drink poison than sit on the panel with a charlatan. Twyla coaxed her into the manager's office for a chat."

"Really? I'm having a problem with rats in my room; they are hogging the bathtub. I believe I need to speak to the manager," Calliope pounded the table with her fist in feigned outrage as she pretended to rise.

Gary guffawed, and Jenna laughed until her sides ached.

After she regained her composure, Jenna asked, "Tub hogging rats?"

Calliope giggled. "It was the best I could come up with on such short notice."

When there was a sudden rush for seats, Jenna said, "Evidently Ms. Drake has been appeased."

A few minutes later, Twyla came into the room; her face grim. She was trailed by Delilah, her expression stern, Victor looking aloof, and Frankie, with a bemused smirk.

After the three panelists were seated at the table in front of their table mics, with Frankie in the middle, Twyla picked up her hand microphone.

"Welcome to our panel session, Shortcuts to Success. I'll introduce our panelists, but please hold your applause until the end."

Jenna wrinkled her nose when Victor glanced at a table near the door and winked.

When a woman at the table giggled, Calliope whispered, "Well, now we know who the wink was for."

"Delilah Drake is the founder of Gravely Gracious Inns and Tours. Delilah was our keynote speaker, so I've already introduced her."

Delilah nodded.

"Victor Grimes who is the genius behind Ghost Realms, Theatrical Paranormal Events hails from New Orleans where he gained fame with his paranormal events in the French Quarter."

Victor rose and bowed.

"Frankie Roberts worked for ten years in the meat department at a supermarket where she conceived her award-winning dynamic innovations to reshape the guest experience and operational efficiency in her now-legendary small boutique hotels. Frankie has repeatedly told us that an entrepreneur learns from experience and dedication."

Frankie smiled.

Twyla led the applause.

"Wow. Did you know that about Frankie?" Gary asked.

Jenna shook her head.

Twyla continued, "We have three questions for our panelists. One panelist will answer the question, and then the other two will provide additional information. To keep us on track with our schedule and to challenge our panel, we have established time limits. Our treasurer, Farah, will be our timekeeper." A slight woman, with her brown hair loosely pulled back into a bun at the nape of her neck sat at the table in front of the panelists' table. She raised her hand without turning around.

Twyla continued, "After we've gone through our three questions, our panelists will have five minutes to discuss one of our questions in more depth. Our first question is for Victor. Victor, you will have four minutes. What is one piece of practical advice you would give to someone who is starting out or struggling?"

When Victor rose, Twyla said, "Your mic is active, Victor. You have four minutes."

"I'm used to being on the stage. I always stand when I speak," he grumbled.

Victor glared at Twyla as he furrowed his brow in thought. "I recommend that anyone who is starting out take the time to write a business plan. Begin with a description of your new company, research your competition..."

Mia slipped in the door and sat next to Gary.

"Is everybody behaving?" she asked.

"So far," Jenna said.

"Victor is pompous, but I guess that's his norm," Calliope said.

"Time." Farah's soft, lilting voice sliced through Victor's pretentious lecture.

Jenna stared at the Farah. *How could a sweet, rhythmic voice like hers carry so much authority?*

"Can I finish my sentence?" Victor growled.

"Five seconds," Twyla said.

"What? Five seconds? That's not enough time for me to recall what I was ..."

"Time."

Victor glowered at Farah and crossed his arms.

"Delilah, you have two minutes to add your thoughts," Twyla said.

"What was the question?" Delilah asked.

Twyla raised her eyebrows, and Delilah's eyes narrowed as she pursed her lips.

The two of them glared at each other until Delilah said, "Everybody knows to start with a business plan, but I would have planned better if I'd known I was going to be the chef, housekeeper, bookkeeper, marketing manager, maintenance guy, and activities director all rolled into one. As it was..."

"Pretty boring, so far," Calliope said.

"Time."

"Frankie," Twyla said. "Your time starts now."

"I would advise anyone who is starting out to focus on their customer, not themselves, and to have a picture in their mind of who their ideal customer is. Draw a picture of them or write a description. How old are they? Are they married? What are their hobbies?"

Mia cocked her head. "That's a good idea."

"Time."

"Delilah, the next question is yours."

"Did you notice the oneupmanship? These are savvy, serious competitors," Gary said.

Twyla read the question. "What was the biggest challenge you have had as an innkeeper, and how did you overcome it?"

Delilah shook her head and exhaled. "One word. Money. I spent three years scraping by with one meal a day, walking instead of driving, and any other way I could think of to cut my expenses to the bare minimum so I could pay for my first house with cash."

"That's determination," Jenna said.

Mia rolled her eyes.

Jenna nodded. "You're right. I forgot for a minute that Delilah was speaking."

"She is convincing," Calliope said.

"Time."

"I don't get it. If I hadn't heard Delilah throw a fit about Victor being on the panel, I would be sitting here thinking the three of them were best buddies and would be going out together for a beer this evening," Gary said.

"Victor. Two minutes," Twyla said.

"My biggest challenge has been countering unethical practices," Victor said.

Mia rolled her eyes. "The president threatened all three of them with revoking their association membership if they stepped out of line, and they knew she would do it. She's not one to toss around idle threats. Victor's teetering on the edge, but if he can refrain from mentioning any names, he should be okay."

Jenna furrowed her brow. "Is association membership that important?"

"It is for them. It gives them creds in the community, including with county departments like zoning, for example. They also have political clout, which benefits them and occasionally helps the association. Twyla obviously considers any dramatics more detrimental to the association than the loss of its political contacts."

"Are we staying for the follow-ups?" Calliope asked.

"We can't all leave at once," Gary said.

"Dibs on leaving first," Calliope said.

"You got it. I'll get a little work done on my computer while we're sitting here," Jenna said.

"If there isn't a group meal planned for this evening, should we still meet in the lobby at six?" Calliope asked.

Gary nodded.

Jenna said, "Good idea. Six o'clock."

Calliope left, and Mia moved to Calliope's seat.

"Mia, did you write the Build a Brand that Haunts book?" Gary asked.

Mia stared at him, then chuckled. "Look at the last page."

Gary opened his book to the last page and furrowed his brow before showing it to Jenna.

Jenna laughed at the handwritten IYKYK. M.

"Why is it funny?" Gary asked.

"It stands for if you know, you know."

Gary smiled. "I feel like a kid in a secret club."

Mia glanced around the room. "People are packing up. I'm going to see if I can waylay them and sell a few more books before they disappear into their rooms."

"Meet us in the lobby at six if you'd like to join us for dinner," Jenna said.

"Thanks. I'd like that; I'll see you at six." Mia quietly left.

Twyla said, "This is our last question. Frankie, what is the most interesting trend you foresee?"

"In four minutes?" Frankie smiled. "Our businesses were typically built through hard work by one, or maybe two people who spent up to eighteen hours a day, seven days a week, growing and then sustaining their business."

"Something's been bothering me." Jenna put her computer on the table.

After she connected to the internet, she searched for the Hughes Signature Event. When she found the auditing company, her eyes widened.

"What did you find, Jenna?" Gary asked.

"See who Twyla lists as her auditors for the Hughes Signature Events?"

Jenna turned her laptop so Gary could see it.

"Is that good or bad?"

Jenna switched her screen to a different tab, and Gary's eyes widened. "Their principal auditor was sentenced for fraudulent filings?"

He shook his head. "Definitely not good."

Jenna nodded.

Frankie continued, "We're seeing a trend, especially among our younger owners, to embrace technology for efficiency. The obvious examples are security, registration, and marketing, but this next year we'll see..."

"Time."

"Frankie got lost in a ramble," Gary said. "I do that when I'm supposed to be delivering a speech."

"Victor, you have two minutes."

"The technology will of course, leap ahead."

While Victor droned on, Gary whispered, "Is he stealing Delilah's thunder? Sounds like he's quoting her. Gary whispered.

"No kidding; look at her face," Jenna said. "Do you suppose his comment about integrity was a dig at her?"

"Could have, now that you mention it."

"Time."

"Delilah, your time starts now," Twyla said.

"The personal touches Victor mentioned..."

"I wish Kendra could hear this. Is this supposed to be recorded?"

Jenna nodded. "They'll send us the link after the conference."

"Time."

"Wow, she is the queen of spin, isn't she?" Gary said.

"The six minutes she had to think about it was an enormous advantage for her, and she listened to what the others said so she could build on their ideas, not duplicate," Jenna said. "I hate to admit it, but that was a brilliant strategy."

"I'm going to stretch my legs," Gary said. "I think I've hit my limit for sitting. See you later."

"Let's shake up our order," Twyla said. "Frankie, you have five minutes. Pick one question and do a deeper dive. Your time starts now."

Frankie nodded at the audience, and a few reflexively returned her nod. "Because most of our members in attendance have at least five years of experience, I'd like to spend more time on the trends we can expect in the next two to four years."

That was an interesting fact. I'd check to see if it's true, but I don't really care.

Jenna slipped her new book and her laptop into her backpack, picked up her coat, and left.

When she was in the hallway, Mia was arranging books on her table. "Did you give up?"

"I heard there was a library. I thought I'd see what I could find."

"I browsed in the library for a while this morning. It's next to the coffee shop. They have a small selection of books about the hotel. If I weren't a responsible person, I would still be sitting in one of their ancient chairs with broken springs poking me while I read with my shoes off and my feet propped up on a rickety footstool."

"That does sound tempting."

When Jenna entered the small, dimly lit library, she inhaled the sweet, earthy fragrance of old books. *This takes me back to all the times I found sanctuary in my elementary school library.*

Jenna closed the library door behind her, and all the noises from the lobby and the coffee shop were muffled. *I've stepped into a different world.*

She smiled as she strolled past the racks of books, then was drawn to the end of the rack where a ring of recessed lights created a halo on a small bookcase.

The lights seem to be concentrated on an old, slim book with a frayed spine. Jenna picked up the book and stared at the title, "Secrets and Sins of the Glenwood Hotel."

She glanced around and spotted an old black leather upholstered chair with splits in the leather seat in a corner with a floor lamp next to the chair.

When she turned on the old lamp, it cast a soft glow as she settled into the chair, the worn cushion yielding to her weight like a soft, well-used glove.

Jenna sighed as she opened the book. An envelope fell out of the book. This must have been used as a bookmark.

After she was halfway through the book, she exhaled and flipped back to check the title of the chapter she had just read. *Spectral Illusions for Stage and Séance.*

She raised her eyebrows. *This book was written to expose an illusionist.*

Jenna checked the copyright page. "Original copyright date was 1897. That's interesting."

After Jenna finished skimming the book, she put the envelope back into the book close to where it had slipped out, then returned the book to the shelf. *I'm glad I found the book before the tour. I'd love to know more about the hotel's trapdoors, rigging, and hidden exits.*

As she strolled toward the door, Jenna noticed a sign she hadn't seen earlier. "Feel free to take the book you'd love to read to your room. We'll retrieve it after you check out. Enjoy your stay!"

Jenna returned to the shelf and slipped the book into her backpack.

When she stepped into the lobby, the line had gone down, and Mia was packing away books.

"There you are," Mia said. "Calliope and Gary were looking for you. The hotel just opened the conference room doors where lunch is being served."

"I'll go find them then. Are you coming?"

"I'm not registered."

"Then don't eat a lot. We'll make room for you."

"I'll be right there."

Jenna hurried into the conference room and smiled at Gary and Calliope who stood at their table.

"Sorry I'm slow. I lost track of time."

"Mia told us you'd gone to the library, so we waited for you while we guarded the table. Is Mia coming?" Calliope asked.

"Yes, she was packing books."

"I'll stay at the table while you two grab your food," Gary said.

Jenna followed Calliope who stepped in front of a woman who smiled.

"Thanks for saving our place in line."

"You're quite welcome. Tell your mom hello for me. This crowd really goes into a frenzy when the food comes out, doesn't it?"

"Sure does."

Calliope whispered, "Jenna, put a little extra on your plate; there might not be much left by the time Gary and Mia make it to the line."

Jenna nodded. When Calliope picked up two plates and stacked one on top of the other, Jenna copied her.

Jenna selected a ham sandwich and a turkey sandwich and put two small bags of chips on top of the sandwiches. They skipped the potato salad and baked beans, but picked up two cupcakes each.

At the end of the line, Calliope grabbed a handful of napkins, and Jenna stuck a handful of condiments into her pocket.

When they returned to the table, Mia was there. "We realized you two were getting our food, so Gary left to get our drinks."

While Mia cleared the table of coats, Calliope and Jenna divided the food onto the extra plates.

"I forgot condiments," Calliope said.

Jenna emptied her pocket. "I picked them up while you got the napkins."

"There's not a bank-robbing gang alive that's as slick as we are," Calliope said.

Mia chuckled. "No kidding."

Gary returned with four bottles of cola. After he set down the bottles on the table, he said, "The drink table is a cluster because people are picking through the coolers. Nobody was interested in this off-brand, but it's wet and cold, so that's what we got."

While they ate, Gary said, "I didn't expect to come away from here with any ideas, but Kendra and I had a long discussion about what our niche might be. There is a popular lake four miles from us, and we're the only bed-and-breakfast that is less than an hour away. An old friend of mine owns a boat rental business. We plan to talk to him about a marketing package of a four-day stay at the inn and a three-day boat rental. Kendra will call my friend's wife to see if we can get together for lunch next Monday."

"I love that idea," Mia said. "If you decide to go with it, hire me for five dollars, and I'll develop the marketing plan for you. Of course, I'd have to stay at your bed-and-breakfast for a weekend so I can capture the right vibe for you."

Gary grinned. "Will you include us in your next book?"

"You might be the star."

"Do you have time for me to pick your brain this afternoon, Mia?" Gary asked.

"I would love it. I'll talk to the manager and wrangle a small conference room for us at three. Does that work for you? Anyone else interested?"

"Mom and I would be. Do you mind if we crash your meeting, Gary?" Calliope asked.

"Not at all. I have all kinds of questions, but I don't know what they are."

"I love collaboration," Mia said.

"Do you write only nonfiction?" Jenna stared at the second half of her sandwich then pushed back her plate.

"Nonfiction is all I have published," Mia said. "I have several unfinished fiction novels."

"Really? What genre?" Calliope asked.

Mia chuckled. "I don't really know, which is probably why I can't finish them."

"On a more serious note, aren't you going to eat the rest of your sandwich?" Gary peered at Jenna's plate.

"No, do you want it?" Jenna slid the plate toward him.

After he reached for the sandwich, she said, "Now I can eat my cupcake." She carefully cut it in half.

Gary's eyes twinkled. "Do I get the second half of your cupcake too?"

"No way. This is my bedtime snack unless Calliope's bath rats come to my room for their snack."

Calliope's mouth was full of cupcake, so she put her hand up to cover her mouth so she could talk without being completely rude. "You can't have my bath rats."

She smiled and finished her bite while the other three laughed.

After Jenna finished eating half of her cupcake, she said, "I expected Frankie to join us. We have enough room."

Mia stared at her cupcake. "I don't think I can resist eating all of mine. Frankie sat with a different group; it's her style to work the room." Mia took a big bite.

"That's interesting," Calliope said. "We enjoy your company, but wouldn't you sell more books if you did that too?"

Mia shrugged and then finished eating her bite. "I might, but I don't care. I'd rather step away from the professional buy-my-book mode and refresh my soul with friends who make me laugh."

She picked up her cupcake. "I hate to eat and run, but I was supposed to clear the book table right after lunch, so I better jump on it."

"Before you go," Gary said, "shouldn't we exchange numbers?"

"Brilliant," Mia said.

After they exchanged numbers, Mia left.

Gary rose. "I'm feeling bad about all the extra work that's fallen on Kendra's shoulders. I'm going to work in my room this afternoon until our meeting with Mia. I'll see you at dinner."

Jenna said, "Don't worry about the table. I'll take care of it."

When Gary left, Calliope said, "Do you mind if I leave you? I want to watch for Mom; she should be here any minute. I'll take the bottles and the trash."

"If you'll take the bottles to the recycle, I'll take all the trash when I take mine to the bin."

After Calliope left, Jenna was alone in the conference room. She smiled at the silence as she savored each bite of her cupcake. After she finished the first half, she sighed, then wrapped up the other half in a napkin.

While Jenna collected the trash, Delilah rushed into the conference room.

"Where's my assistant?" she growled. "She was supposed to wait for me at the book table, but she's gone, and so is the table."

"She probably took the books to her car."

Delilah clutched an overstuffed, nine-inch by twelve-inch padded envelope to her chest. "These are all my notes for my second book, and I can't be carrying them around like some poorly paid office clerk. It completely ruins my image."

Delilah started toward the door then turned back and marched up to Jenna's table. Jenna braced herself in anticipation of Delilah's overpowering perfume, but caught only a whiff of a floral scent.

Delilah held out the padded envelope toward Jenna. "Make yourself useful. Give this to my assistant and tell her she should not be careless for a change and leave it lying around where just anybody could pick it up and read it, and tell her my bottle of perfume is missing too. I reported it to the hotel management, and they said I must be mistaken, but they will check with housekeeping, so now I need a good lawyer. Who is yours?"

Jenna glared at her. "I don't have a lawyer."

Delilah snorted. "Of course, you don't. What was I thinking? Let her know I'm holding her personally responsible if someone else gets hold of this and publishes it before I do, especially that old crook, Victor. He'd just love to get something on me, but I'm not the fraud, so it must be him."

After she slammed the envelope on the table, Delilah stormed out of the room.

"You forgot to say please," Jenna called out. *I guess she was moving too fast to hear me. Just as well.* Jenna looked at her cupcake, then took a big bite.

Chapter Five

Jenna polished off her cupcake before she picked up Delilah's envelope. She immediately dropped it onto the table when she was nearly smothered by intense sadness. She stared at the envelope. *What was that all about?*

She quickly stuffed the envelope into her backpack and slung the strap over her shoulder. She sighed as she gathered the trash and picked up her coat.

After Jenna carried her trash to the bin, Frankie came into the room and waited for Jenna at the door.

"Are you still going on the tour, Jenna?" Frankie asked as they walked out together into the lobby.

Jenna furrowed her brow. *I don't remember discussing the tour with Frankie. Maybe she saw the hotel's list.* "Probably not. I have some unfinished work I'd like to catch up on. What about you?"

"You'll be missing out on a great opportunity." Frankie smiled. "Twyla's trying to get a count for dinner tonight. Are you going?"

"I hadn't heard anything."

"There's a sign-up sheet at the registration desk." Frankie rolled her eyes. "Delilah, Victor, and I were supposed to get the word out, but I haven't seen them around. I'd appreciate it if you'd help me spread the word. Sorry, but I have to dash. I'll see you later."

Frankie hurried out the front door.

Jenna raised her eyebrows. *She didn't answer my question.* Jenna shrugged. *She probably didn't hear me; she seemed really distracted.*

Jenna joined the line at the registration desk. While she waited behind a woman who sighed heavily every few minutes and muttered about the slowness of the line, she sighed too. *Am I speaking too softly? Delilah didn't answer me, and neither did Frankie.*

When it was her turn, the clerk smiled as Jenna approached the desk.

Jenna returned Lucy's smile. "Isn't this early for you?"

"The hotel's a little shorthanded today, and the hotel manager couldn't figure out how to clone anybody, so here I am. I saw the electrician a few minutes ago. He said he fixed your light, but when I asked him what the problem was, he told me I wouldn't understand. I gave him my best glare, and he ran off. I can only hope he was in tears." Lucy peered at Jenna, and Jenna chuckled appreciatively.

Lucy continued, "I suspect the lights didn't flicker when he turned them on, so he's taking full credit for fixing them. Let me know if you're still having a problem. So, that's my news. How can I help you?"

"I was told there was a sign-up sheet for dinner tonight."

"There was, but the president pulled it because she said she had a headache and couldn't deal with it."

"I'm not surprised. She was herding rattlesnakes, not cats, all morning." Jenna turned to leave. "Are you still assisting with the tour?"

"Sure am."

"Good." Jenna strolled to one of the comfortable lobby chairs and sat where she could see the registration and the clock.

After she settled in her chair, she stuffed her backpack next to her side and sent a text to Morgan. "Good day so far; how are you?"

Her phone rang. *Morgan.*

"Hey, Jenna, are you okay?" Morgan asked.

Jenna frowned. "Yes, why? You sound worried."

"It was probably a prank, so I didn't say anything to Shane or Ethan. There was a voicemail message on the inn's phone, and the voice of the caller sounded mechanical, you know, like they disguise voices on the true crime shows. Anyway, whoever it was said to tell Jenna to mind her own business because busybodies have short lives. Just from the echo of the background noise, I'm pretty sure they were calling from the lobby, but I also heard bells jingle."

Jenna furrowed her brow. *The elevator?* "Did the bells sound close?"

"I don't know. They were clear, and the conversations weren't, if that helps."

Helps a lot. "If it's a prank, it isn't funny."

"I agree. I checked, and the phone number was for the hotel where you're staying. Just be careful."

"It sounds like I'll be fine if I just mind my own business. That won't be hard to do."

"Are you kidding me?" Morgan snorted. "That's almost impossible for you to do. Do me a favor and don't be brave. So, now that we have that straight, what's on your agenda for this afternoon besides minding your own business?"

"I'm going on a guided tour of the hotel. Lucy is assisting on the tour and will fill in the details that are being sanitized because the guests are delicate or management is hiding something. You know which way my vote would go."

"I'm jealous."

"Drop everything and come join me."

"I'd love to, but Boss Lady would fire me."

Jenna giggled. "What a tyrant."

"Speaking of which, I was in the middle of updating the registration book for this weekend; I want to get it updated before Darlene checks it. I'll talk to you later. Wait a minute; Katy's staring at me. Tell her hello."

"I miss you, Katy." Jenna brushed back a tear.

"Eww. Katy licked my phone, so I think she sent kisses," Morgan said.

Jenna smiled. "Good girl."

After they hung up, Jenna's eyes widened as Delilah and Victor came into the hotel from outside. *Why are they smiling?*

Jenna gaped when they hugged, then Delilah headed toward the hall to the elevator and stairs, while Victor beelined to join the small group gathered in front of the registration desk. *Wow.*

Jenna sent a text to Ethan. "Strange day so far. I miss Katy and you."

She chuckled as she read his reply. "We miss you more."

Her phone rang. She glanced around, but no one was nearby as she answered.

She whispered, "You made me laugh."

Jenna could hear the smile in his voice. "We aim to please, ma'am. How was your morning?"

"I'm surprised at how much I'm learning, and I have three friends, so I don't feel like I'm here alone."

Ethan exhaled. "Shane and I are at his office. I'm sorry, but I thought I'd have a few minutes to talk. Our client has shown up early; I wish it were you instead. Are you sure you can't leave early?"

Jenna sighed. "It's tempting, but I should stay. It would be rude to leave early since they gave me a scholarship."

"You're right." Ethan hung up.

Jenna frowned. *That was abrupt. Was he in a hurry, or does he think I'm wasting my time?*

Jenna glanced at the small group that had gathered near the reception area. Victor had eased away from the group then slowly turned and strolled toward the hallway for the main floor rooms then stopped and scanned the room.

A small group of elderly women came into the hotel with their luggage and made their way to the registration desk. By the time all of them were through the long line and on their way to their rooms, Victor was no longer in the lobby.

An overweight, middle-aged man in a short-sleeved white dress shirt, gray flannel slacks, and a paisley tie that ended three quarters of the way down his shirt came out of the hotel office. After he motioned for the behind-the-scenes tour group to follow him, Jenna gathered up her backpack and coat and joined the group.

"I'm here," Lucy whispered from behind Jenna. "Marvin is the tour guide. Let the group get a few steps ahead of you."

Marvin led the small group of six past the large conference room and two small conference rooms. "We will take the freight elevator because it is large enough for our group."

He stopped in front of the wide elevator doors and tapped the control panel with his hotel ID before he pressed a button. When the doors opened, he stepped inside, and the group followed him. Lucy was on Jenna's right and pointed to the back corner on the right side. Jenna strolled to the corner, and Lucy followed her.

When the elevator stopped at the fourth floor, the elevator groaned, then swayed slightly. There was a collective sigh of relief when the front and back doors of the elevator opened.

"This way, please." Marvin stepped out the front door and flipped on the lights. Jenna followed Lucy out the back door.

Jenna shivered and put on her coat.

After the elevator doors closed, Lucy said, "The fourth floor isn't heated. Marvin will show his group a guest room that has been staged with mannequins. I think it's creepy, but it's supposed to be a peek into the life of a couple that would have stayed in the hotel in the late 1890s. The clothing and furnishings aren't authentic, but they are true to the era. We'll catch up with the group in just a second, but I wanted to show you what the Glenwood Hotel was really famous for."

Jenna glanced at the surroundings. "Smells musty, like it's been closed up for a long time. What's that light, sweet smell?"

Lucy bit her lip. "It's bat guano, but Marvin claims it's the lingering perfume of flappers."

Jenna giggled. "Seriously?"

Lucy shrugged. "He told me bat guano sounded too esoteric. I think he doesn't know what it is."

Jenna peered down the dimly lit hallway. "When were the low wattage hall lights installed?"

"I think they were installed in the mid-1990s as part of a complete renovation of the hotel. The original plan was to recreate the entire fourth floor as a reproduction of the hotel in the 1890s, but after the huge budget overrun for the renovation of the first three floors, all work stopped."

As Jenna followed Lucy down the narrow hallway, Lucy said, "When prohibition swept the country, part of the theater on the third floor was blocked off and turned into a hidden room with a pull down staircase in the ceiling. The speakeasy was on the fourth floor."

Lucy stopped at a door, then pulled out a small flashlight from her pocket. "This was the speakeasy."

When they went into the room, Jenna stared at the dust-covered bar with a brass rail.

"Hotel management still talks about moving the old bar to the first floor since they have a license to sell alcohol, but it's one of those things that never became a priority."

"That bar is absolutely gorgeous. I wish I had a dustcloth and some wood oil." Jenna sighed.

"I agree completely. I'd like you to see something else; let's go behind the bar."

Lucy shined her light on the floor behind the bar. "What do you see?"

A mouse ran to the wall.

"Besides the mouse?" Jenna giggled.

Lucy chuckled. "There are probably quite a few mice up here. When we turned on the lights, they hid."

Jenna peered at the floor. "Just an ordinary wooden floor." Her pink opal felt warm against her skin. *Different board.*

Jenna slowly scrutinized the floor, then pointed. "This floorboard is different."

"I don't know how you found it, but you're right." Lucy pulled out a multi-tool from her pocket and carefully pried up the board then pulled the handle that was underneath it and lifted a three-foot by three-foot section of the floorboards.

"Wow." Jenna gazed at the room below. "Was this an escape hatch?"

"It certainly was." Lucy pointed at the iron ring attached to the bottom of the boards she had lifted. "There would have been a sturdy rope attached to the ring by a slipknot."

"How can you lift those boards so easily? They look like they'd be heavy."

Lucy nodded. "And they are, so look closer."

Jenna narrowed her eyes. "I see a rod on the side. It's hydraulic, isn't it?"

"Good eye." Lucy closed the hatch, then put the board that hid the handle back into place. "Are you ready to join Marvin and the group? I have more to show you on the third floor."

Jenna and Lucy found Marvin and the group in front of the freight elevator.

"The plan to renovate this floor and restore it to its original roots is on schedule for next year." Marvin pressed the button for the elevator.

Jenna raised her eyebrows as she and Lucy exchanged glances. Lucy rolled her eyes, and Jenna smirked.

When the freight elevator doors opened, everyone filed in. As the door closed, the woman who stood nearest to Marvin asked, "Does the rest of the fourth floor have guest rooms like the one we saw?"

"Exactly as we saw, minus the mannikins and most of the furniture, which has been moved downstairs. You'll see some of it in the library."

"He doesn't have a clue," Lucy whispered, and Jenna nodded.

When the elevator doors opened on the unfinished, dimly lit third floor, everyone filed out.

"This section of the third floor is blocked off from the updated guest rooms," Marvin said. "It was once a movie theater. The plan for next year is to convert it into guest rooms. As you can see from the length of the hallway, our accommodations will be greatly expanded. If you'll return to the elevator, we'll end our tour with a surprise for you."

Lucy pointed to an alcove, and she and Jenna stepped back into the shadows.

The group murmured their approval and quickly returned to the elevator.

"Has Marvin even been to the rest of the fourth floor?" Jenna asked.

Lucy snorted. "Obviously not."

After the elevator doors closed, Lucy said, "This half of the third floor used to be a ballroom, but before that it was a vaudeville theater with a stage."

Lucy opened the door to the former ballroom Marvin had described as a movie theater and turned on her flashlight. "If you look closely at the ceiling, you'll be able to tell me where the speakeasy was."

"It was there." Jenna pointed.

"That didn't take you long," Lucy said.

As they headed back to the elevator, Jenna said, "My inn included a successful speakeasy during Prohibition, so I probably have a soft spot in my heart for a good speakeasy."

Lucy chuckled.

"We'll skip the freight elevator and use the service elevator. It's the one the staff uses, so look like staff if anyone joins us."

Jenna nodded. *Wait until I tell Morgan the hotel let me be staff.*

As they rode to the first floor, Lucy asked, "What are your plans for this evening?"

"I'm going to dinner with friends."

Lucy nodded. "People you knew before you came here?"

Jenna side-glanced at Lucy. *She sounds like Ethan and Morgan.*

"No. I met them here."

"Calliope?"

After Jenna nodded, Lucy smiled. "Calliope is excited about her mother coming."

Lucy already knew who my friends were. "I'm looking forward to meeting her."

While Lucy rushed to the hotel office, Jenna sat in what was becoming her favorite chair in the lobby, which gave her a view of the front door, registration desk, and hallways to the guest rooms. She pulled out her library book and began reading.

When she reached a page with an artist's rendition of the speakeasy that was dated 1932, she smiled at the accuracy of the bar.

"What are you reading?" Gary sat in the chair across from her.

Jenna put her book down on her lap. "I guess I was really engrossed in the book. I didn't realize you were sitting there. I found this in the hotel library; it's the history of the hotel."

Gary cocked his head. "Sounds dry, but I read thrillers to relax."

Jenna patted the book. "I'm an accountant, so I love data and details."

Gary chuckled. "Kendra's the same, which is why she takes care of the books, and I fix things that are broken or better yet, before they break."

"There's Jenna and Gary," Calliope said.

Jenna closed her book and glanced toward the guest rooms as Calliope and a middle-aged woman who was slightly shorter than Calliope strolled toward her. The woman's long, ash-brown hair was pulled back into a low ponytail, and she wore a silky, emerald green, low-cut blouse under a dark brown leather jacket, and jeans tucked into her western boots. Her brown leather crossbody purse had fringe along the sides.

Jenna raised her eyebrows. *Delilah described Sara as average. I think Delilah's jealousy streak must operate in overdrive.*

Jenna put the book in her backpack and smiled as she and Gary rose to greet them.

"Mom, this is Jenna and Gary," Calliope said.

"I'm Sara, and it's nice to meet both of you."

"You too," Jenna said.

After Sara and Gary shook hands, she smiled at Jenna. "Love your boots, Jenna."

Jenna returned her smile. "Yours too."

"Where are we going?" Gary asked.

"I made reservations for us at Mom's favorite place," Calliope said. "It's only two blocks from here."

"It's a diner that serves down-home Southern cooking. We can order individual dinners or family style. I recommend family style. I'd say their specialty is fried chicken and seafood, but that's true of most of the restaurants in Savannah." Sara's chuckle reminded Jenna of the chimes.

Calliope said, "If we order family style, fried chicken is one entrée then we pick one or two others. Is everybody okay with family style?"

"Jenna?" Gary asked.

"I am; what about you?"

"I live for family style." He grinned.

"Oh, good," Sara said. "I recommend only one additional entrée for the four of us. We'll pick two sides; our meal will include hush puppies and cornbread. Each of us orders the dessert we want, and they will automatically pack our desserts to go."

I think I'm homesick. Jenna sighed as she rested her hand on her pink opal pendant, then put on her coat.

As they strolled to the diner, Gary and Sara led the way with Jenna and Calliope close behind them.

"How was the tour?" Calliope asked.

"I really enjoyed it. I've been reading a book that I found in the library about the history of the hotel, so the tour brought sections of the book to life for me."

"Sara, I've been wondering, how do you deal with security?" Gary asked.

"I want to know too," Jenna said.

"Maybe I should postpone answering until we're at the diner." Sara asked.

"Makes sense to me," Gary said.

Before they reached the diner, Sara said, "I should warn you; it looks noisy and chaotic, but it isn't. We'll ask to be seated in the dining room, which they call the old folks' section."

Jenna rolled her eyes. *I've gone from barely old enough to buy a beer to sitting in the old folks' section in less than a day.*

When they stepped inside the diner, Jenna inhaled the heavenly aroma of fried chicken but cringed and gritted her teeth to keep from covering her ears with her hands.

Sara spoke to the host who led the four of them to the back of the diner and opened a door to a hallway.

"Last one in, close the door behind you."

"That's me," Gary said.

After Gary closed the door, Jenna relaxed.

The host continued, "The restrooms are on your left. The old folks' section is on our right."

She opened the door, and they went into a large dining room with wide booths along the walls and tables that seated only six and were covered by white tablecloths. Couples and small groups were sitting in the booths or at the tables, but their conversations were muffled by the heavy drapes over the windows and the carpeting on the floor.

After they were seated, and everyone had a menu, the host disappeared.

Sara said, "The service is a little slower back here, but nobody is in a rush. The menu is the same as at the front of the diner, except it's served family style. I think food tastes better when there's a tablecloth on the table."

"So, what's our main dish besides fried chicken?" Calliope asked.

"Jenna, you pick. I can't decide," Gary said.

Jenna stared at the long list of entrées on the menu and sighed. "I'm not sure I can either."

"How about the seafood casserole?" Calliope whispered.

"Seafood casserole," Jenna said.

"My first choice." Gary grinned.

Sara and Calliope chuckled.

Jenna smiled. *Calliope inherited her mother's laugh.*

After Sara ordered for the group and their server left, Jenna said, "I think I'm officially an old folk. This is wonderful."

"I'm glad you like it," Sara said. "Gary, you asked about security."

"Do you mind if I take notes?" Jenna asked.

"Go right ahead."

While Jenna pulled out a notebook and pen from her backpack, Gary asked, "Will you share your notes?"

Jenna nodded as Sara explained her current security plan and the changes she had in mind.

When their food arrived, Jenna put away her notebook and pen. "No talking business while we eat because I can't eat and take notes."

While they passed the platter of chicken, Gary asked, "So when did you go purple, Calliope?"

Her eyes twinkled. "After I tired of green."

Gary chuckled. "I should have known."

"What about you, Jenna? Did you ever go through the color rebellion?" Sara asked.

"When I was seventeen, everyone was going purple, except it wasn't pretty like Calliope's. It was kind of muddy back then."

Sara nodded. "I remember that color. I think it was supposed to be a pastel."

"I told Mom I'd rather be sparkly. Do you remember when the hairsprays had sparkles in them? I wonder if there are any still around."

"There are," Calliope said. "Sounds like a great idea to me."

"What about you, Gary?"

He took a swig of tea. "Remember the mohawk era? I had a mohawk before anybody even thought of color."

Sara smiled. "An original."

"Your turn, Sara," Gary said.

"I think I might still have my crimper somewhere. It was difficult and time-consuming, and I burned my fingers and singed my hair. But in style."

"What was crimping?" Calliope pulled out her phone, then wrinkled her nose. "Eww, Mom."

"What if it makes a comeback?" Jenna asked.

Calliope shrugged. "Then I'll have my own expert."

"I know Jenna's an accountant. What about you, Gary?" Calliope asked.

"I was a World War Two fighter pilot."

When they laughed, he raised his eyebrows and launched into a story about his amazing feats in between bites.

After he ended his story, Jenna said, "Accountant sounds too boring. I need an exciting background story like Gary."

After they finished eating and wrapped up their stories of their former fantasy occupations, they ordered dessert.

Sara said, "Thank you, everyone. I don't know when I have had this much fun. Tonight is my treat."

She interrupted Gary who tried to protest. "It's already done."

Gary narrowed his eyes. "You really are a sneaky espionage agent, aren't you?"

Sara beamed.

"This has truly been fun," Jenna said. "I've been so wound up with work that I'd forgotten there is life outside of the business world."

As they headed to the front door, Jenna heard Frankie call out her name. *It's too noisy in here. I don't want to stop to talk.*

She continued to follow Calliope and Sara out the door with Gary close behind her.

After they were outside, Gary whispered, "I heard her too. I knew you wouldn't want to get into a conversation in that part of the diner."

Jenna exhaled. "Thanks."

As they strolled back to the hotel, a distant rumble of thunder interrupted Sara's story about her least favorite professor in college.

"I didn't think there was any rain in the forecast," Calliope said.

"I didn't either." Gary pulled up the weather on his phone. "But the forecast has changed."

"Am I going to get soaked?" Sara asked. "Because I'm too stuffed to run."

"Looks like we have about forty-five minutes. If you planned to work tonight, download it to your computer in case we lose our internet connections."

As they approached a drugstore, Jenna said, "I'd like to stop and buy a flashlight."

"Good idea. I don't have one either," Gary said.

After they bought flashlights and batteries and were on their way back, a nearby crack of lightning, then the boom of thunder made them jump.

"I guess the forecast changed again," Gary said.

"I'm still not running, but I'm going to walk this last half block as fast as I can," Sara said.

"You set the pace; we'll keep up," Jenna said.

After they reached the hotel, Sara, Calliope, and Gary headed toward their rooms.

Lucy, who was alone at the registration desk, waved and smiled. Jenna returned her smile as fat drops of rain slammed the sidewalk, then turned into a heavy downpour.

Jenna strolled to the desk.

"Do you have a flashlight?" Lucy asked.

"Yes, we stopped at the drugstore on our way back and bought flashlights and batteries."

"Good. I was going to offer you one in case you might need it. The hotel doesn't have a generator."

Jenna pulled out her flashlight. "Do you have scissors so I can put my flashlight together before I head upstairs?"

"Sure." Lucy pulled out scissors from a drawer and put them on the counter.

While Jenna cut open the package, she asked, "What was the purpose of those built-in ladders along the walls on the unfinished side of the third floor?"

Lucy smiled. "I thought you noticed them. I was going to bring them up myself, but you just stole my thunder."

Lucy was interrupted by a flash and a loud boom that made the windows shake.

She shuddered. "I guess I shouldn't have said that. All the rooms on the third floor have a wide space between the walls of an adjoining room. In the space there were ladders that went between the third and fourth floors. The third floor was the discreet bordello in the posh hotel from the 1920s through the late 1950s. The entertainers, as they were called, visited their clients by going down the ladder from the fourth floor and entering through hidden doors in the third floor rooms. The entertainers were never seen in the hallways."

"Are the doors still there?"

"Of course, but they are boarded up."

"Are you sure?"

Chapter Six

Lucy stared at Jenna. "No. Check your room and let me know if I need to bring up some clean towels, nails, and a hammer."

"I will."

"When Marvin said the movie theater area on the third floor was blocked off from the guest room areas, he was partially right. There is a door with a keypad that opens with a code. I keep trying to convince Marvin to change the four-number code, but he won't. I think it's because he's afraid he'd forget a new code."

As they strolled up the stairs, Lucy said, "Let me know if you need clean towels, ma'am." She handed Jenna her personal business card and pointed at her cell number.

"Thank you." Jenna hurried to her room.

When she went into her room, Jenna turned on the light. She waited, but it didn't flicker.

"So far, so good."

She examined the outside wall, starting at the heater unit and working her way toward the opposite corner.

When she was three feet from the corner, she caught a whiff of a familiar sweet aroma.

Jenna examined the wall where the aroma was the strongest. *I don't see anything, but I feel it.*

She lightly slid her fingers across the wall. When she found a slight gap that felt like a clean slice in the wallpaper, Jenna ran her hand down the slice to the baseboard and found a small peg that was painted the same color as the baseboard. When she pulled the peg toward her, a door opened, and cool, sweet air brushed her face. She pushed the door closed and picked up her phone.

She sent a text to Lucy. "Clean towels please."

"Two minutes."

She patted her pink opal and furrowed her brow. "Lucy seems more like an investigator to me than a desk clerk and a housekeeper."

She smiled when a sudden gust rattled the window. "I miss the chimes."

Her opal warmed under her hand. "Thanks, Nettie."

Jenna heard a light tap on her door. She hurried to the door and peered through the peephole. Lucy held up a fluffy white towel with the hotel's logo embroidered in gray.

Lucy dropped the towels on the bed. "Where is it?"

"I'll show you."

"Show me how you found it too." Lucy furrowed her brow as she gazed at the wall.

"Walk toward that corner and tell me what you smell."

When Lucy neared the corner, she glanced at Jenna. "Here?"

Jenna nodded.

Lucy leaned close to the wall and inhaled deeply, then coughed. "That was a mistake. Flapper cologne, right?"

Jenna giggled. "Exactly."

Lucy ran her fingers across the wallpaper. "Ah ha."

"That's exactly what I did. There's a peg on the baseboard."

Lucy found the peg and pulled. When the door opened, she exhaled. "Wow."

She closed the door then unfolded the towel and pulled out the hammer she had wrapped in the towel. After she pulled nails out of her pocket, she kneeled down and angled the first nail from the baseboard on the door toward the baseboard on the wall and hammered it in at the angle to toenail the door to the wall. Next, she toenailed a second nail in the same way from the wall to the door.

Lucy rose. "I'd like to have a board across the baseboard too, but I might have trouble scrounging one up tonight."

Jenna cocked her head. "In the meantime, could you help me push the chair so it will block that door? It's really heavy."

"Excellent. It would take a lot of pushing to move the chair away from the wall, and there's no space between the walls for leverage."

After Lucy left, Jenna called Ethan.

When he answered, Jenna sat in the overstuffed chair.

"I want to hear about your day. My day was crazy," Jenna said.

"My partner is a workaholic. I told Shane that after you get back, we're going to slow down because I'm going to spend more time with you than with him, and he needs to slow down too, or he'll burn out."

Jenna stared at the phone. *That doesn't sound like someone who thinks I'm wasting my time.*

"I think I need an attitude adjustment too," Jenna said. "I've been immersed in the conference."

"Being at a conference gives you a pass. Actually, you get a pass whenever you like because you're you."

A tear slipped down her cheek. *That was so sweet.*

Her opal pendant was warm against her skin.

Jenna told him about dinner with Sara, Calliope, and Gary and about the tour of the hotel with Lucy.

"What are you leaving out, babe?" Ethan said.

"Just a hidden door."

Ethan was silent.

Jenna bit her lip. "I could have phrased that a little differently."

Ethan said, "When the phone rang, I had a stern conversation with myself about staying calm for a change. I'm trying to ignore my tendency to come unglued when you tell me something that triggers my instinct to jump into my truck and drive all night."

"I need to work on that," Jenna mumbled.

Ethan exhaled. "Please don't. I count on you to tell me what's going on despite how ridiculous I'd react.

Although sitting at the foot of your bed with a shotgun while I guard you is not out of the question. I have my truck keys in my hand. Now, start from the beginning."

"When Lucy and I were on the tour, I noticed something she didn't mention and asked her about it this evening after supper."

Jenna told him about the ladders in the walls between the fourth and third floors, finding the door in her room, Lucy's fix, and the chair.

"Tell Lucy to reserve a room for me."

"The hotel is fully booked, and I'm fine."

"Tell Lucy to put a rollaway bed in your room."

A flash of light was immediately followed by a crash of thunder with a boom, and the streetlights and the lights in her room went out.

"Just a minute. I have to find my flashlight."

"Did your lights go out?"

"Yes; streetlights too." Jenna fumbled in the dark until she reached the table. She felt around for the flashlight and knocked it onto the floor. "Dang it. Give me a minute; I dropped my flashlight. I knew you wouldn't be happy, but it's completely unnecessary for you to come here."

"Calliope's mother came to the conference; why can't I?"

Jenna narrowed her eyes. "I don't need your protection. I can take care of myself."

"Fine, then I promise I won't protect you. I'll be in your way and say all the wrong things."

Jenna chuckled as she sat down on the floor. "Now, that's tempting."

She felt around under the table. "Ha, I found my flashlight."

Jenna turned on the flashlight and exhaled. "I propose a truce. I'm fine for tonight, and it's not a good night for traveling. The weather is horrible."

"I'm listening. What's the truce part?"

"Give me a minute. I'm having trouble because I keep thinking how silly it is for us to have my car and your truck here. It doesn't make sense for me to follow you back to Paisley."

Ethan groaned. "You're right. I'd want you to ride with me."

"There are just two more days of the conference."

"But three nights," he muttered.

"I could leave after the banquet on Wednesday, but you'd be unhappy I was driving by myself at night."

"Tonight's out because of the weather, so let's sleep on it. There must be a solution. Call me if anything at all happens, no matter what time it is."

"Will you sleep tonight if I promise to call?"

"Of course."

"Me neither. It's a deal." Jenna sighed. "I miss you, and I saw you yesterday." *I'll ask Lucy about a rollaway bed for me when I see her tomorrow.*

"Seems like weeks," Ethan said.

"If we keep..." Jenna tried to stifle a yawn. "I'm sorry. I was going to say if we keep talking, we'll pass each other on the highway because I'll be headed home, and you'll be on your way here."

Ethan chuckled. "That sounds right, but if you're actually considering it, please don't."

"I am in my heart, but I'll stay put." Jenna yawned again.

"Text me when you wake tomorrow or if you can't sleep," Ethan said. "Good night, sweet thing."

"Good night, cowboy."

After they hung up, the lights came on, and Jenna blinked and shielded her eyes. *The lights are almost too bright after being in total darkness.*

"Katy and I should be going for a walk, and I should have gotten a goodnight kiss," she muttered as she took off her boots then padded to the alcove for her pajamas.

She stared at the shelves. She had stacked her clothes with her pajama pants on the bottom of the stack, but her pajama top was underneath the pants.

Jenna's hands shook as she called the front desk. When Lucy answered, Jenna said, "I'm sorry to be calling so late, but I need a towel, please."

"I'll be right there." Lucy hung up.

Less than a minute later, Lucy tapped on the door. "Housekeeping."

When Jenna opened the door, Lucy whispered, "Are you okay?"

Jenna nodded.

After Lucy closed the door, she asked, "What was the call for the towel for?"

"Somebody searched my room. My clothes that I stacked on a shelf were rearranged."

"Nothing taken?"

"No, but I had my backpack with me all day."

Jenna furrowed her brow at the gadget Lucy pulled out of her pocket. *That looks like a miniature television remote.*

Lucy strolled around the room with her gadget. After she waved her gadget in the bathroom, she returned the gadget to her pocket and shrugged. "New toy."

"A sensor?" Jenna asked.

"Sure is; can you tell if anything has been taken?"

"All my clothes are here, and the toiletries are untouched. I don't have any jewelry other than the necklace I wear, and I had my backpack and computer with me all day."

"Let's talk." Lucy pulled out the desk chair and sat down while Jenna sat on her bed.

Lucy said, "I have a vacant room on the first floor, but it hasn't been decorated with period furniture. I didn't think you'd mind. Are you okay with moving?"

"I think I'd sleep better, and it would make Ethan happy."

Lucy raised her eyebrows. "Who's Ethan?"

"A good friend."

"Oh, so you're not a couple?" Lucy cocked her head. "How quickly could you be ready to move?"

"All I have to do is put my clothes and toiletries in my roller bag."

"I'll wait."

While Jenna packed, Lucy said, "Where is Paisley? Is it anywhere close to Macon?"

"Not all that close; something like almost two hours away."

"My cousin claimed her heart was broken by a man named Ethan, and I think she said he was from Paisley, but she told me it was close to Macon, which is where she lives."

"It wasn't Ethan Bentley, was it?" Jenna closed her bag.

"No, and I think it was Liam, not Ethan. Anyway, her stories tend to be a bit farfetched, and it's always hard to sort out what's true and what's an embellishment." Lucy turned away.

Jenna peered at Lucy. *Lucy's hiding something.*

Jenna scanned her room, then checked the bathroom. "Okay, I've got everything."

"I'll take your roller bag, and we'll go to your new room."

Jenna followed Lucy down the stairs to the guest rooms on the first floor.

When they were close to the end of the hall, Lucy stopped at a door and unlocked it. "I'll bring you your room key."

Lucy handed Jenna her roller bag as Jenna went inside the room.

"I'll be right back." Lucy closed the door as she left.

Jenna smiled as she examined the pale gray-painted walls, the wide dresser with a television mounted above the dresser, and the two queen-sized beds. "This is a welcome change."

She opened the bathroom door and snickered. "It's a regular hotel bathroom with a tub and shower."

Jenna opened the sliding mirrored door that was next to the door to the hall. "I can hang up my clothes and store my roller bag in here." Before Jenna put her backpack on the desk, Lucy tapped on the door. "Housekeeping."

Jenna opened the door, and Lucy came into the room. "Here's your key. What do you think?"

"I loved the concept of the room on the third floor, but this is heaven."

Lucy nodded. "I've explained to management that if people want atmosphere, they'll go to a bed-and-breakfast. When people come to a hotel, they expect a well-appointed hotel room."

Jenna gazed around the room. "I might have argued with you at one time, but not now."

"This room is not included on the list for housekeeping. Would it be okay with you if I leave it off?"

"That's fine with me."

Lucy furrowed her brow. "I think I'll spread the word that the next time a big shot shows up, we'll put him in our best third floor room. I'll see you tomorrow."

After Lucy left, Jenna turned the deadbolt on the door and shuddered as she stared at the lock. *I completely missed that the third floor room didn't have a deadbolt lock on the door.*

Jenna unpacked her roller bag and changed into her pajamas.

While she plugged in her laptop to charge, a bright flash outside and a clap of thunder announced another thunderstorm.

She pulled out her flashlight and put it on the bedside table then sent Ethan a text. "I moved to a room on the first floor. It's roomier, and I have a deadbolt lock on the door."

She furrowed her brow when her phone rang. *I should have just called him.*

"Did something else happen? Why did you have to move? I already have my bag packed. I'll see you in three hours."

"Wait; nothing happened, and it's four hours not three because I'd never speak to you again if you drove that fast especially in a storm."

Ethan exhaled. "Okay, four hours, so why did you move?"

"Lucy knew the room made me nervous, so she found me a room on the first floor. It's larger, so it feels less claustrophobic, and it's not decorated like a room in a haunted hotel. I feel much better."

"Good. Do you think you'll be able to sleep?"

"I think so. Good night."

"Thanks for letting me know. Good night, babe."

After they hung up, Jenna turned off the lights and snuggled under the covers. *It's a good thing Katy wasn't here. She would have given me a look for not telling Ethan the entire story, but he deserves a good night's rest.*

She rolled over and fell asleep to the rhythm of wind and rain.

Chapter Seven

When Jenna woke, her room was still dark. She padded to the window to open the heavy curtains, but they only partially opened only a quarter of the way on each side. She gazed at the sky as it changed from dark blue to pale purple.

When it was light enough to see what was behind the hotel, Jenna snorted as she scanned her view of the alley with overturned trashcans, debris, and ripped garbage bags with scattered contents. *No wonder the curtains don't fully open. That's not a scenic view I'd want my guests to see.*

She sent a text to Ethan. "Good morning."

Her phone rang. "I didn't know if it was too early to call," Ethan said. "Thanks for the text. How did you sleep?"

"After we talked, I went right out. The bed is almost as comfortable as mine at home. What about you?"

"I planned to stay awake all night so I could worry about you, but I kept thinking about how much I enjoyed hearing your voice, and then it was morning."

"What are your plans for today?"

"I did plan to mope because you weren't here, but if it warms up a bit, I might pick up Katy and take her to the job site this afternoon. They're going to be surveying and will probably need Katy's supervision. Have you had any coffee?"

"Not yet."

"I'll talk to you later. Thanks for the text."

Jenna smiled as they hung up.

After she showered and was getting dressed, she heard a low hum near the window. She rushed to the window and stared at the heating and air conditioning unit then held her hand near the vents and felt the warm air. *I was ready to leave last night. I can stay after all.*

Before she left her room, Jenna quickly made her bed and then pulled back the curtains. After she adjusted her carry piece in its holster, she put on her ball cap and grabbed her backpack.

When she strolled past the room with the vending and ice machines, a mockingbird trilled outside the window. Jenna stopped and glanced toward the window but didn't see it. *It must have flown away.*

A housekeeper she didn't recognize stood near the ice machine. The tall, muscular woman glanced at Jenna, and her face drained of color. She quickly stuffed something small into her uniform shirt top pocket. In her rush to leave the vending room, the housekeeper jostled Jenna who lost her balance and bumped against the wall.

Thief. The word was so loud, Jenna gasped. "What did you say?"

"Sorry," the woman mumbled as she hurried away.

Jenna shook her head and continued to the café.

As she crossed the lobby, Calliope called out from behind her. "Hey, Jenna; wait up, and we'll have coffee with you."

Jenna smiled as Calliope and Sara joined her.

After they were seated in the café at a table for four and placed their orders, Calliope said, "We were really glad we had flashlights last night. You were a genius to think of them on our way back from dinner."

Jenna felt her face grow warm. "Thanks."

"How did you sleep?" Sara asked.

"Better after the worst of the storm was over. How about you?"

"It wasn't my bed, but I'll sleep better tonight," Sara said.

"Mom fell asleep before I did, but I had some catching up to do online. I stayed in the bathroom so the light from my phone wouldn't bother Mom," Calliope said.

Sara nodded. "I am a light sleeper. I thought I heard someone pacing on the floor right above our room, but I don't think it's occupied. What about you, Jenna?"

"I really miss my dog, Katy. This is the first time I've ever been away from her. Yesterday when I talked to my friend Morgan, who is keeping Katy, Katy sent me kisses."

"Did she lick the phone?" Calliope's eyes twinkled.

Jenna snickered. "Yes, she did."

"We have two orange cats," Sara said. "I called my sister this morning. She said they didn't miss us at all."

Calliope giggled. "They're such fickle girls. They love whoever has possession of the can opener."

Jenna raised her eyebrows when Frankie came into the café and glanced around.

Sara snorted. "Don't look now, but Frankie just walked in. She's wearing her red silk blouse. She's definitely running for the open board position because she once told me that red was her lucky color."

When Gary joined them, the server brought him coffee and took his order.

"The agenda says the panel this morning is about how to integrate a service partner into your business model. Do you suppose they could have made it any more boring?" Gary chuckled.

Jenna smiled. "I know, but I'm really looking forward to it. We had a real disaster with our first and only experience of using a caterer."

"Really? What happened?" Sara asked.

Jenna told them about their problems with the inexperienced caterer, but left out the detail of the chef being murdered. "After that experience, I'm very wary of hiring a caterer, but it really stretched us thin when we took over the event. We'd rather not do it again, so I'm supposed to learn what to look for so we can make smarter choices."

"What did your guests think of the event?" Gary asked.

"They loved it."

"That's what matters," Sara said.

Gary furrowed his brow. "Our neighbor asked if we'd like to buy his property that is next to ours. It would take some work to turn the building into an event venue.

Kendra has lined up three contractors for estimates, but I'm not sure how long it would take to break even."

"My calculations are rough, but I think it will take us four years to recoup the costs of upgrading the barn, assuming that we rent the space six times a year. We've slowed down our advertising, though, until we find a reliable caterer," Jenna said.

Frankie strolled into the café and pulled up a chair to the corner between Jenna and Gary. "What are we talking about?"

"The panel this morning. Are you going to be on the panel?" Gary asked.

Frankie furrowed her brow. "Which one is it?"

"Coffee?" the server asked.

"No, thank you. I just stopped for a second," Frankie said.

"Integrate a service provider into your business model. How have you been, Frankie?" Sara asked.

Frankie flinched. "Hi, Sara. Good to see you." Frankie cleared her throat and rose. "I'm supposed to meet with Delilah this morning. I should probably wait near the registration desk, so I'll see her when she comes down from her room. See you later."

After Frankie left, Gary said, "Frankie seems to run hot and cold, or is it just me?"

Sara shrugged. "Frankie and I go way back. She obviously didn't see me before she sat down."

"From the way she acted, Mom, you must have given her a time out," Calliope said.

Sara narrowed her eyes as she gazed at the empty lobby. "Something like that."

"Back to your barn, Jenna; would you do it again knowing what you know now?" Gary asked.

"If you had asked me right after the weekend was over, I'd have said no. I would like to, but I have more questions than answers. Ask me after the panel."

The server brought their food and refilled their coffee cups, and the only sounds at the table were the clinking of silverware on the plates.

After they ate and paid for their breakfasts, Calliope said, "I'll grab our table in the conference room after I check a few things."

"I'll be there soon," Gary said. "I told Kendra I'd call her after breakfast."

As Jenna and Sara left the café together, Jenna said, "Calliope is a beautiful name; is it a family name?"

"It is. My husband's family was Greek. His mother asked us to name Calliope after her mother, and I thought it was a lovely idea. We always called her Poppy, but after she started high school, she switched to Calliope. I sometimes slip, but I'm proud she's honoring her great-grandmother."

"That is so sweet."

As they headed toward the conference room, two police officers strode into the hotel. Marvin's face was red as he rushed to greet them.

"The panel starts in ten minutes," Sara said.

"I'm ready to get situated and watch all the stragglers try to sneak in. What about you?" Jenna asked.

"Sounds like a good time."

After Jenna and Sara were seated, Gary rushed in.

"Do we expect Mia?" he asked.

"I don't know. Have you seen her this morning?"

"She told me she was taking the books home and would be back early this morning. She was looking forward to the panel discussion. I'll send her a text," Calliope said.

While Gary sat, Calliope sent the text.

Calliope's phone buzzed with a text, and her eyes widened.

She whispered, "Mia's car had a flat tire last night. She said she ruined her rim driving as far as she did on the flat, but she didn't want to stay on the side of the road. She spent the night in the parking lot of a closed gas station. The tow truck picked up her car about half an hour ago, and she has a rental car now. She said she'd be leaving the gas station in a few minutes and would be here as soon as she could."

"She should have called one of us," Gary said. "We could have picked her up."

"Right; we can scold her when she gets here," Calliope said.

"That man's going to blow a gasket," Sara said.

"Who?" Calliope asked.

"The manager."

Jenna narrowed her eyes at Marvin, who stood in the conference room doorway scowling at Victor who stood next to a table of six women. Victor was laughing as he winked at a woman. She giggled and fluttered her eyelashes.

Twyla strolled into the room, followed by a woman and two men that Jenna didn't recognize.

After the three sat at the panel, Twyla picked up the microphone and raised her eyebrows at the young woman who sat at the table with the audio-video equipment.

When the young woman nodded, Twyla said, "Good morning."

After the audience responded appropriately, she said, "This morning our panel will discuss hiring caterers and other service providers."

While Twyla introduced the three people, Jenna's phone buzzed a text from Morgan. She glanced at her phone and picked up her backpack as she whispered, "Be right back."

When she stepped into the lobby, she called Morgan.

"Thanks for calling, Jenna. I wanted to tell you what's going on. I took Shane to the hospital. He was in terrible pain. The doctor told me it was appendicitis, and Shane's in surgery right now. Katy is with Ethan. Shane will be in the hospital for at least two days. I'm hoping that's all, but nobody is telling me anything. I can't even pull out the wife card, so I have to throw my weight around as the bossy girlfriend."

Jenna smiled. "Shane has the best on his side."

"Thanks; I try," Morgan said. "Is your internet access at the hotel good enough to keep an eye on the registration system? Wendy said she'd keep the registration book up to date if you'll text her with any changes."

"I can do that, but please don't worry about the inn. I can leave now if you'd feel more comfortable."

Morgan sighed. "No, I trust Wendy and Darlene. Wendy told me they can take care of everything at the inn until you return on Thursday."

"We have the inn covered, so you can focus on Shane," Jenna said.

"Thanks; I knew you would, and Wendy said the same thing."

After they hung up, Jenna shook her head. *Poor Shane. I know Morgan's worried sick, but the hospital better not get between her and Shane.*

As she headed toward the conference room, two more police officers came into the hotel and strode to the registration desk.

My nosy streak wants to sit in the lobby to see what's going on. She slipped into the conference room and sat at the table.

"What did I miss?" Jenna asked.

"Staff replacement plans, staff experience, and onsite coordinator," Calliope said.

"All goes in the contract," Gary added.

"I'm taking notes." Sara had her laptop on the table as she typed.

"Everything okay?" Gary gazed at Jenna.

Jenna nodded. "Staff issues."

Marvin came into the conference room and motioned for Twyla's attention. Twyla frowned. After Twyla whispered briefly to Farah and handed the speaker notes to her, Twyla joined Marvin at the door and left with him.

Farah rose to the podium. After she read the notes, she raised her eyebrows. "This is an interesting twist to our previous question. How can event coordinators help caterers?"

The three panelists exchanged glances, then the woman said, "I may not be speaking for the group, but the number one area I need as a contractor is to have a single contact for the event. We're frequently put in the middle trying to decide who is in charge: the event coordinator, the owner of the venue, or the mother of the bride."

The two men nodded.

Sara's phone buzzed with a text. Her eyes widened as she read it.

Jenna glanced at Sara and felt a sudden shock, like a painful, powerful jolt of electricity.

Jenna tapped her fingers on the table. When Sara glanced at her, Jenna gritted her teeth as she motioned to the door, and Sara nodded.

"We'll be right back," Sara whispered. She followed Jenna into the lobby.

Sara cleared her throat. "Let's go to the library; it's more private."

Jenna shuddered as she followed Sara. *This is bad.*

After Sara sat in a chair near the door, she asked, "How did you know?"

"Know what? I felt like you were badly shocked by your text."

Sara nodded. "It was literally a shock. A friend of mine sent me a text that a housekeeper found Delilah deceased in her room this morning."

Jenna gaped at Sara. "Delilah? She seemed fine yesterday."

"My friend said Delilah took her own life."

"Delilah? That can't be true."

Sara stared at the door to the lobby. "That must be why the manager pulled Twyla out of the meeting. Do you think they're going to cancel the convention?"

"I don't know. I don't see how it could continue. Delilah is, was, a longtime member of the association. I wonder if Mia's okay?"

Sara raised her eyebrows. "You know Mia is Delilah's niece?"

Jenna nodded.

"Few do." Sara rose. "Ready to go back?"

As they strolled back to the conference room, Sara said, "Delilah and I were once close friends. I was pregnant with Calliope, and my husband and I decided we'd found the perfect home for us to raise a family. It was an old house, so we revisited our dream of a bed-and-breakfast that I could manage so I could be home with our baby and still bring in a little income."

"Is that where you live now?" Jenna asked.

Sara shook her head. "It was the Thorne house. We had applied for a loan, and our lender, who was a good friend of ours, called us one evening and told us the board had refused our loan. He said there was nothing wrong with our credit, but one of the board members heard a previous house inspection had revealed the house was infested with rats, and he was worried about me and rats carrying disease because I was pregnant."

"Your loan was denied because of a rumor?"

Sara sighed. "There's more. You want the kicker? The board member was Delilah's cousin."

"He was worried about your health? What a crock. I heard Delilah bought the Thorne House right before it went into foreclosure."

Sara snorted. "In a roundabout way, yes. You heard the story about the elderly owners and foreclosure from Frankie, didn't you?"

"It isn't true?"

"No. Frankie, Victor, and Delilah got into a bidding war. Frankie dropped out because she didn't have the collateral for a loan. Delilah didn't either, but the bank gave her a loan. Victor put up a big stink, but Delilah paid him off, so he was happy. Or as happy as a crank like him could be."

"Is that why you don't trust Frankie?"

Sara smiled. "Not really. When Frankie didn't get the Thorne House, she tried to tell me she was bidding on it so she could sell it to us at her cost. I was skeptical, but when I found my current house after my husband died and Calliope was born, she tried to go in with a low-ball bid. I had already bought the house and had kept my purchase quiet. She went off the deep end and claimed I was sneaky and cheated her out of her house."

"Wow. Good move."

"I'm not fond of being around any of them, though, which is why I was happy Calliope agreed to represent our business at the annual meetings. There really is a wealth of useful information when you get all the experts together. If for no other reason than they're all trying to outdo each other."

"Calliope told me you'd inherited your house from her grandparents."

Sara nodded. "In a way, we did. It's a long story, but the short version is my grandmother was tricked by an old friend into signing the house over to him, and then he sold it to pay his gambling debts. When we searched the deed, we discovered the house had been in my family for a long time."

When they reached the conference room door, Jenna asked, "Are you ready to go in?"

Sara nodded. "I'm okay now."

When Jenna opened the door, she heard two men arguing.

They slipped into their seats, and Calliope grinned. "We hit a nerve. The topic was besides food safety, what was the biggest risk for events, and the panel is arguing about blind imitation and poor pricing strategies."

"Blind imitation means you don't know who your customer is or what they want," one man said.

"But until you're in business long enough..." Jenna tuned them out and pulled out her computer.

She searched for the address of Thorne House and then searched for the property tax records. She furrowed her brow. *The online records only go back 15 years. I need an old book.*

Jenna checked the registrations and approved the two that were pending. *We're full for the coming weekend beginning on Friday.*

After she sent Wendy a text with the information, she checked her email.

She stared at her computer. *What do you do if you want to research the ownership of an old house?*

She closed up her computer and glanced around the room. *Calliope and Gary are the only ones taking notes; Sara and only a few others are listening.*

The speaker's voice cut through her reverie. "That's old school."

Jenna rolled her eyes. *That's it. I have to go old school. How far are we from a library?*

She opened her computer. *Not far, but too far to walk.*

She exhaled. *I'll check the hotel library. I should have thought of that first.*

Jenna put her computer in her backpack, then whispered to Calliope. "I have to take a quick break. I'll be right back."

Calliope nodded as she continued taking notes.

Jenna picked up her backpack and slipped out of the conference room. When she closed the library door, she inhaled the aroma of books and smiled at the absolute silence.

She beelined to the section where she had found the book on the history of the hotel and bit her lip to keep from squealing at the three books she spotted with Thorne family or Thorne house in the titles or subtitles. As she pulled the books off the shelf and stuck them into her backpack, a three-ring notebook that was next to the books she had pulled dropped with a thud into the now-vacant space.

When she opened the notebook, she did squeal. *These are copies of legal documents.*

"Jenna, are you okay?" Gary's voice boomed in the silence.

Jenna jumped and stifled a scream that came out as a squeak.

He joined her in the back corner. "I thought I heard a mouse. Is that what you saw? This is an old hotel."

Jenna exhaled. "I think that's what it was. It's gone now, but it startled me. What are you looking for?"

Gary looked away from Jenna. "Just browsing."

Jenna narrowed her eyes. Gary glanced at her and ducked his head.

Gary just confirmed we're having a meeting of the liars' club.

"The genealogy club I told y'all about got me interested, so I was looking for some genealogy books," Jenna said.

Gary nodded. "I would have looked in the history section too."

He glanced away, then shuffled his feet. "I was looking for a basic accounting book. I don't have any background in it at all and would like to understand what Kendra is telling me."

Jenna smiled. "I know where the accounting section is. I can help you find a book that covers the basics."

Gary stared at her. "I forgot you were an accountant. I'd like to get caught up on the basics, and then maybe we could talk. We might have an opportunity to grow, and Kendra thinks we can do it, but I'm worried we'd be getting in over our heads. I'd like to take the stress off her and propose some cheaper alternatives."

"Anytime. The accounting books are close to the front." Jenna set down her backpack.

After Gary left with the two books Jenna recommended, she returned to the back corner and stuck the three-ring notebook into her backpack. Before she left the corner, she spied a spiral-bound diary with pages that had turned yellow with age. When she opened it, she squinted at the cramped, tight handwriting in the dim light. *Definitely a diary.* She stuffed the diary into her backpack then held the two sides of the zipper together while she struggled then zipped it closed. *I have plenty to keep me busy.*

Jenna hurried back to the conference room and sat next to Calliope while the panelists rehashed what they'd talked about before Jenna left the room.

Calliope whispered, "I heard from Mia. She's running late."

Finally, Farah rose. "Thank you, panelists, for the lively discussion."

Calliope whispered, "Ouch. Talk about sarcastic, or should we call it tongue in cheek since her voice sounds so sweet?"

Sara smiled, and Jenna snickered.

Gary strolled into the room and sat down.

Farah turned toward the group. "Lunch will be served here in forty-five minutes. Our discussion topic for our afternoon panel is 'Marketing on a Budget.'"

Sara said, "Calliope and I are going to a diner for lunch. Anyone else care to go along?"

"I can't," Gary said. "I have a few things that need to be done today, and if I can get them done, I can go to dinner this evening with a clear conscience."

"Same for me," Jenna said. "We are still planning on dinner, aren't we?"

"Of course," Sara said. "Does anybody have any ideas? We'll make our reservations if we can nail down where we want to go."

"I know a place with great food that isn't very expensive," Gary said. "It doesn't have that fancy, la-de-dah atmosphere, which is a bonus, at least for me, and they don't take reservations, but they aren't busy on Tuesdays, so we can probably walk in and sit down."

"Is it far from here?" Sara asked.

"It's half a block west of where we ate Sunday night."

"I'm game," Jenna said.

Calliope nodded.

"Sounds like a plan. Our usual six o'clock?" Sara asked.

Gary nodded. "Might as well. No reason to change what works."

After Sara and Calliope left, Gary asked, "I'll check in at home, then do a couple of things. I'll come back here for lunch. What about you?"

"I'll be here too."

"Good; I already have some accounting questions for you. Do you mind?"

"Not at all. You don't know anything about hiring caterers, do you? I thought that was on the agenda when I signed up, but I think the planned agenda has gone by the wayside."

"I'll ask Kenda if she knows of any resources."

Gary picked up his computer bag and left, and Jenna headed toward her room. When she passed the registration desk, Lucy came out of the office and walked with Jenna toward the hallway.

"I heard about Delilah," Jenna whispered. "Did you find her?"

Lucy shook her head. "What do you think happened to her?"

"Accidental overdose, maybe, but not suicide," Jenna said.

"You and I are the only..." Lucy was interrupted by angry voices behind them near the elevator. "I need to see what's going on. I'll be right back."

Lucy hurried to the elevator, and Jenna followed her, then stopped when she recognized Frankie's voice.

"You aren't the injured party here, Victor. You can't call someone a fraud and expect to walk away clean."

"It was supposed to stay buried," he growled.

When Victor stormed toward the front door, Frankie snorted. "Old fool."

The elevator doors closed, and Lucy joined Jenna.

"For a minute I thought that argument was going to turn physical. I don't think the gentleman is as frail as he looks, though. My first impression of him yesterday was that he was a bully. This isn't the first time those two have squared off; there must be a longstanding feud between them. Weren't they on a panel yesterday? How did that go?"

"Polite sniping," Jenna said.

Lucy nodded. "To answer your question, our newest housekeeper, Raelynn, found her. It was a surprise because she was assigned to the second floor, not the third. She's on work release, so I'll have to talk to her later. Anyway, what I was going to say was Delilah raised a big fuss over a missing bottle of perfume with the manager. An hour later I was at the desk, and she told me the thief had returned her perfume."

"Do you think it was really stolen and returned?"

"No, but when I asked her if she was sure she hadn't overlooked it, she became irate and told me I should be fired. I really wanted to tell her I would appreciate it, but I just told her I was glad she found it. Did you sleep okay last night?"

"Yes, I did. I don't need the white noise machine anymore. I'll drop it off at the desk on my way out this evening. I meant to do it this morning, but I was totally focused on coffee."

Lucy smiled. "I completely understand."

"What was your cousin's name? The one who had her heart broken?"

"Paige Adams, which reminds me, I meant to call her so I could ask about her boyfriend, Allen, or whatever his name was. I see so many names every day, I've lost my ability to remember names without a face." Lucy shook her head.

"Paige is a pretty name. I thought you said the boyfriend was Liam or Ethan."

"No, I've completely forgotten; I better get back to the desk. Thanks for the break."

Jenna's stomach churned as she hurried down the hall. *Breakfast must have been too rich for me. It's none of my business if Ethan and Paige broke up ages ago.*

When she walked into her room, she smiled. It took very little effort to straighten her room and open the curtains before she left, but the sunlight streaming into the room and the still lingering scent of her foamy shower wash welcomed her. *This feels like a palace after that dark, cramped room upstairs.*

As she removed the books from her backpack, Jenna noticed the overstuffed envelope Delilah had given her.

I'd forgotten about that. I'll give it to Mia as soon as she returns.

Jenna sent a text to Morgan. "How's Shane?"

Morgan replied, "I'm waiting for the verdict. The doctor said Shane might be released tomorrow. Will let you know."

Jenna signed onto the registration system and then raised her eyebrows. *Three reservations for the end of the month.* She sent a quick text to Wendy, then picked up the notebook with the three-ring binder and the diary.

Wendy replied, "Thanks. We miss you. W & D."

Darlene would know.

Jenna sent another text to Wendy. "Ask Darlene if Ethan had a girlfriend, Paige Adams? I met her cousin."

After she pulled her desk chair close to the soft chair so she could put up her feet, she opened the diary. The first page said, "Beware. This diary is protected by magic. All snooping floozies, especially you, Reba M., will suffer a horrible fate." The letter 'B' was signed with a flourish. *I'm not a floozie or Reba M., so I'm okay. Our Miss B. sounds young.*

Jenna turned the page and read. After half an hour, Jenna carefully closed the diary. *Miss B. was not impressed by her drunken magician, but was certainly fond of the drummer, Willy. I'll ask Lucy about the trapdoor on the stage that drops to the basement.*

Jenna's phone buzzed with a text from Wendy. "Long answer from Darlene. You'll hear it next time you talk to her. Short answer. Yes. But it's complicated."

Jenna frowned. *That's not what Lucy said.*

The elevator stopped at the main floor and jingled before the doors opened.

Ethan's a good man.

The pink opal felt like hot coals on her skin.

"You're prejudiced just like Darlene, Nettie," Jenna growled and removed the necklace.

A crow landed on the window ledge and tapped on the window.

"What do you want?" Jenna growled.

The crow tapped again.

Jenna put the necklace back on. "Are you happy?"

The crow flew away, and the elevator jingled its arrival.

Jenna exhaled, then carefully wrapped the diary in one of her shirts before she put it and the three-ring notebook into her backpack.

She opened the door to go to lunch, then glanced at the books on the desk. *I can't carry all of them, and I can only read one at a time.*

She rested her hand on her pink opal pendant and sighed. *I can't wait to go home.*

Jenna picked up the Miss B.'s diary and headed toward the conference room for lunch.

As she strolled toward the conference room, two women came out of the elevator.

One woman said, "Well, I heard Frankie has been trying for years to expand her hotel boutique business by buying inns to turn into guest houses."

"My cousin told me Frankie approached her, but she wasn't interested in her lowball offer."

"Are you saying Frankie is cheap?"

"I'm not saying anything, but there are things going on we don't always know about." The second woman sniffed.

Chapter Eight

As Jenna continued across the lobby to the conference room, Mia came in the front door, pulling a blue canvas cart with a large cardboard box in it.

Mia glanced up and smiled as Jenna headed toward her. "It's so nice to see a friendly face; the hotel wants me to pick up Delilah's things since the investigators are finished with her room."

"Do you need any help?" Jenna walked alongside Mia toward the conference room.

Mia pointed to the large box. "I'd really like to sell the rest of these books, but I have to tackle Delilah's room first. Know where I can get a clone?"

Jenna smiled. "I need one of those myself sometimes."

"The hotel was supposed to set up the table again so I could hide the box under it while I packed up Delilah's room. I don't think anyone will notice them."

The elevator jingled, and Jenna touched her pendant. *Help her.*

"Seriously?" Jenna muttered, then exhaled. "If you tell me what to do, Mia, I could sit at the table and sell books. Actually, I suspect they'll sell themselves, and this is a perfect time because the association members will be here soon for lunch."

Mia stared at her and then shook her head. "That's too much to ask."

Jenna rolled her eyes. "You might be right, but I didn't hear you ask."

Mia glanced at the carton of books. "Are you sure?"

"That I can sell them? I never even had a lemonade stand when I was a kid, but who knows? I might have an aptitude for sales."

Mia exhaled. "Okay, but only on the condition that you shut down anytime you want and put the remaining books in the box under the table."

As they strolled toward the conference room, Mia said, "I don't accept cash because that would make me a target for thieves. I'll install my sales app on your phone. All you have to do is tap in the number of books, and the app takes care of everything else. I'll show you."

"Sounds perfect. Are you going to be around to go to dinner with us tonight?"

"I'd like that." Mia parked the cart near the wall. "Let me see your phone."

After Mia installed the app on Jenna's phone, she showed Jenna how to use the app for sales.

Jenna smiled. "I think I've got it; it's similar to our registration system."

"Text me if you have any problems. I won't be that far away, and I'd definitely appreciate an interruption. I'll check the status of the table."

Jenna stared at the books. "I don't know how to sell books," she hissed.

The elevator bell seemed to be stuck as it jingled.

Jenna rolled her eyes. "I'm glad you're enjoying this, Nettie."

The elevator dinged twice.

While Mia stopped at the registration desk, a maintenance man with the hotel logo on the pocket of his shirt rolled a dolly with a six-foot table and a folding chair strapped onto it. Lucy followed him; she wore her housekeeping uniform and carried a crisp white tablecloth in her hand.

After the clerk gave Mia a key, Mia said, "I'll help you set up, Jenna."

Jenna waved her on. "I'll be okay. Take care of your other tasks."

"Thanks." Mia hurried to the elevator.

The maintenance man set up the table near the conference room. "You got this, Lucy? I have to check that darn elevator."

Jenna couldn't stop the smile that crept across her face.

"Yes, thanks for your help, Roy."

As Roy left, Lucy put the tablecloth on the table. "Will there be anything else, ma'am? A pitcher of ice water?"

Lucy glanced around, and her eyes twinkled as she whispered, "A nice bottle of wine with a straw?"

Jenna smiled. "That's tempting; I am totally out of my comfort zone with this."

"You're a good person, Jenna. Not everyone..."

Lucy was interrupted by Victor who shouted from the office, "I'm not going anywhere. These accusations are all lies. I'll bet Delilah planted them herself. She's spent years siphoning business away from me, but this is an outrageous ploy for attention, even for her. She was a spiteful..."

A man said, "Mr. Grimes, nobody is accusing you of anything. We'd just like to talk to you somewhere that is more private."

"I need to make a quick change into my alter ego." Lucy dashed to the registration desk and disappeared for a moment and then reappeared wearing her registration clerk jacket over the housekeeping top. She had pulled her ponytail into a bun with a claw hair clip holding it in place before she dashed into the office.

"That's a great idea." Jenna pulled her hair clip out of her backpack and pulled her hair back into a messy bun and anchored it.

Jenna set her backpack on the chair and stacked all the books on the table, counting as she unloaded them from the box. "Seventeen books." She glanced at the people going in and out of the front door. *I miss Katy. She always enjoys greeting people.*

"Mr. Grimes, I don't blame you at all for being distraught, but no one could possibly have the insights you do," Lucy said.

"That's true, isn't it?" Victor said. "I'm well known for my keen observation skills and my caring nature."

Victor came out of the office wearing his signature black suit and a scowl; he was accompanied by a large man with a comb-over who wore khaki pants, white shirt, and a navy suit jacket. The right side of the man's jacket had the imprint of a pistol.

"Just questions?" Victor asked.

"That's right, Mr. Grimes, and we appreciate your cooperation."

Victor growled, "I think it's a waste of time. Delilah would do whatever it takes to frame me."

The man side-glanced at Victor. "Sir, you understand we did confirm she is deceased."

Victor snorted. "Proves my point."

Jenna shook her head as the two men left the hotel.

Lucy joined her. "Mr. Grimes and Ms. Drake must have had a long history of rivalry; it sounds like he doesn't believe she's dead."

"It heard that, but I don't know why. Do you suppose he's in denial? You did a good job of appealing to his ego."

"I knew it would work. Thank goodness that's not my case, but something else has popped up." Lucy sighed.

Jenna furrowed her brow. *Your case? That doesn't sound like a housekeeper or a registration clerk. Isn't that what a cop would say?*

Lucy continued, "It's a complication I brought on myself. I mentioned to Mom that you were from Paisley. I probably shouldn't have because my family talks and word got back to my cousin Paige who lives in Macon. Paige called me twenty minutes ago and told me she had rearranged her schedule so she could visit me today and meet you because she loves Paisley and would enjoy talking to you. I tried to tell her now was not a good time, but she insisted and will be here later this afternoon. Can you join us for dinner?"

I'm not sure I want to meet cousin Paige. Jenna furrowed her brow. *I should have told Lucy about Ethan.* "I'm sorry, but I already have plans."

"I understand; it really is short notice, isn't it? It's not all that convenient for me either. I'll send her a text and ask her to cancel."

Jenna nodded. *Good. I'm not ready for another complication.*

Lucy glanced at the conference room. "They'll be opening the doors for lunch soon. I'll fix you a plate so you don't starve."

"You don't need to do that; it won't hurt me to miss a meal." Jenna smiled.

Lucy returned her smile. "I'm in the running for this month's customer service award. I'll be right back."

Jenna sent a quick text to Wendy. "My friend's cousin Paige might be here this afternoon. Do I avoid her?"

A few minutes later, Wendy replied, "Darlene said to stay away from her. I think you should talk to Ethan or see for yourself."

Jenna stared at her phone, then put it in her backpack when one of the association members approached the table.

"That's such a shame about Delilah," the woman said. "Are these her books?"

"Yes, her assistant hired me to sell them. They're signed by Ms. Drake, so her assistant thought the members of the association would be interested in having a copy."

"Really? I'll take two. Do you accept credit cards?"

"We certainly do." Jenna smiled.

After the woman's credit card was approved, Jenna slipped the books into a sack with the Gravely Gracious Inns and Tours logo. The woman rushed into the conference room, and five women and two men hurried out.

While the line formed, a woman said, "Did you hear about Delilah's jewelry? It was fake."

Her companion snorted. "Everybody knows that. I heard she sold it years ago but didn't tell the insurance company."

It didn't look fake to me. Jenna shrugged. *Not that I'm an expert.*

A woman whispered, "They've arrested Victor; my neighbor told me her cousin's best friend works at a pizza parlor, and he said he heard Delilah and Victor ran a money-laundering scheme, but she got greedy."

One of the association members stood in the middle of the lobby wearing a black wool coat while her friend hurried to the conference room with a navy blue coat slung over her arm. When the woman wearing the black coat returned, she said, "She's not in there. Let's give her another five minutes."

Jenna sold two more books.

The woman with the navy coat said, "Here she is."

Jenna raised her eyebrows at Frankie, who was wearing a black turtleneck shirt and carrying a deep purple and green plaid long-sleeved flannel shirt as she strode toward the conference room.

"We've been waiting for you, Frankie. I made the reservation at the café you said you liked so much, but we're going to have to hurry because they won't hold it much longer." The woman put on her navy coat.

"You two go on. I'll catch up with you. I have a critical meeting I can't skip." Frankie rushed past them and down the hallway past the conference room.

"That was rude." The woman in the black coat glared toward the hallway.

The other woman snorted as she linked arms with the first one. "Let's go. I'll submit our meal receipts to her highness for her to pay; after all, she invited us."

They cackled as they hurried out the front door.

"Excuse me?" The woman standing in front of Jenna tapped her fingers on the table. "I'd like to buy a book. Will you take a credit card?"

"Of course," Jenna said. "Tap your card on my phone."

While the woman waited for Jenna to slip her book into the sack, the woman said, "I heard Twyla was jealous because she learned Delilah and Victor were putting on a show so nobody would know they were, you know, like a couple." The woman raised her eyebrows, and the woman behind her twittered.

After twenty minutes, all the books were gone.

Jenna sighed with relief as she leaned back in the chair. *I survived, but it will be awhile before my ears recover. I've never heard so much wild gossip crammed into such a short amount of time.*

Jenna sent Ethan a text. "I just sold seventeen books to strangers."

She smiled when her phone rang. *He always calls.*

"That's great, babe. I know what it took for you to do that. What's going on?"

She told him about Delilah and Mia.

"Untimely death? Did she have a medical condition?"

"You wouldn't believe how many stories the gossips have going around. I don't think anybody really knows."

Ethan exhaled. "You're there. It's murder, isn't it?"

She gritted her teeth. *Why does he always think the worst?* "Nobody knows. I have to go. I'll talk to you later."

Jenna hung up and crossed her arms.

The elevator buzzed, dinged, and then chimed.

"What?"

He's right.

"You always take his side," Jenna grumbled.

She gazed at the lobby's high ceiling, and her eyes widened at the ornate molded plasterwork of octagons. *Why haven't I noticed that before?"*

Jenna sighed. "But I was a little abrupt, wasn't I?"

She sent a text to Ethan. "Nettie agrees with you."

Her phone rang.

When she answered, Ethan said, "Oh good. You're still talking to me. Congratulations on the book sales."

Jenna rolled her eyes. "Thanks."

"I'll talk to you later, babe."

"I know."

She smiled as they hung up.

Lucy came out of the conference room with two plates and peered at the box. "You sold all your books?"

"Sure did."

"I fixed two plates so I could keep you company but my plan to go through the line quickly fizzled. Would you like to eat in the conference room or go with me to my office?"

"Your office, if you don't mind. I'm just Mia's assistant she hired to sell her books. I'd rather not get into any more conversations for a while."

Lucy chuckled as they went into her office. "Assistant to the assistant?"

Jenna giggled. "Sounds official, doesn't it? It wasn't as bad as I thought it would be. There was actually a rush to buy the books, so all I had to do was charge their credit cards, put their books into a sack, and move on to the next buyer. Oh, and not roll my eyes at all the theories about Delilah's death."

When Jenna entered Lucy's office, her eyes widened at the plush taupe carpeting, the enormous mahogany desk, and the wooden visitor's chair with arms and padded back and seat. "This is a spacious office."

"It's supposed to be the general manager's office, but he's never here, so it's mine. Marvin covets it because it has a lock on the door and it's almost twice the size of his office, but he's stuck with his hotel manager's office."

Jenna chuckled. "I can see Marvin being envious of the larger office."

After Lucy closed the door, they sat at the small round conference table. The pale gray padding on the backs and seats of the three armless chairs around the table complemented the tan and gray herringbone pattern on the visitor's chair.

"So how are you doing?" Lucy asked.

"I miss Katy, my golden retriever." Jenna took a bite of her sandwich.

"I know exactly what you're saying. I miss my German shepherd, Bear."

"Is he staying with your mom while you're in school?"

A fleeting shadow crossed Lucy's face. She nodded and bit into her sandwich.

Jenna raised her eyebrows, then focused on her sandwich. *That wasn't true.*

"You said Raelynn found Delilah. Is she a tall, muscular woman?" Jenna asked.

Lucy narrowed her eyes. "Yes, why?"

"I saw her earlier this morning on my way to breakfast."

"Really? Where did you see her?" Lucy reached for a pad of paper and a pen.

"She was in the vending room, but she left." Jenna removed her hair clip and stuck it in her backpack.

Lucy fiddled with her pen, then tapped it on the pad. "What time was that again?"

Tell her.

Jenna sighed. "I'm very sensitive to things and people, kind of like an empath, but a little more intense. For example, I know you're a cop or an investigator."

Lucy raised an eyebrow but didn't flinch and remained quiet.

Told you. Cop.

Lucy exhaled. "So, what does that have to do with Raelynn?"

"When she saw me, she stuck something small into her shirt pocket and in her rush to leave, she bumped into me. I sensed the word thief so strongly I thought she'd said it. So where is Bear, really?"

Lucy examined Jenna's face. "He's with a close friend, and the two of them are probably eating junk food and staying up later than they should watching movies while I'm away, and I'm jealous."

Jenna nodded. "I know Katy's vet will have a fit over the weight she's gaining this week from all the treats."

"Could you tell what Raelynn stuck in her pocket?"

"I didn't really see it, but I'm positive it didn't belong to her."

Lucy polished off her sandwich and stuck her cookies into her pocket. "I have to go look for her."

After they rose to leave, Lucy's phone buzzed with a text. "Well, fiddle. Paige took three days off work to come here." Lucy exhaled. "Maybe she'll be okay if we get together for coffee during one of your breaks."

The elevator jingled. *Tell her.*

Jenna bit her lip and shook her head.

Lucy narrowed her eyes as she examined Jenna's face. "I might not have the sensitivity you do, but my radar tells me you're holding something back that I need to know. What is it?"

Jenna sighed. "Ethan Bentley is a friend of mine."

Lucy raised her eyebrows. "What kind of friend? I know I've already asked you this, but are you a couple?"

Jenna glared at Lucy. "I'll take my lunch to the conference room."

Before she reached the door, Lucy said, "I told you about Bear."

Jenna leaned against the door. "Isn't that blackmail or enticement or something?"

"Probably. So tell me about Ethan."

Jenna shrugged. "He's a good friend, but it's complicated."

"So when Paige goes into one of her rants about what a jerk he is, are you going to deck her?"

Jenna giggled. "Maybe, or maybe I'll top her story."

Lucy smiled. "Either way, I'm on your side. She's the most annoying relative I have, and that's saying a lot."

"Coffee sometime would be okay." Jenna opened the door.

Lucy followed her out and locked the door behind them. "Thanks for telling me."

After Lucy rushed across the lobby to the stairs, Jenna dumped the rest of her sandwich in the trash but kept her cookies.

Gary stood near the conference room door. When she joined him, he said, "I was in the conference room, but all the gossip about Delilah was more than I could take. I need fresh air. You want to go for a walk?"

Jenna nodded. *Gary needs to talk.* "Sounds good to me; maybe we'll come across a store that sells gloves. You want a cookie?"

Gary smiled as he took the offered cookie. "Thanks. We were supposed to look for gloves, anyway."

Jenna buttoned up her coat and then slipped her arms through her backpack straps before they went outside.

As they strolled along, Gary polished off his cookie in two bites while Jenna munched on hers.

Jenna stopped to peer into the display windows of the small shops. "Am I walking too slow? I'm watching for gloves. That last store had knit caps with pom poms on top and baseball caps but no gloves."

"You're fine." Gary cleared his throat. "Mia's lawyer called Kendra a little earlier to talk about the Thorne House. He offered to give us a first right of refusal contract if we were interested. He said Mia expects the vultures to circle and make the value of the inn and the rest of Delilah's properties plummet so they could snatch up a bargain. Kendra thinks we should go ahead with the property we wanted to buy and sign the first right of refusal contract. I can't believe she wants to do both. She scares me sometimes, but we went over our finances last night and talked more about money again today. I agree we can afford it. I'm just not sure I'm ready to become a company with employees, which is what we'd end up doing."

"What did your wife say when you told her that?" Jenna stuck her hands in her pockets as the wind became stronger, and the temperature dropped.

"She said we're a team, and we'd be fine, but she always says that. You have employees. How do you do it?"

"I have a great staff, but it did take a while for me to learn to get out of their way so they could do their jobs. As an accountant, I was used to doing everything myself."

"See, that's where I am."

Jenna nodded. "I understand it's hard to let go, but I was so stretched trying to do everything myself that I was accomplishing nothing. Even after I had good people in place, I still had to learn to let them do their jobs so I could do mine, but I didn't have a choice because I was in danger of having a breakdown, walking away, or causing the inn to fail."

"Right, and none of those are acceptable choices," Gary said.

As they neared the end of the block, Jenna said, "Do we want to keep going?"

"Let's take a left. We haven't been down that street."

When they turned the corner, their breath was taken away by an icy blast of wind. Jenna clutched her cap with both hands to keep it from blowing away.

"Go back," Gary said.

They immediately turned around.

After they turned the corner and were sheltered again from the wind by the buildings, Jenna said, "That was a shocker. What are you really worried about?"

Gary exhaled. "The conversation in the conference room turned from why Delilah committed suicide to speculation over who killed her. For what it's worth, the amateur detectives in the conference room think Delilah was a fence for stolen jewelry. I don't want Kendra to be the target of a killer, so I don't want to do anything until we definitely know it was suicide, or the killer is caught. Kendra thinks I'm too cautious."

Jenna bit her lip. "I hope you don't mind me saying that I wouldn't mention Mia and the lawyer to anyone else."

"I understand. Sara and I go way back, and I trust her, but there's no reason to burden her with this, and there's nobody else I'd talk to."

As they neared the hotel, Gary said, "I did hear one interesting tidbit that is probably completely false. Someone said that Delilah's earrings and her necklace were missing when the police arrived. Even I know her necklace was worth thousands of dollars."

"Wouldn't that imply a robbery?" Jenna asked.

"Maybe that was the killer's plan to hide his real motive, which is another theory from the conference room."

As they went inside, Jenna breathed in the warm air. "Ahh. Maybe my toes will thaw."

Gary chuckled.

"So what was the conference room's consensus on the real motive?" Jenna unbuttoned her jacked.

"Nobody liked Delilah," Gary said. "I don't think they realized they just admitted their guilt in the conspiracy of the entire association to do away with Delilah."

Twyla and Farah hurried through the lobby toward the conference room.

"Looks like we're going to have an afternoon meeting after all. I was concerned that it was all going to fall apart," Jenna said.

When they went into the conference room, Jenna exhaled when Calliope waved from what was becoming their table.

As they joined her, Calliope said, "Mom said she wanted to check a few things, but I told her she had to bring her computer here and not hide out. She seemed a little irritated, but she agreed."

When Twyla rose and picked up the hand microphone, the young woman who sat at the audio table nodded, and Twyla turned on the mic.

Sara slipped into the room and smiled as she sat down.

Twyla held up her hand, and the room became quiet. "We have a slight change to our schedule. We will have a brief exercise this afternoon in our small groups. We are hosting appetizers for happy hour here at five thirty, and the hotel will provide a cash bar. Dinner will be buffet-style beginning at six fifteen to allow a little extra time for our happy hour. After dinner, I'm pleased to announce that the president of the South Carolina Association will be with us. He will speak on a topic of his choice, but many of us have heard him speak before, and he is a wealth of knowledge and wit."

"She's right," Sara whispered while quite a few other members nodded.

Twyla continued, "We will have the scheduled panel tomorrow morning at nine, and our afternoon program will be another small group exercise. Tomorrow's dinner is our banquet, and our after-dinner speaker will be an innkeeper from Montana who has managed five working dude ranches for over twenty years and will share his experiences with us."

A few people applauded, and then the rest joined in. The applause was replaced with a buzz of conversation at all the tables.

Sara said, "I'm impressed. Twyla really hustled to keep the meeting going. I don't know who the Montana rancher is, but he sounds interesting."

"I'm certain I'll learn a few new things," Jenna said.

"Twyla just guaranteed nobody will consider leaving before tomorrow evening, didn't she?" Calliope said.

Twyla raised her hand for quiet. "I will use your responses from this afternoon's exercise on our website's blog. You'll need a recorder at your table who will email your group's responses to me so I can compile them. Do I have two kind volunteers who will hand out our questions?"

A man and a woman hopped up, and Twyla gave each of them a small stack of papers.

After everyone had a sheet, Twyla joined Farah at their table.

"I'll record our answers," Calliope said.

Sara read the first question. "Décor at bed-and-breakfast inns is typically themed, historic, or modern. What is the décor for the rooms at your inn? If you were going to change your theme, to which type would you change?"

"She should have added to reply with wrong answers only, but if we're being serious, I'll start," Gary said. "Our décor is straight from the thrift store, and our guests call it historic. I call it prehistoric, and I wouldn't change a thing."

Calliope giggled. "That was your serious answer?"

Jenna smiled at the lively discussions and occasional laughter in the room as everyone dived into the exercise.

She furrowed her brow as she scanned the room.

"Something wrong, Jenna?" Sara asked.

"I don't see Frankie. Do you suppose she went home?"

Sara snorted. "I doubt it. There's an opening on the board. If she's not around, it will go to Victor by default."

"I saw her earlier," Calliope said. "She must have stepped out."

"Victor or Frankie? What a choice. Why aren't you running, Sara?" Gary asked.

"I didn't come here to be nagged." Sara glared at Gary and pushed away from the table so abruptly that her chair fell backward. She stormed out of the conference room.

Gary's eyes were wide as he righted her chair. "Why did asking her about the board make her so mad?"

Calliope shrugged. "I don't know. I mentioned it last year, and she laughed it off. I don't know why she was so mad this time."

"I'm going to talk to her," Jenna said.

Calliope shook her head. "I don't think that's a good idea."

"Don't you think it would be better to let her cool down first?" Gary asked.

"Probably." Jenna picked up her backpack and left the conference room. When Jenna didn't see Sara in the lobby, she went into the library and found Sara sitting in the corner in the black leather chair.

Chapter Nine

Sara glanced at Jenna. "I suppose I owe Gary an apology. He didn't deserve to be snapped at like that."

"You're right."

Sara snorted. "Pull up a chair; I need to talk."

Jenna dragged a chair away from the nearest table and sat near Sara.

"I have no patience for the politics, but Twyla's been after me to be on the board since she became president. I'd be absolutely miserable serving on the board. The only reason I would run would be to spite Frankie, and I don't like that side of me."

Sara shook her head. "I'm really torn because if I don't run, Frankie will be a shoo-in, and she'd take advantage of the position. Delilah was loyal to the association and a great buffer; nobody could fill her shoes. She'd never let Frankie or Victor pull anything shady."

Jenna nodded. "I see your point."

"Gary's smart; he should run for the board."

Jenna leaned forward. "No disrespect intended, but I think Gary is too nice."

Sara smiled. "You have a point. If I ran, my campaign slogan would be Not afraid to kick butts."

"That would work, or maybe you could go with something like If you need a friend, find a dog."

Sara laughed.

Jenna examined Sara's face and waited while Sara appeared to sink into deep thought.

Finally, Sara exhaled as she rose from her chair. "Okay, let's go back into the conference room. I have to talk to you and Gary."

As they strolled across the lobby, Sara said, "Do you see the housekeeper who is pushing the cart from the elevator toward the first-floor rooms?"

Jenna glanced up as Raelynn hurried out of sight. "Yes, why?"

"When I came out of the conference room, she was standing near the elevator. I thought it was odd because the housekeeping carts are too big for the elevator, and it was strange to me she was still there until after we were talking."

Jenna shrugged. "Maybe she was taking a break."

When they went back inside, Calliope raised her eyebrows, and Gary glanced at Sara and then quickly looked away. She sat next to him.

"I apologize for lashing out at you, Gary. You asked a perfectly logical question, and I responded with a tantrum that rivaled a two-year-old. I am truly sorry."

Gary examined her face.

When Sara smiled, he returned her smile.

Sara exhaled. "I'd like to answer your question, Gary."

"Only if you want to, Sara; it's really none of my business."

Sara continued, "I do think I should run, but only under one condition. Gary, I'd like you and Jenna to agree to be my advisors. I have baggage that will be difficult for me to shed when it comes to association business, and sometimes I'm a little short-tempered, so I need you two to be sounding boards for me."

"Sometimes, Mom?" Calliope giggled. "Your idea is brilliant."

Jenna frowned. "We wouldn't have to go to meetings, would we?"

"Not at all," Sara said. "I just need to know I could send a text or call for a reality check. Anytime I'm taking too much of your time, I'll have to trust that you'd tell me."

Jenna and Gary exchanged a glance.

"Why don't we make this a three-way support system?" Jenna asked. "I'd like to have experts on my side."

"And I'd like to know I can ask questions too, especially about finances, at least until I have more confidence," Gary said.

"I can set up a group chat-type system for you," Calliope said. "You'll be able to ask questions and get answers without trying to coordinate being available at the same time."

"That would be perfect," Sara said. "I could drop in my questions, and y'all could answer when you had time."

Twyla stepped up to the podium with her microphone. "Thank you, everyone. We've received all your responses and will post them this afternoon. I do have a surprise for you. The board and I met, and for those of you who live close to Savannah, we would like to invite your spouse or partner to join us at the banquet tomorrow evening as a special thanks from us for taking care of business so you could be here."

She smiled at the enthusiastic applause. "I'll see you at happy hour at five thirty."

"I have to call Kendra," Gary said.

"I have a question," Calliope said. "Are we still going out to dinner, or are we going to stay here?"

"Have you already made reservations, Gary?" Jenna asked.

"Yes, but I can easily cancel," he said.

"Let's not cancel. We have the banquet tomorrow," Sara said.

"Sounds good to me," Gary said.

Jenna and Calliope nodded.

"Good, then we'll still meet at six o'clock," Sara said.

"Calliope, you'll be the administrator of the chat system, right?" Jenna asked.

"See, that was a question I wouldn't have known to ask," Sara said.

"Of course." Calliope beamed. "I'm glad I can help."

Frankie walked into the conference room carrying her flannel shirt. "That sounds interesting. Help with what?"

Jenna smiled. "Calliope was our recorder for the team exercise and did a wonderful job."

"Ready to go, Mom?" Calliope closed her computer and rose.

Sara nodded as she glared at Frankie.

While Jenna and Gary packed up their computers, Frankie said, "I was looking for Twyla; do you know where she is?"

"She said something about grabbing a coffee," Jenna said.

"I should have known." Frankie hurried out of the room.

"That was slick," Gary said.

Jenna patted her hair. "People who annoy me bring out my ornery side."

"Was I the only one who noticed she wasn't wearing her lucky red blouse?" Calliope asked.

"I noticed her black turtleneck earlier. I assumed she changed because the turtleneck is warmer than her silk blouse," Jenna said.

Sara's eyes flashed. "I'll be back in a minute."

Sara darted out the door.

"That's not good," Calliope said.

"Why not?" Gary asked.

Sara's going to confront Frankie. Jenna snatched up her backpack and rushed out of the room.

She slowed down when she saw Sara standing alone at the front door.

Sara exhaled when she saw Jenna and smiled. "Care to sit for a minute?"

While they sat in the upholstered chairs in a corner near the front door, Sara said, "Frankie saw me coming and threw on that flannel shirt and took off. I scared her, and that flannel shirt isn't nearly warm enough to wear outside for long, so I'm happy."

"I'm glad you're happy, but I don't understand."

"Frankie always made fun of Delilah when she wore black, which was frequently. She was being disrespectful."

Jenna narrowed her eyes. "There's more to it than that."

Sara sighed. "I don't know where she got that purple and green plaid shirt, but that was a direct dig at Calliope and me. It was childish of me to react so strongly, but I haven't had that much fun in ages."

Jenna continued to examine Sara's face. *That's not it. There's something else.*

Jenna shifted her gaze toward the conference room. *It's not my business.* "What are you going to tell Calliope?"

"What I told you, but I might wait a few years before I do."

Jenna smiled. "It's good to come clean, isn't it?"

Sara grinned as she rose. "I'll go talk to Calliope and Gary so they won't worry about me. We're still on for dinner at six, aren't we?"

"Absolutely."

"Don't you love Gary made reservations for us? We're lucky he's a foodie."

After Sara left for the conference room, Jenna pulled out Miss B's diary to read.

She became wrapped up in the scandalous tale of a girl who was picking pockets in the speakeasy and hiding the money in a secret drawer in the mahogany bar. 'A pair of C's was the goal for getaway cabbage. With that, she would be on easy street. She was fixing to skedaddle, but Reba M. stole it. Time to call in a chit.'

Jenna raised her eyebrows. *Miss B. is talking about herself. A pair of C's is two hundred dollars. That was a lot of money back then. Miss B. probably had some tough friends. It does not look good for Reba M.*

She was startled by a loud voice. "Jenna?"

"Sorry, I didn't mean to scare you," Mia said. "I guess you didn't hear me at first. What are you reading?"

"It's a gossipy diary from the early 1920s." Jenna opened her backpack to put away the diary and saw the padded envelope Delilah had given her.

"Sounds interesting." Mia exhaled. "It's been an exhausting day. I've cleared out all of Delilah's things except for her makeup, perfume, and things like that." She pointed at the hotel cart with suitcases and a large cardboard box. "I told the desk clerk they can throw out everything I left."

"I almost forgot. I have some papers Delilah gave me."

Mia's phone buzzed with a text. She groaned as she read it. "I can't believe it. I have to go to the lawyer's office right away, and I just left there. He has more paperwork that has to be signed today."

She's overwhelmed.

Mia's eyes welled up. "Let me take a quick peek."

Jenna pulled the icy envelope out of her backpack, and Mia removed a few pages.

Mia glanced over the top three pages. "I don't even know who Leo is. These look like old bank records. I don't know why Delilah had them because her accountant has all her bank records. She was never a packrat, so I don't know." Mia rubbed her forehead. "Just toss them. I'm sorry, but I have to run upstairs and get my coat."

Mia handed the pages back to Jenna.

Jenna quickly slid the cold papers back into the envelope. "Don't worry about the papers. I'll take care of them."

"I can't thank you enough for all you've done for me today." Mia brushed away a tear, then hurried to the elevator.

"Bad timing on my part," Jenna muttered as she passed a housekeeping cart next to an open room.

"Busybody," a woman behind her growled.

Jenna turned and glanced at Raelynn who glowered at her. When Jenna cocked her head and met her gaze, Raelyn ducked into the room as she continued to mumble under her breath.

I can't tell Morgan Raelynn called me a busybody. She'd throw Shane into her car and drive here without stopping. Jenna furrowed her brow. *No, it's worse. She'd tell Ethan.*

After she was in her room, she dropped her backpack next to her chair and took off her boots. Jenna relaxed in the chair and wiggled her toes before she pulled the diary out of her backpack and read.

She raised her eyebrows when she came to a page about the entertainers. 'You had to be a flapper to get down them ladders. Some marks liked big girls, but they were left out in the cold.'

I'd love to see if that's true. I wonder if Lucy would be interested too.

Jenna's phone buzzed with a text from Morgan. "We're home. Call when you can."

Jenna called her.

Morgan said, "Shane wants me to set up an office for him in the living room so he can see his clients because he can't drive for at least two weeks, but it might be three."

"Are you going to do it?"

"If I don't, he'll sneak out while I'm at the inn. I hid his keys, but knowing him, he has a spare set somewhere."

Jenna nodded. "Of course, he would. He's Shane."

Morgan sighed. "I called Mr. Moore. He has an old desk and a comfortable office chair we can borrow. Ethan will pick it up for us in the morning and bring it here."

"How's Mr. Moore doing?"

"I think he's finally recovering at least a little from his loss. He told me he'd be happy to be Shane's assistant until Shane is back on his feet."

"That's wonderful news."

"Exactly; he's the only one Shane would trust to check an insignificant detail no one else would care about and could keep Shane from disappearing to check it himself."

After they hung up, Jenna picked up the diary. She chuckled at the deviousness of Miss B.'s antics from putting henna into a blonde rival's bottle of shampoo to adding hot sauce to the boss man's coffee. "You were a prankster, Miss B."

When Jenna heard a backup alarm outside her window, she went to the window to see what was going on and disturbed the mockingbird that sat on her windowsill. The bird flew to the rooftop of the building across the alley and trilled another chorus of backup alarms.

Jenna chuckled then scanned the alley and its usual trash. Her eyes widened at the figure lying face down next to the dumpster like a child's discarded doll.

Her heart pounded. "It's a woman."

While she snatched up her room key and threw on her coat, she called Lucy.

When Lucy answered, Jenna was running down the hall and was halfway to the emergency exit that went to the alley. "There's a woman on the ground in the alley behind my room. Can you meet me there?"

"Slow down. Did you say a woman on the ground? I'll come to your room. Wait for me."

"I'm already outside." Jenna hung up and clutched her phone as she ran down the alley from the exit toward her room to find the woman.

When she reached the tall, muscular woman who wore a housekeeper's uniform, she froze at the sight of the widespread pool of blood surrounding the body.

Raelynn. She gasped, then gagged at the overwhelming metallic odor of blood.

"Jenna, where are you?" Lucy shouted.

"Here," Jenna's voice squeaked.

She cleared her throat and forced herself to shout, "Here!"

When a feral cat yowled and hissed from inside the dumpster next to her, Jenna put a hand over her mouth to stifle a scream as it leaped out and raced away.

Jenna felt her knees weaken, so she moved close to a trash bin and leaned against it for balance.

"Toughen up, buttercup," she growled.

She stared at Raelynn's body. Her lanyard for her hotel ID lay in the pool of blood, but Jenna saw the lanyard had been cut and Raelynn's ID was gone. *The killer had no qualms about having blood on his hands.*

Bile rose in Jenna's throat, and she clung to the trash bin while she heaved.

When she regained her composure, Jenna wiped her face with her shirt and shivered. *My feet are cold.* She stared at her feet. *No wonder. No boots.*

When Lucy reached Jenna, she asked, "Did you check her?"

"I didn't go close to her because of the blood, but I know it's Raelynn."

Lucy continued closer as she examined the body but stayed clear of the blood as sirens howled in the distance. "Tell me what happened."

"There's not much to tell," Jenna said. "I looked out of my window, saw her, and called you."

Lucy nodded. "You don't have to stay out here. I'll come talk to you later."

"Thanks," Jenna headed toward the emergency exit.

"You can't get in through the emergency exit. You'll have to go around to the front."

Jenna peered down the alley and shuddered at the debris that partially blocked it. *It will be dark by the time I get back to the hotel. I wish I'd brought my flashlight.*

"No, wait. I wasn't thinking," Lucy said. "You don't even have any shoes on. I'll text Roy to open the employee entrance door for you."

Lucy pointed in the other direction. "It's near the other end of the hotel where the freight elevator was. You'll see the door."

Jenna exhaled in relief. "Thanks."

When she reached the door, Roy was waiting outside for her. "Lucy told me you went out the emergency exit, but I didn't know you were wearing only socks, Mrs. Ross. It's a wonder you didn't step on any glass. I've told that worthless Marvin we needed to put up a sign to let guests know there's no re-entry at that door and another sign outside with the hotel phone number so guests know they can call us if they accidentally go out that way. I'll ask Lucy to order them; she'll take care of it."

"Thank you, and that's a great idea. I didn't realize I couldn't get back in."

Roy nodded as he led her through the storage area to the hall that went to the conference room. "You aren't the first."

Jenna strode past the conference room and through the lobby to her room.

When she was in her room, she removed her coat and socks. *My feet are freezing.* She rubbed her feet to warm them, but they just made her hands cold.

Now what? Jenna turned on the shower. After a hot shower, she exhaled. *Better.* She glanced at her phone while she dressed. *It's almost six. I missed happy hour. I'll get over it.*

Before she left her room, Jenna put Miss B.'s diary in her backpack. *Calliope will get a kick out of some of Miss B.'s misadventures.*

When Jenna reached the lobby, she smiled and returned Calliope's wave. A slender blonde wearing high-heeled boots, gray wool slacks, and a long-sleeved, deep blue blouse, stood next to Gary. She was three inches shorter than Calliope and at least three years older than Jenna. Her hair was styled in the latest fashion, and her makeup was flawless. She laughed when Gary spoke and put her hand lightly on his arm.

Gary's eyes narrowed, and with a subtle shift, he stepped behind Sara.

Jenna raised her eyebrows. *Who is that?*

Calliope beamed when Jenna joined them. "Jenna, this is Paige. She's Lucy's cousin. Lucy has to work, so Paige decided to join us for dinner."

Paige's smile was a plastic imitation of joy. "It's nice to meet you, Jenna. I've heard so much about you already." She raised an eyebrow and smirked. "Nice hat."

Jenna's face mirrored the sincerity of Paige's smile. "Thank you." *And thanks to Mia for being a model for deflection of sarcasm.*

Gary cleared his throat. "Jenna and I will visit my mother in the hospital after dinner, Paige, so we will have to leave immediately after we eat."

When Paige's face fell, Sara nodded. "We're positive she'll be much better by the end of the week."

"Well, we should really get moving. It's walking distance to the restaurant, isn't it?" Calliope looped her arm through Paige's. "We'll follow you and Jenna, Gary."

"I'll walk with you too, Gary. We'll let the kids follow us," Sara said.

Jenna turned away to hide her smirk when Paige's face tightened with annoyance.

After they were outside and headed toward the restaurant, Calliope called out, "Victor's back."

"Who's Victor?" Paige asked.

Calliope said, "One of the old-timers; he had a medical procedure today. He'll have stories galore with all the details about his procedure and the diagnosis. He's hilarious."

Sara whispered, "Would you have guessed Calliope didn't like how Paige talked about you before you joined us?"

Jenna smiled.

After they had walked half a block, Paige asked, "Do you have to walk so fast? How much farther is this restaurant?"

"It's only five more blocks," Jenna said.

"We usually walk a few more blocks than that, so we may have to take the long way back to get all our steps in for the day," Sara added.

"Oh no, I completely forgot. I apologize, but I can't go to dinner with you after all," Paige said.

Jenna, Sara, and Gary turned to watch as Paige hurried back toward the hotel.

"She lasted longer than I expected," Calliope said.

After walking another block, they reached the restaurant.

"That was a fast five blocks," Sara said.

"This is an old-fashioned diner," Gary said. "The food isn't fancy, and neither are the prices. They do have a nice selection of wine, though."

After they ordered and were munching on hushpuppies and crawfish dip with crackers while they sipped their wine, Sara said, "Now tell us all about Ethan because Paige said you stole him from her."

"It actually was a fascinating story," Calliope said. "You were so devious when you took over the inn that you conned Ethan into taking care of everything for you. In fact, because he was so busy fixing up your barn, he had to hire people to do the work for his lawnmower business."

Jenna giggled. "Ethan and I had a rough start and still clash mostly because he's pigheaded, and I'm the nice one."

Sara's eyes twinkled. "Like me?"

"Exactly."

Gary rolled his eyes. "Poor Ethan."

Jenna snorted. "Now the lawnmower business part is almost true, except he had a landscaping business, which is a little different. Ethan is a general contractor, and he and his partner picked up the contract to upgrade the barn when circumstances prevented the original general contractor from continuing. They have grown their business, so they did have to hire more people."

"It's almost like she took every other word out of the true story, isn't it?" Sara asked.

"I've known people who have kept just enough of the truth in their story to make their lie believable," Gary said.

"It's called paltering," Calliope said.

When the other three stared at her, Calliope said, "I learned about it in psychology class, but I never expected it to come up in a normal conversation."

Jenna giggled. "I'm not sure anyone in your psychology class would define any of our conversations as normal."

After they ate and were on their way back, Sara said, "I'm glad we walked because I need to walk off the five pounds I probably put on."

"Are we going back the long way for the extra steps?" Gary chuckled.

Jenna giggled. "That was an excellent touch, Sara."

"It was amazing how quickly Paige dumped us," Calliope said. "What an amateur."

When they reached the hotel, Gary said, "I'm skipping tonight's speaker. I'll see you in the morning. I have work to do."

"So do we," Sara said, "but I might show up late just to see what's going on."

"I'm skipping," Calliope said.

Jenna nodded and headed toward her room. As she passed the offices, Lucy joined her. "How are you doing?"

"I'm glad I went to dinner with the group; I'm doing fine."

"The hotel has snacks and drinks in the conference room for guests. I think they're trying to keep the guests separated from the staff; not that I blame them. There aren't many people in there, so we can talk. Can I buy you a hot tea?"

"That sounds great."

On the way to the conference room, Jenna asked, "How was Raelynn murdered?"

Lucy stopped and spoke softly. "Her throat was cut with a single swipe; she bled out in seconds."

Jenna shuddered at the memory of the sight and smell of all the blood. "She was slender but obviously worked out. She was not a weak, helpless woman."

Lucy exhaled. "No, she wasn't. She must have known her assailant because there was no evidence of a struggle. She had a note in her back pocket that said, 'back alley in ten minutes.' That will be on the news by morning."

When they went into the conference room, the conversations were surprisingly subdued, despite the number of people who were in the room.

Jenna glanced at her usual table, and it was empty; she smiled. *Everybody knows who sits where.*

After they had their hot tea and cookies in hand, Lucy asked, "Where would you like to sit?"

Jenna pointed to a table near the door and the podium. "No one ever sits there."

After they were seated, Lucy said, "The police found Delilah's earrings in Raelynn's front pocket, which is another detail the newscasters will announce in the morning as late-breaking news."

The elevator dinged twice.

"Did Raelynn have her necklace too?" Jenna asked.

"No." Lucy sighed. "The elevator is driving Roy crazy trying to figure out how it is making sounds it is not wired to make."

Never blackmail a killer.

"Never blackmail a killer," Jenna murmured.

Lucy stared at Jenna. "What?"

Jenna blinked at Lucy. "It was just a random thought. Did I tell you about the diary I found in the library?"

"I don't think so."

"It was written by one of the young women who lived in the hotel in the 1920s. It's gossipy, but she said a few things that interested me. She said the ladders from the fourth floor to the third could only be used by flappers, and I think she meant slender women because she also said some marks liked big girls and they were out of luck."

Lucy raised her eyebrows. "If that's true then you, for example, could go down the ladder and return, but I could not. Do you want to check it out?"

"I'd love to. I'd hate for a brilliant theory to go unproven. The other thing she mentioned was that there was a trapdoor in the stage that went straight down to the basement. I don't know if we care, but maybe that's something else we could look at before I leave."

"I agree. I'll bet it has at least a ladder if not stairs because that would be some drop from the third floor to the basement. Why don't we plan to check the ladder and the trapdoor tomorrow right after breakfast? Did you find anything else?"

"Not yet, but I'm not even halfway through. I'll be reading more before bed tonight, and checking things out right after breakfast sounds perfect."

"Where did you go for supper? Paige told me she was going to tag along. Did she?"

"No, it was too far for her to walk." Jenna told her about the restaurant and the food.

Lucy furrowed her brow. "That's not all that far away; she must have come up with something else she'd rather do. Just as well."

While they chatted, Paige came into the conference room with four other women who were members of the association.

Jenna raised her eyebrows. Paige was wearing a rustic rose ball cap with a brown bird embroidered on the crown.

She must have stopped at the hat store on her way back.

When Paige saw Jenna, she pointed at her and snickered. "I told you she would have copied my hat."

The women with her stared at Jenna, and two of them tittered. The other two glared at Paige.

Lucy leaned forward to rise out of her seat.

"Let her go," Jenna said. "She's not worth causing a fuss over."

"True."

"But she's been wearing her peach blossom cap since Sunday," a woman said.

"Yes, but see how new it looks?" Paige asked. "My hat has been around the block."

"Yours looks new to me," another woman said.

Paige smiled. "Thank you. I wear it all the time, but I keep it clean by handwashing it." She glanced around. "They closed down the bar."

"There's a bar across the street," a woman said.

"Sounds good to me. Who's game?" Paige asked.

Two of the women left the conference room with Paige.

"I'm embarrassed by her attitude," Lucy said. "I'm calling Mom tonight."

The two women who remained whispered and then strolled to Jenna's table.

"Jenna, we apologize for what that woman said. She's not a member, and we've never seen her before. She joined us for dinner when we were leaving the hotel. She implied she was related to you when she told us her cousin was here, but then later she said you stole her boyfriend, and her cousin was an undercover cop. You aren't an undercover cop, are you?"

The other woman rolled her eyes. "Of course she isn't. Paige was just trying to make herself sound important. Anyway, Jenna, we were mortified by what she said to you."

"Thank you, but don't blame yourselves. She seems like she's a lonely person and says whatever pops into her head for attention."

The two women nodded and then left the conference room.

"Well done, Jenna." Lucy furrowed her brow. "I don't know if Paige knows how dangerous it is for her to claim to be related to an undercover cop. I'll talk to Mom.

Maybe she can convince Paige to return home before she causes some real damage."

After they rose and cleared the table, Jenna said, "I'm going to call it a night. I'm looking forward to changing into comfy clothes and reading Miss B.'s diary. I'll see you in the morning."

Lucy nodded.

After Jenna was in her room, she changed into her pajamas and then texted Ethan. "In my room."

He replied in a text. "On my way home. Will call you in ten minutes."

Jenna frowned at her phone. *Why was he working so late?*

She put up her feet and opened the diary.

After she had read two pages, she chuckled. *At least I know he isn't with Paige.*

Jenna furrowed her brow. *I thought I wanted to know the full story of Ethan and Paige, but now that I've met Paige, I really don't care.*

She answered her phone on the first ring. "I can't wait to hear your excuse for working so late, except you'll just blame Shane, won't you?"

Ethan chuckled. "This time it really was. Morgan told you about Mr. Moore's office furniture, didn't she? I'm going to pick it up tomorrow, but Morgan's been under a lot of stress, and isn't her usual organized self. She called me in a panic because she realized right after supper that almost everything in the living room would have to be moved to other rooms, but she didn't think it through, so it took several tries to get everything the way she wanted it. So that's what I've been doing. Now I want to hear about your day."

"It was a little rough."

"Like how rough?"

Jenna bit her lip. *There's too much to just dump on him this late at night. I should tell him in person. Maybe I'll go home tomorrow night after the banquet.*

"Paige Adams is Lucy's cousin, and I spent most of my day dealing with her. Lucy had innocently mentioned I was from Paisley, so Paige came to Savannah and made a pest of herself. I don't know if I'm complaining or confessing, but she got on my nerves."

"What did she say?"

"She claimed to be my cousin, told a group her cousin was an undercover cop, and then told them I stole her boyfriend, who she claimed was Ethan from Paisley. I swear she said all that in practically the same breath, if you can believe that."

Ethan groaned. "Actually, I can. Do you want to hear the story?"

"Not really," Jenna said. "I don't know if she's a pathological liar or has to make up lies for attention, and I don't much care."

"Thanks for telling me she was there. A buddy of mine took her out one time, and my date, who was an old friend from school, and I ran into them. My buddy dropped her after that one date, but she told everyone it was because I flirted with her all night. My old friend was the one who told me what Paige was saying. She told me to ignore Paige, but I thought I knew better and asked Paige to meet me so we could clear up the misunderstanding."

"Ouch; not a good move. Your heart was in the right place, but she's a snake," Jenna said.

"You're right." Ethan exhaled. "I guess I'm still paying for that mistake."

"What do you mean?"

"You know...with you."

"Not at all. In fact, I have a little more to tell you about Paige."

Jenna told him about Paige inviting herself to dinner, Victor's infliction, and the five blocks to the diner.

"I like your new friends; they definitely jumped in and had your back, didn't they? But if I didn't know Paige, I wouldn't have believed she'd broadcast her cousin was an undercover cop, whether or not it was true."

Jenna's pendant quivered, and the elevator dinged three times.

Jenna sighed. *Okay, Nettie.*

"Well, it's actually true because when I found a housekeeper who had been murdered, Lucy took over the investigation."

Jenna held her breath. *Thanks a lot, Nettie.*

The elevator chimed.

Ethan exhaled. "That was today too?"

"Yes."

"Anything else?" Ethan asked.

Jenna closed her eyes. *Wasn't that enough?* "No, that was the gist of my rough day. The rest can wait until

Thursday when I see you." Jenna unsuccessfully stifled a yawn.

Ethan's voice softened.

"Right, Thursday. You need to get some rest. Good night, Babe."

"Good night, cowboy."

After they hung up, Jenna gently stroked her pendant. "I'm glad I told him, Nettie. Thanks for the nudge."

Jenna picked up the diary and began reading about the floozy who tried to steal away the drummer, Willy, from Miss B.

"I would call this section of the diary Miss B.'s revenge." Jenna stretched, then paced as she mumbled, "She put Fletcher's Castoria, which I'm pretty sure was a laxative, in the floozy's flask and permanent red ink in her perfume bottle."

Jenna's eyes narrowed. "Sprays of red ink would look like a rash. The combination of the effects from the laxative and the suspicious skin rash would have guaranteed a significant cut in the floozy's income."

She shook her head. "Miss B. definitely fought dirty."

Jenna tried to read more, but her head and her eyes drooped.

After Jenna closed her book, she glanced down at floor before she stood up. "I forgot that Katy's not here for me to talk to. At least nobody knows I've been talking to myself."

She rose from her chair and checked to be sure she had locked the deadbolt, then climbed into bed and turned off the light.

She listened to the faraway rumbles of thunder while she drifted off thinking about Miss B., her rivals, and Willy the drummer.

Chapter Ten

Jenna woke and stretched. *I need coffee.* She glanced at the time and groaned. *Five in the morning. The hotel has coffee around the clock in the lobby.*

She glanced down at her white-and-peach plaid pajama pants and her long-sleeved, solid rose T-shirt pajama top. *Nobody cares.*

After she brushed her hair, she slipped on her fuzzy pink slippers and picked up her backpack. *Roy will be proud of me. I'm wearing something besides socks on my feet.*

The hotel was eerily silent except for the soft murmuring of long-gone voices and the moans and creaks of the old building. As she drew closer to the lobby, the voices became whispers of forgotten secrets. Jenna smiled. *It's nice to know the renovations have not removed the past from the hotel.*

The lone night clerk was heads-down, closing out the books for the previous day. No one else was in sight. The coffee machine gurgled as she approached it.

"I just made that pot, ma'am," the night clerk called out. "I'm sorry to say you missed the six-hour old coffee."

"Thank you. I'm sure I'll adjust to the two-minute old coffee."

The night clerk chuckled. "Me too. Don't tell anybody, but I made it ahead of schedule as my reward for finishing early."

Jenna smiled. "Well-deserved, and I appreciate it." Jenna sipped her coffee. "How long have you worked here?"

"Three weeks," he said. "I like it. I understand most people don't like working nights in an old hotel because it's too quiet. It suits me."

Jenna refilled her cup and then headed across the lobby toward the hallway to her room. As she passed the registration desk, she heard a scream and a thud from the stairwell. When she set her cup on the registration desk, the night clerk's eyes were wide. "Did you hear that?"

"Yes."

The two of them ran to the stairwell. The young man beat Jenna to the door and flung it open. The stairwell was dark except for the light coming from the lobby.

Paige was splayed out on her back with her right leg at an awkward angle. Jenna kneeled next to her and exhaled in relief. "She's breathing."

"I'll call an ambulance." The night clerk blocked the door open so there would be light on the landing, then raced away to his desk.

Jenna pulled out her phone and texted Lucy. "Paige fell down the stairs at the hotel. Unconscious but breathing. The lights were out in the stairwell."

Paige opened one eye and hissed, "You pushed me."

Jenna gaped at her as the night clerk returned with a flashlight. He flicked the light switch, but the lights didn't come on. When he shined the light on the landing, Jenna narrowed her eyes at Paige's new dusty rose ball cap that was in the corner.

"Is she your older sister, ma'am?"

Paige grunted.

"No, why?"

"You two look so much alike," he said.

The sound of a siren ripped through the night, and the night clerk rushed to the front door to open the door for the ambulance crew.

While the crew rolled Paige out of the hotel, she groaned, and Jenna sighed with relief. Lucy joined Jenna in the lobby.

"What happened?"

"I woke up early and came out for coffee. On my way back to my room, the night clerk and I heard a scream and a thump. When we ran to the door, we saw Paige on the landing. The stairwell lights were off. I didn't see anyone else. I don't think she's as bad off as she's acting."

"Probably not. What do you mean?"

"She opened one eye and told me I pushed her."

"I'm not surprised. I need coffee."

"I could use a warm-up." Jenna glanced down. "And then I probably should get dressed."

While Jenna refilled her cup and put the lid on it, she said, "Her dusty rose ball cap was in the corner and probably still is. The night clerk asked if we were sisters."

Lucy narrowed her eyes. "I don't see it. Does anyone know you changed rooms?"

"Just Ethan, but no one here unless they have access to the hotel registration system. I haven't had any reason to mention it."

"Your first floor room is registered as VIP, which is used for hotel upper management when they are here. You're still officially registered in your third floor room, which is the room I gave to Paige. I'm going to check her phone and her room. Do you have anything else for me?"

"No. Are we still going to do our after breakfast check?" Jenna asked.

"I think we should." Lucy headed toward the stairs.

Jenna carried her coffee to her room, locked the deadbolt behind her and put her cup on the table.

The night clerk's words echoed in her head, "Is she your older sister, ma'am?"

Her knees buckled, and her head spun. Jenna grabbed onto the upholstered chair and dropped into the chair.

Did someone think Paige was me? She put her head between her knees to stop the spinning.

When she felt calmer, Jenna picked up her coffee, but her hand shook, so she clutched it with two hands and returned it to the table.

She stared at her cup, then removed the lid and sipped her coffee. "I'll wear my peach blossom hat. If somebody pushed Paige, maybe I'll shake them up."

After she showered and dressed, Jenna put on her necklace and her peach blossom cap. *I could ask Lucy to shred Delilah's documents.* She exhaled and pulled the envelope out of her backpack and onto the small table so she could examine the files.

Jenna raised her eyebrows at the handwritten note on the top page. Delilah had printed "For LEO." *That's why Mia said she didn't know who Leo was. Delilah intended for these to go to a Law Enforcement Officer.*

While Jenna inspected the bank statements, they warmed to room temperature. She studied the details and took notes while she organized them as she would have in her auditing days when she was a corporate accountant.

After she had pored over the stack of papers, she glanced toward the window and blinked. *It's sunrise!*

She slipped the papers back into the envelope and put the envelope in her backpack. *Follow the money.*

She texted Ethan. "Good morning."

Jenna was ready when her phone rang.

She relaxed her shoulders when she heard his voice.

"I was hoping you'd sleep in, but I should have known you wouldn't. I'm leaving the house as soon as we hang up. There's another furniture crisis at Shane's. We moved his file cabinet in front of the window, but now he is complaining because he can't see the driveway. Have you had your coffee?"

She smiled as a sense of calmness washed over her. *I didn't realize how tense I was.*

"Yes. I sneaked down to the lobby a few minutes ago in my pajamas."

"Have you decided when you're coming back?"

"I'll leave in the morning after breakfast. I'll be home for lunch."

"Are you sure you won't be leaving today? What if the sessions end early?"

"I'm positive."

"Okay, I'll see you later, babe. I miss you."

"I miss you too."

Jenna sighed as they hung up. *One more day.*

When Jenna strolled into the lobby, the night clerk was still there. He motioned for her to join him at the desk. "Mrs. Ross, I'm working a double. Lucy asked me to tell you she'll meet with you later this morning."

"Thanks."

Jenna glanced at the elevator as it creaked then dinged as the doors opened. Her eyes widened when three people rushed out of the small elevator followed by Sara and Calliope, whose face was pale.

On the way to the hotel coffee shop, Calliope shuddered. "The elevator was as awful as I had imagined. I couldn't believe it when the door to the stairs had a sign saying out of order taped on it. Was it like that when you came down? How can stairs be out of order? I tried the door, and it was locked. They need a second decent set of stairs."

"I think they should retire that old elevator and install a new one," Sara said. "Jenna, on our way down, a woman told her friend not to eat breakfast because she heard a national linen supply company is picking up the tab for a buffet breakfast. Of course, we all politely pretended not to hear, so we don't know how true it is. Do we want to take our chances and just get coffee?"

Jenna shook her head. "I can't; I planned on an early breakfast because I have some things I have to do before the meeting begins."

Sara nodded. "Since we don't have any details, we don't know if they'll push back the start time for the meeting or have the buffet available during the meeting."

"I don't mind winging it," Calliope said, "but I'd rather eat now. Although if they have cinnamon rolls, I'll have one to be polite."

Jenna smiled. "Excellent idea. I'll adjust my plans to include a cinnamon roll."

When they went into the coffee shop, Gary was sitting at a table with his accounting book. While they sat down, he said, "I've already ordered; this accounting stuff is deeper than I thought. I'm going to focus on accounting today."

"I learn better with no distractions too," Jenna said.

The server rushed to them with coffee, then quickly returned with Gary's breakfast.

After they ordered, Calliope asked, "Did you hear about Paige?"

The hair rose on the back of Jenna's neck. *I wasn't ready for this quite so early.* She picked up her coffee. "No, what?"

"She went to a restaurant with a group from the hotel, then dumped them to go bar-hopping with another group that was sitting at the table next to them."

"She didn't know them?" Sara shook her head. "That is downright reckless. How did you hear about it?"

"The first group returned last night before I went to my room. One of them and I had chatted during a break on Monday, and she saw Paige talking to us earlier. She asked if I knew her."

"What did you say?" Gary asked.

"I told her Paige had introduced herself to our group, but she wasn't a member of the association."

Just as their breakfast orders arrived, Gary finished eating and grinned as he rose. "I hate to eat and run, but that's what I'm doing."

Calliope took her last bite and glanced toward the lobby. "My new friend from last night is alone; she must be waiting for her friends. I wonder if she's heard anything more about Paige. I'll see you in the conference room."

As Calliope rushed to the lobby, the elevator chimed. *Ask her.*

Jenna furrowed her brow. *It's none of my business.*

The elevator chimed again.

Jenna glanced toward the elevator. *Okay, but I'm going to lose a friend.*

Jenna said, "When we were talking about Frankie last night, you told me about purple and green, but there's more, and it's something you'll never tell Calliope."

Jenna put her hand on her pink opal pendant when Sara's face contorted as though she was in intense pain.

Sara stared into her empty coffee cup, then put it down.

"Only Delilah knew, and she stood by me. She was a conniving liar and a self-serving cheat, but she was my best friend. Isn't that strange?"

"Sometimes we don't pick our friends; they pick us," Jenna said.

"That is so true. Delilah told me once I was her hero because I was so passionate. When I argued with her, she laughed and told me I was a calculating hot-head which made me average."

Jenna furrowed her brow, then giggled. "Oh, I get it. Calculating the average. What a play on words."

"That was Delilah. People thought she was stuffy, but she wasn't at all. She enjoyed playing the role of an overbearing matriarch because it was a brilliant cover for her criminal activities. For example, after she bought the Thorne House out from under me, she told me the house would be mine, but the time wasn't right yet. I thought she was just making excuses. I know you asked about Frankie, but you had to understand Delilah first."

Sara glanced at the line forming outside the coffee shop. "We should leave so someone else can have our table. I'll tell you the rest later."

After they paid and strolled into the lobby, Jenna glanced toward the registration desk. *Lucy's back. Her office door is open.*

"I'll be in the conference room," Sara said. "Calliope is probably waiting at our table."

"I'll be awhile, but hopefully I'll make it to the conference room before the meeting starts."

When Jenna reached the registration desk, the night clerk said, "Lucy's in her office waiting for you, Mrs. Ross."

Lucy met her at the office door and furrowed her brow. "Are you still okay with checking the ladders?"

"I think we should."

Lucy picked up the heavy-duty flashlight she had on her desk, then handed a flashlight to Jenna. "Clip this onto your belt when you go down the ladder."

As they strolled toward the freight elevator, Jenna asked, "Which room are we checking? Delilah's or mine?"

"I thought we'd check both."

When they reached the freight elevator, Lucy tapped the control panel, and then pushed the button for the elevator.

On their way up to the fourth floor, Jenna clipped the flashlight to the belt loop on her jeans.

When the freight elevator stopped at the fourth floor, they stepped out. Lucy scanned the surrounding area with the aid of her flashlight.

Jenna glanced at the wide dust mop with clumps of dust bunnies clinging to it and then shined the light ahead of them. "Is there a reason someone would have used that dust mop to create a path toward the guest rooms?"

Lucy narrowed her eyes at the cleaned walkway with heavy dust on both sides. "I can't think of a better way to hide footprints."

As they slowly continued past area that had been gutted except for the still-intact walls between the long-abandoned rooms, Jenna steeled herself against the whispers of warning and the dread from the shadows that wavered, and then hid from the brightness of Lucy's flashlight.

Lucy scattered the threats when she spoke. "An old friend called me last week and told me you'd be here and to stay close to you. I talked to her again yesterday; she said you'd know who she was."

Jenna exhaled in relief at the break. "It had to have been Georgia."

Lucy chuckled. "She also told me to ask you when you knew I was a cop."

"When the detectives took Victor Grimes in for questioning and you said you were glad it wasn't your case."

Lucy rolled her eyes. "The second I said it I knew I'd slipped, but then I hoped you didn't catch it because nobody else would have."

She led the way to the ladders that went down to the guest rooms on the third floor. "We'll start with Delilah's room and then come back this way to your room."

Lucy stopped and pointed to a gray cleaning cloth near the ladder. "This is Delilah's room; I dropped the cloth off earlier to mark it."

When they lifted the hinged wooden cover of the opening, Jenna shined her flashlight down the ladder. "Nobody has been on this ladder in years, Lucy. Look at the cobwebs."

Lucy exhaled. "Well, now we know no one went into Delilah's room using the ladder. It points to someone using the housekeeping key, which we can't confirm. When Marvin checked the records for tracking room access yesterday, he told the police they had been corrupted, probably by a power surge during the storm."

"That's convenient."

Lucy narrowed her eyes. "A little too convenient."

The shadows darkened, and whispers groaned. *Perfume.*

Jenna cleared her throat. "Mia took only what she wanted from Delilah's room. Has housekeeping cleaned the room?"

Lucy examined Jenna's face. "I intended to do that today. Why?"

Jenna coughed from the dust they had stirred up when they lifted the hatch door.

"Let's talk later," Lucy said. "Will you be okay if we check your room before we leave the fourth floor?"

Jenna nodded as she strode away from the settling dust.

After she caught her breath, she said, "Let's do that."

As they headed toward Jenna's old room, Lucy said, "I should have thought about the dust and brought dust masks."

"Hopefully this is a onetime experience."

When Jenna saw the housekeeping cloth, she strode to the ladder.

After they lifted the wooden cover, Jenna shined her light down the ladder. "Lucy, there are no cobwebs."

Lucy peered down the opening. "You're right, and I could easily climb down that ladder. I expected it to be much narrower after what your Miss B. said, didn't you?"

"Their big girls must have been more than just curvy," Jenna said.

Lucy snorted. "My ego's in better shape now that I see I could be a flapper after all."

"Do you want me to see how far I can go down the ladder?" Jenna asked.

"I don't think we have to. We know somebody used the ladder recently, but now the access to the room is nailed shut."

"Maybe whoever used it to search my room knows it's blocked off now, too."

Lucy exhaled. "Right, which means no one had access from the fourth floor to your old room. Let's check out that escape route from the stage to the basement."

As they headed back to the freight elevator, Jenna asked, "You told me my room on the first floor was off the list for housekeeping; does anyone in housekeeping have access to my room?"

"The VIP room key is equivalent to a hotel staff ID, but a VIP room cannot be accessed by hotel staff. No one has access to your room except you and me."

"How would someone who doesn't work for the hotel get to the fourth floor?" Jenna asked.

"They would have to have a hotel staff ID for access to the freight or staff elevators or to the stairs. Unfortunately, Marvin does not keep a record of the IDs, so he can't cancel a lost ID or the ID of a former employee."

"There are stairs for the staff?"

"They're not lit and rarely used, and I see where you're going. There's a real possibility our killer is using the stairs. I'll see how quickly I can get a camera set up on the entrance to the staff stairs."

When they reached the freight elevator, Lucy pushed the button.

After they exited the elevator on the unrestored area of the third floor, they strolled to the former vaudeville theater and went up the five steps to the stage. Their footsteps on the stage echoed eerily in the cavernous room.

"I think we're onto something because the stage doesn't have any dust," Lucy whispered. "Why am I whispering?"

"Because it's so spooky." Jenna tiptoed toward the back of the stage.

"Here's our trapdoor." The hinges creaked as Jenna lifted the door by its heavy iron ring, and then she and Lucy gaped at the set of stairs that led down.

"Are you game?" Lucy turned on her flashlight and stepped down three steps and stomped. "They're as sturdy as they look. Follow me, but not too close in case there's a faulty step. No sense in two tragic deaths by an unfortunate fall." She shuddered as she clutched onto the rickety iron pipe that served as a handrail.

Jenna turned on her flashlight and closed the trapdoor behind her as she followed Lucy who tried each step before she put her full weight on it. Jenna cringed at the overwhelming smell of mildew and stale air and shivered at the oppressive dampness.

After Lucy reached the second floor, she picked up her pace, and they were soon in the basement.

"Now what?" Jenna asked.

"I'll show you." Lucy strode to a large laundry area with two commercial sized washers and driers and pushed the button on a service elevator. After they were inside the elevator, it went up one floor, and the doors opened to the laundry room on the first floor.

"The laundry area in the basement is no longer used; instead, a commercial supplier provides the clean sheets and towels for the hotel."

"This elevator has no control pad," Jenna said.

"Right, so it's possible to go from the first floor to the basement and to any other floor from there without a hotel ID for access. I've never thought about it."

"Who would know about this?" Jenna asked.

"Anyone who has ever worked for the hotel. The orientation isn't much, but everyone is told the elevator goes to the basement, and there's nothing down there but rats. It's an effective deterrent to the curious."

As they strolled to Lucy's office, Jenna said, "Delilah gave me a large envelope stuffed with papers to give to Mia. Mia glanced at them and told me I could dispose of them because she didn't know who Leo was or why Delilah would have kept old bank statements. Delilah had written 'For Leo' on the first page."

Lucy froze. "What did you do?"

"I'm an accountant; I examined them like an auditor. I think I know what they are. They're in my backpack in your office."

After they were in Lucy's office, Lucy closed the door. When Lucy sat at her desk, Jenna handed her the envelope.

While Jenna sat in the visitor's chair, Lucy examined each page carefully. "Tell me what I'm seeing, auditor."

"These are records of funds moving from one bank to another. The sums are significant, and the money eventually ends up in foreign banks. The account owners are holding accounts."

Lucy shook her head. "Delilah knew she'd gotten too close. Her information has been key in the investigation I've been working on for a while."

Lucy rose from her chair and paced. "Delilah told me once that she lived for drama, and nothing matched the intrigue of being an informant and outwitting a criminal."

"The more I learn about Delilah, the more amazed I am at how complex she was."

"I do have one more..." Jenna was interrupted by a knock at the door.

Lucy swept the papers into a drawer and locked it. "Yes?"

Marvin opened the door. "We have a problem with the caterer. The coordinator wants to talk to you."

Jenna rose. "Thanks for the help."

"I'll call the plumber this morning, Mrs. Ross; thank you for bringing this to my attention, and I'll let you know immediately when it's repaired."

"Thank you; I really do need to talk to you before the room is cleaned."

Lucy's eyes widened. "Yes, ma'am. I'll keep you completely informed."

Jenna exhaled. *Good; she knows I'm talking about Delilah's room.*

Marvin crossed his arms and glowered at Jenna as she headed toward the door.

She smiled as she passed him. "Good morning."

Marvin mumbled, "Good morning, Mrs. Ross."

On her way to the conference room, Jenna's phone buzzed with a text from Mia. "Call me when you can."

Jenna strolled to the entrance of the library and called Mia.

"Jenna, I hate to bother you, but that large box that I thought was books is more bank records, and it's marked for Leo. What do I do with it?"

"Can you have a courier bring it to the hotel to the attention of Lucy Adams? She'll dispose of them properly."

Jenna sent a text to Lucy. "Box coming to the hotel to your attention. Marked LEO."

Chapter Eleven

Jenna stopped outside the conference room and sent Morgan a text. "How is everything going?"

"Shane is a terrible patient. I'm going to ask the hospital for a refund."

Jenna chuckled. "Good luck today."

"Thanks. I'll need it."

When she went into the conference room, Jenna smiled and joined Sara at their table.

"Where's Calliope?"

"In the buffet line with Twyla. Those two have really hit it off. Can you believe that?"

"I can see Twyla would love to mentor someone, and Calliope is a sponge for learning."

Sara nodded. "I've thought about it, and I can tell you the rest of the story about Frankie."

Jenna examined her face. "Only if you want to."

"Did you notice when Paige flirted with Gary how slick he was when he rebuffed her advances?"

Jenna nodded. "Very impressive."

"Frankie was just as flirty as Paige, but my husband was weak. It was before Calliope was born, and Frankie had her eye on the Thorne House. Frankie's plan was for us to buy the house so she could convince my husband to give the house to her."

Jenna gaped at Sara. "Would he have done that?"

Sara nodded. "Probably. After we learned Delilah had bought the house, I wanted to search for another one, but my husband said he wasn't sure that was the right thing to do. He packed a bag and told me he was going away for the weekend to think things over. I assumed it was his way of rekindling our marriage and started packing too, but he went into a rage and accused me of not caring about my unborn baby."

"Were you shocked by such an extreme reaction?"

"Not really." Sara sighed. "Frankie had dropped her usual not-so-subtle hints, so I checked the business credit card, and he had charged four nights at the Sweethearts Lodge for Mr. and Mrs. Nikitas. On his way to pick up Frankie for their getaway in the mountains, he tried to beat a train at a railroad crossing. He died at the scene, and as far as I'm concerned, Frankie killed him."

"I am so sorry."

"It's been over twenty years. You'd think I'd have gotten over it by now, but I never will never forget how she targeted such a vulnerable man while pretending to be my friend."

"What about Victor Grimes? Is he really as pompous and out of touch as he appears, or is that his façade?"

Sara raised an eyebrow. "Don't let Victor fool you. He's more cunning than people realize. He was a successful accountant and ran his own firm for years until he decided there was more money to be made in the paranormal world. He is still the owner of the accounting firm and has two or three long-time clients, but he quit accepting new clients years ago. He has at least six accountants who manage clients at the firm."

"I wouldn't have guessed that at all." Jenna furrowed her brow. "He sounded like he didn't believe Delilah had died when the police wanted to question him."

"Frankie and Victor are showmen to the core. Nothing they do is ever accidental or impulsive; their moral compasses are broken, and neither of them has any respect for authority, but if you're wondering if they would harm Delilah, they might, but the price would have to be right."

Jenna rolled her eyes. "It's a good thing I'm not an investigator. I'm stumped, plus Delilah's necklace is still missing. Do you suppose someone drugged her to steal the necklace?"

"I wouldn't think so."

Jenna raised an eyebrow. *Why did Delilah give the necklace to Sara?*

Calliope hurried to their table and sat down. "They had cinnamon rolls. Did you know Twyla was an interior designer? She's going to send me a copy of her favorite book on interior design and a subscription to an interior decorator magazine she likes."

While Calliope talked about what she'd learned so far about interior design, Jenna's phone buzzed with a text from Lucy. "Come to my office when you can. I need auditor help."

Jenna whispered, "I have to step out for a few minutes."

Sara nodded.

When Jenna went to Lucy's office, the door was open.

"Come in and close the door behind you."

After she closed the door, Jenna's eyes widened. Lucy's computer and desk accessories were on the floor, and papers were scattered across the top of her desk.

Lucy rose from her seat and gazed at Jenna. "I forwarded the box from Mia to the auditing team, and they were excited to hear they were getting more data. You accounting types are beyond my understanding."

Lucy clutched a spiral notebook to her chest as she pointed to her desk with her pen.

"I scanned the pages in Delilah's envelope and sent them to auditing earlier, but they estimate it will take weeks to uncover who is behind the money laundering. When I complained, their supervisor told me they were open to any suggestions, but she didn't sound all that sincere. I've been trying to organize the records, but I need help."

Jenna sat in Lucy's chair and pulled out her notes and handed them to Lucy. "This is how I started. I recorded them by date and account numbers and then looked for layering."

Lucy examined Jenna's notes. "What's layering?"

"Unusual transactions like rapid transfers between multiple accounts, same-day deposits and withdrawals, and accounts that transfer funds to each other."

Lucy exhaled as she handed the notes back to Jenna. "So instead of organizing the normal transactions, you searched for abnormal transactions."

"Right. I wasn't trying to prove anything, which is what I suspect would be the goal of a forensic accountant. I was just trying to see if there was any pattern of abnormal practices."

"That makes sense, but I won't stop pressuring the accounting group." Lucy's eyes twinkled.

While Lucy picked up the papers that were on her desk, she said, "Paige is being released from the hospital later this morning. She had a mild concussion and a broken leg, but you probably guessed that. She told the investigator that you chased her to the stairs, started an argument, and then pushed her."

"What?"

Lucy nodded. "The detective asked her if she knew the penalties for filing a false police report because he knew exactly where you were when she fell. When she tried to bluster her way through, he asked her if she wanted him to record her statement so he could charge her without wasting anyone else's time."

Jenna shook her head as she rose to leave. "You don't think she'll come here, do you?"

"A prudent person would go home."

"Right." Jenna sighed. "Before I go back to the meeting, I have something for you."

Lucy set the papers down and leaned against her desk. "You have my undivided attention."

"I have another story courtesy of Miss B.'s diary. She put red ink in a rival's perfume bottle. When her rival sprayed herself with perfume, her neck would have looked like she had a rash."

Lucy cocked her head. "That would not be a good look for an entertainer."

"The entertainer's popularity and income would definitely plummet."

"Perfume." Lucy narrowed her eyes. "I get it. Delilah claimed the housekeeper had stolen her perfume, and then later said it had been returned to her room. I thought she'd just overlooked it, but what if someone took it and added a lethal substance that absorbed through the skin before returning it to Delilah's room? I'll notify the lab to pick it up and let them know our suspicions."

Before Jenna left, Lucy grinned. "Because of you, I'm gaining the reputation of being a busybody who constantly tells other departments how to do their jobs."

Jenna furrowed her brow as she hurried toward the conference room. *Raelynn called me a busybody, and Morgan said there was a voicemail message on the inn's phone that said busybodies have short lives.*

As she returned to her table, Twyla picked up the microphone.

"Good timing," whispered Sara. "The panel is Victor, Frankie, and Farah, and the topic is ethical accounting standards."

Jenna snorted. "Seriously?"

Sara's eyes twinkled. "I wouldn't miss this for the world."

Twyla nodded at Victor, Frankie, and Farah, who took their seats at the panel table.

Twyla beamed as she surveyed the audience.

"Twyla is pleased with how many members are still here," Calliope whispered.

"You all know Victor, Frankie, and Farah. Our topic this morning is ethical accounting standards."

Twyla held up a soup bowl. "We have four slips of paper in the bowl, and each panelist will draw one before they speak. Each speaker will have fifteen minutes total. They can use their time however they like."

Twyla turned to the panel. "I suggest you take a few minutes to ponder the question you've selected and possibly take notes before you speak. You may want to allow at least five minutes toward the end of your time for questions."

Jenna side-glanced at Calliope and smiled. *This was her idea.*

"We'll begin with Farah." Twyla held the bowl in front of Farah who selected a slip.

"Transparency." Farah smiled.

While Farah spoke, Jenna realized she was sitting on the edge of her seat. She glanced around the room. *I'm not the only one enthralled by her voice and impressed by the depth she gives to what appeared to be a simple concept.*

When Twyla called time, applause broke out, and Farah nodded in acknowledgment.

"Frankie, you are next." Twyla held out the bowl.

Frankie selected a slip. "Integrity."

Sara snorted. "This is rich."

Frankie closed her eyes in thought for a few moments, then began. "A person's integrity is revealed by their actions..."

Sara glared at Frankie as Frankie continued to expound on integrity.

When Frankie glanced at Sara, Frankie stumbled over a few words and rambled for a bit, but she cleared her throat and recovered.

When Twyla called "time," Frankie sighed in relief.

"Mama, you rattled her," Calliope said.

"Isn't that just too bad?" Sara's eyes twinkled.

"Victor, pick your topic." Twyla held the bowl while Victor considered the two slips of paper, then picked one.

As Victor unfolded the paper his eyes narrowed. He glared at Twyla, and then with a raised chin and a commanding voice, he said, "Accountability."

Jenna and Sara exchanged a look.

"Accountability is the cornerstone of accounting ethics..." Victor's voice was a monotone, and his bored facial expression suggested the topic was beneath him.

"Do tell, Victor," Sara muttered.

Jenna smiled as Twyla glanced at Calliope and winked.

Calliope rubbed her forehead to stifle her giggle.

"Gary's going to be sorry he missed this," Jenna whispered.

Calliope grinned, then surreptitiously pointed at the AV expert who stood next to the AV table with a camera on a tripod.

"Do the panelists know?" Jenna asked.

"They should. The panelists' contracts granted the association the right to photograph, video, and audio record the conference." Calliope snickered.

"Farah would have read the contract before she signed it, but not Frankie or Victor," Sara said.

After a few minutes, Jenna smiled at Victor's increased enthusiasm for the topic when the inflection in his voice became more animated, and his tone brightened.

Sara elbowed Jenna. "Now, we'll hear the story of Victor, the man and the legend."

Jenna smiled as Victor continued. *Sara got it right.*

Twyla said, "Time."

Victor's eyes twinkled. "And be accountable for your time."

The audience laughed and then applauded.

"That was a genius ending of a true showman; I'm impressed," Sara said.

Twyla smiled as she picked up her mic. When the applause died down, she said, "Thanks to our panelists for sharing their diverse experiences with us. Lunch today is on your own. The registration desk has coupons for nearby cafés and diners, so we can show our support to our fellow small businesses. We will reconvene at two o'clock for our small group exercise, which I know you'll enjoy, and we will begin this evening with happy hour with light appetizers and a cash bar at five o'clock to be followed by our banquet at six. If you brought your western boots wear them because our speaker will have us all imagining our own dude ranches out west. Enjoy your lunch, and I'll see you at two."

Twyla nodded and smiled at the applause.

As groups filed out of the conference room, Calliope said, "I'd like to have lunch with Twyla, if you won't feel like I'm abandoning you. We talked about a working lunch."

"That's fine," Sara said.

Calliope rushed to join Twyla who stood near the panelist table while she chatted with three members.

Jenna smiled. "Do you suppose we're allowed to go to lunch without Gary's recommendation?"

Sara returned her smile. "It's too late; he sent me a text while Victor was rambling and suggested a diner that is a block away and has great tamales."

Sara buttoned up her dark brown leather jacket and slipped the strap of her brown leather crossbody purse over her neck. Jenna buttoned up her navy blue wool coat and flipped the hood over her head before she slipped her arms through her backpack straps.

When they stepped outside a blast of icy wind took away Jenna's breath; she covered her mouth with her collar and put her head down as they hurried toward the diner.

After they were inside, Jenna heard the sizzle and savored the aroma of meat, onions, and peppers on a hot grill and inhaled the warm, earthy, and spicy scents mingled with the citrusy bite of lime.

Sara asked a passing server, "Where's the best place to sit away from the door?"

The server, a heavy-set woman who was surprisingly nimble, whirled around and smiled. "Follow me. Ya'll will get the best service because it's my booth."

Jenna stared at the tall backs of the booth seats that gave them a sense of privacy. She led them to a corner booth. "What would you like to drink?"

"Coffee for me," Sara said.

"Iced tea," Jenna said.

The server smiled. "Southwest Georgia, am I right?"

"You're right." Jenna returned her smile.

The server cackled. "I could hear it. Menus are right there by the napkin holder. I'll have your drinks here shortly."

Jenna reached for the menus and gave one to Sara.

Sara's eyes widened. "This is going to be hard. There are a lot of choices."

Jenna nodded.

The server brought their drinks along with a basket of tortilla chips, a large carafe of salsa, and two small bowls. "Are you ready to order?"

"Not yet," Sara said.

While they nibbled on chips and salsa, the diner began filling up with customers, but the booth was isolated from the noise.

"How about this booth?" Victor asked as he unknowingly sat behind Jenna.

"Perfect, Mr. Grimes."

Jenna widened her eyes. *That's Farah.*

"Can you hear the people who sat behind me?" Jenna asked.

"Not at all, which is good because it means they can't hear us either."

Maybe. Jenna nodded as Sara studied the menu and then glanced at the nearby tables to see what other diners were eating.

Jennie stared at her menu while she tuned out the constant buzz of conversations in the diner so she could listen to Victor and Farah.

The server stopped at Victor's booth. "Your menus are next to the napkin holder. What can I get you to drink?"

"Coffee," Victor said.

"Nothing for me; I'm not staying," Farah said.

"Gotcha," the server said.

As the server hurried away, Victor said, "This is a nice place..."

Farah interrupted him. "What was the favor you wanted? I don't have a lot of time, so get to the point because I have to meet our guest speaker at the hotel in thirty minutes."

Jenna raised her eyebrows. *Farah might have a sweet voice, but she has the soul of a shark.*

Victor cleared his throat. "I don't feel like I can trust just anyone. I have an offer I'd like someone to consider, but it's a delicate issue, so I want to remain anonymous until..."

"I don't care about your feelings or your motives; get to the point," Farah said.

When Victor didn't respond immediately, Jenna pursed her lips to keep from smiling. *I wish I could see his face; I'll bet he's ready to explode. Victor has met his match.*

He grumbled, "Here's a sealed envelope. Put it on the panelists' table."

"You said you'd pay me two hundred dollars. I'll take the cash now."

"I can write you a check."

"I don't have time to play. Enjoy your lunch."

Sara asked, "What are you going to order?"

Jenna furrowed her brow as she examined the menu. "I'm still deciding."

"Fine," Victor growled. "Here's your cash."

"Okay." Farah left.

"Your coffee, sir; are you ready to order?" the server asked.

"I changed my mind. Sorry for the trouble."

When the server shifted to Jenna and Sara's booth, she stuck a folded twenty-dollar bill into her pocket. "Ready to order?"

He didn't want a scene. "I'd like the tamale lunch special," Jenna said.

"That sounds good; I'll have the same," Sara said.

"Good choice." The server refilled Sara's coffee and left.

Sara sipped her coffee. "Calliope asked me for our lawyer's name this morning; she said she and Twyla are discussing the possibility of Calliope joining Twyla's event management business. Calliope suggested creating a new business and including Farah because of her accounting expertise."

Jenna raised her eyebrows. "A new business? I'm impressed; that would be the only way Calliope could be a partner, not an employee taking orders from Twyla. How did Twyla react to that?"

Sara chuckled. "Calliope didn't say, but I would guess Twyla was a little resistant."

"Whatever they do, I can see how successful they would be with Twyla's contacts and experience with events and Calliope's energy, vision, and business experience; adding Farah was genius."

Sara nodded. "Our bed-and-breakfast wasn't much of a challenge for Calliope. I had stepped back so she wouldn't feel cramped, but I've been bored. I think she was too because it wasn't a fulltime job even for me, and she spent extra time on updating the website and beefing up our marketing."

Jenna smiled. "Going on the board will help keep you busy."

Sara chuckled. "It's worse than that. Calliope hinted Twyla plans to ask me to take over as president of the association."

Jenna's eyes widened. "What do you think?"

"I might consider it if you or Gary would come on the board."

Jenna shook her head. "I'm too green. Gary would be perfect."

Sara nodded. "I'll wait to see what Twyla comes up with, but you're right about Gary. Kendra is another possibility."

Their server returned with their food and refilled Sara's cup.

While they ate, the server led three women to a table on the other side of the room.

A woman glanced up and waved, and Sara returned her wave.

"I am seeing people I haven't seen in ages. I didn't know I actually missed being social." A tear slipped down Sara's cheek, and she brushed it away. "I don't know where that came from. I'm usually not sentimental."

"It's been an intense few days," Jenna said. "I knew Delilah only briefly, but even I feel her loss."

Sara set down her fork as she became lost in her memories. "Delilah didn't trust anyone, but for some inexplicable reason, we clicked. She absolutely adored Calliope and in fact, insisted on paying for her college expenses. I wouldn't see Delilah for years, but we stayed in touch with texts and weekly phone calls."

Her eyes welled up then tears streamed down her face. Sara pulled a tissue out of her purse and wiped her eyes and face. "Sorry," she mumbled. "I told myself I'd cry later."

Jenna felt the gut punch of Sara's sorrow.

Sara picked up her fork and poked at her tamale and then spooned up some guacamole and put it on her plate.

While Sara stared at her plate, Jenna said, "I didn't know Delilah very long, but I sensed how complex she was, and I enjoyed her offbeat sense of humor. I found it interesting how hard she fought Twyla for Mia to introduce her."

Sara's smile was weak. "Delilah told me once she'd be a terrible mother, so she had to be the eccentric aunt. Delilah always had a soft spot for her niece and Calliope too, but she would never have admitted it."

"I did get the feeling Delilah's complaints about Mia and Calliope hid a sense of pride."

Sara nodded. "When Calliope was thirteen, she decided she was too smart for school. When I dropped her off one morning, she slipped out the back door and went to the coffee shop with two of her friends who were also too smart for school. I grounded her for two weeks. Before I took her phone away, she texted Delilah and told her she was a prisoner in the house for no reason at all."

Jenna chuckled. "Nobody does drama like a thirteen-year-old."

Sara smiled. "So, Delilah told her she'd fix it."

"Did you get a call?"

"No, Delilah came to the house with a gift bag and asked me to give it to Calliope. There was a note inside that said, 'Here's your tiara to wear in your tower.' Calliope was highly insulted, but she wore her tiara until she wasn't grounded, and she still has it."

Jenna chuckled. "Sounds like Delilah and Calliope clicked too."

Sara nodded as her lip quivered. "I'm really going to miss her."

When Sara placed her hand on her upper chest near her throat, Jenna heard the clear three-note call of the sandpiper, "weet-weet-weet."

Jenna put her hand on her pink opal pendant, and it warmed under her hand. *Thanks, Nettie.*

On their way back to the hotel, Sara said, "Did you notice Delilah's necklace and earrings?"

Jenna nodded. "Beautiful craftsmanship."

"Delilah's brother owned a large beach house. When Calliope and Mia were young, we'd all go to the beach for a week. A friend of Delilah's made the sandpiper necklace and earrings for her and a necklace with a bottlenose dolphin for me. I gave my bottlenose dolphin necklace to Calliope when she graduated from college."

Jenna side-glanced at Sara. "The sandpiper necklace is for Mia."

Sara nodded, then bit her lip. "Delilah sometimes had visions and premonitions. People thought it was for show, but I knew better. She gave Calliope a small box on Sunday evening and told her it was for me, and I would understand."

That's why she gave me the envelope of papers for LEO.

As Jenna opened the hotel door, she said, "So many talents; what a remarkable woman."

Sara exhaled. "I'm glad we talked. I have to run for the board, don't I?"

Jenna heard the clear three-note call of the sandpiper, "weet-weet-weet."

She smiled. "Yes, you do."

Chapter Twelve

When they went inside the hotel, Jenna was startled by the bustling noises from the past as footsteps clicked across the wood floor in front of her, voices next to her shouted for a baggage rack, and a rowdy group in the corner roared in laughter at a bawdy joke.

She froze, blocking the door.

Sara spoke softly. "Jenna, can you step to the side?"

Jenna blinked, and the noises became muted except for one voice. "You're in the way."

Then all was quiet.

Sara asked, "Jenna, what was it?"

Jenna furrowed her brow as she glanced around at the empty lobby. She exhaled and then headed toward the conference room. "I'm in the way." *A busybody would be in the way.*

Sara followed her into the conference room where a few tables were occupied by members who were focused on their laptops while they finished eating their lunch.

"Can I get you something? A drink? A cupcake we can share?" Sara asked as they sat at their table.

Jenna examined Sara's earnest face. "I'm fine; this hotel was really popular back in the day, and sometimes I feel it more strongly than I expect."

"You said you were in the way."

"There's more to it, but I don't know what." Jenna bit her lip. "I need a distraction; let's check the desserts."

While she surveyed the desserts, Jenna saw an envelope near the coffee machine. She casually picked it up and turned it over. *Nothing written on either side.* She set it down.

Jenna returned to the dessert table and selected a vanilla cupcake with peach cream frosting.

"I'm having trouble deciding." Sara continued to examine the desserts. "I've been thinking about my niche. Do you feel like talking?"

"I'd love it."

"I'll go with chocolate." Sara picked up a chocolate cupcake with black cherry cream frosting, and they returned to their table.

While they ate, Sara said, "I can't say anything to Calliope, but I'm nervous about managing our bed-and-breakfast alone if she joins Twyla's event company. It's not that I want to stand in her way, but she's been a big part of the inn since she was old enough to walk."

"I understand," Jenna said.

"For example, two members I recognized but don't really know were exiting the elevator and began talking about décor and the difference between authentic and out-of-date. I really wanted to follow them to hear more."

"I would have been interested in that too. I thought I was doing fine at the inn until I came to the conference. I can't believe how much I've learned."

"I knew you would understand. I'll watch for them; maybe we can chat with them during a break."

Lucy opened the conference room door and peered inside.

Jenna glanced at Lucy and rose. "I won't be long."

Sara pulled out her laptop and nodded.

"Do you have a few minutes?" Lucy asked.

"Sure; your office?" Jenna asked.

"Let's go."

Jenna followed her.

After they were inside the office, Lucy sat at her desk, and Jenna made herself comfortable in the visitor's chair. A crow outside Lucy's window cawed, and other crows echoed the call.

Lucy glanced out of her window. "There's a cat in the alley. I guess that's why the crows are warning the neighborhood."

Jenna peered out the window. "We need a crow."

Lucy nodded. "That would be nice; however, your Miss B. is amazing. I don't have the details, but I got an unofficial call from the lab that Delilah's perfume bottle contained a high concentration of a substance that was lethal if inhaled or touched the skin. After Delilah sprayed her perfume in the air, she set her perfume bottle on the table, and then collapsed and died. It was that fast."

"What about Mia?"

"The exterior of the bottle was clean, but we didn't know that until after it was tested at the lab," Lucy said. "In hindsight, we should have removed the bottle before we allowed Mia to remove Delilah's belongings. I realize nobody's perfect, but it could have been tragic if Mia had taken it home with her."

"You didn't know."

"That's no excuse." Lucy rubbed her forehead. "Delilah also had a larger bottle of the perfume at her home that she obviously used to refill her atomizer for travel, so the lab tested it too. That bottle was fine, so we know that only the perfume she had with her at the hotel was contaminated."

"What about Raelynn?"

"She had a plastic self-closing bag with latex exam gloves turned inside out in her pants pocket, and the gloves had traces of the substance on them. She must have been warned to be careful. I'm positive someone paid Raelynn at least a thousand dollars to remove the perfume from Delilah's room and replace it with the tainted bottle because we found a thousand dollars in an envelope in her car. We haven't completed the investigation, so we don't know if there was more."

"Why was Raelynn murdered?"

"We don't know, but my theory is she got greedy and insisted on more money. It's like you told me, never blackmail a killer. Where did that come from?"

Jenna shrugged. "Something from Miss B.'s diary must have made me think of it."

Lucy examined Jenna's face. "Oh."

The elevator chimed.

Jenna cleared her throat to keep from smiling.

Lucy shook her head. "There goes the elevator again. Roy swore he fixed it. After you finish reading Miss B.'s diary, I'd like to have it. I have a feeling she's going to be the source of a new training manual at the academy."

"She seems so flighty in her diary; I'm sure that must have been her reputation. I wonder if anyone ever truly grasped the depth of her thirst for revenge."

Lucy chuckled. "I'd hire her, but I'd never turn my back on her."

"Have you heard anything more about Paige?" Jenna asked.

"She hasn't been released yet. Someone requested a psychiatric evaluation after she insisted you pushed her down the stairs, but I don't know if that will happen. If she's smart, she'll claim she was confused for a moment and you weren't around her at all, because that's the only way she could be released by her doctor today."

Jenna giggled. "Miss B. might suggest I visit your cousin at the hospital to take her flowers and offer my sympathy on her unfortunate fall."

Lucy laughed. "That would certainly set her off, wouldn't it?"

"Thanks for filling me in."

Lucy's face turned somber. "You be safe."

Jenna nodded. "It's number one on my list."

As she strolled across the lobby, Jenna paused, then texted Mia. "Do you have time to talk?"

Mia replied, "GMTA."

Jenna stared at her phone. *Great Minds Think Alike? Is she going to call me?*

When she strolled into the conference room, her eyes widened at Mia, who sat at their table with Sara.

Jenna giggled as she hurried to the table. "I didn't expect to see you."

Sara nodded. "That's what I said."

Mia smiled. "Oh, you know how great minds think alike. I just dropped by to chat for a minute. Have you talked to Lucy?"

Jenna examined Mia's face. "Sure did."

"I have some of Delilah's perfume from her house. I found an extra bottle that she must have had as a reserve that hadn't been opened yet." Mia raised her eyebrows as she peered at Jenna.

"I understand."

"I thought you might like it to flush out any hard feelings." Mia handed Jenna a two-ounce amber glass spray bottle inside a reclosable plastic bag.

Jenna's eyes brightened with understanding. "You know I would; thank you."

Sara stared at them. "Are you two talking in a secret code?"

"Yes, ma'am." Mia rose. "Jenna, let me know if there is anything else I can do."

"Hold on," Sara said. "I'll walk out with you."

Jenna stared at the door after they left. She waited and listened with anticipation.

Jenna smiled when she heard the clear three-note call of the sandpiper, "weet-weet-weet."

Jenna touched her pink opal pendant while the elevator chimed, dinged, and chimed again, and a tear slipped down her cheek.

Sara's eyes were red-rimmed when she returned to the conference room.

When she sat next to Jenna, Jenna put her hand on Sara's and felt Sara's loss of her friend, and her joy of giving Mia the sandpiper. Sara's smile was weak.

Jenna removed her hand and brushed away an errant tear. "It was the right thing to do."

Sara sniffled as she nodded. "Mia told me to tell you I'm ready for the answer to the secret code."

Jenna raised an eyebrow. "Mia gave me a spray bottle of Delilah's perfume."

Sara gazed at Jenna and then smiled. "This is going to be wonderful. What are you going to do?"

"I'm not sure yet, which is probably why Mia told me to tell you the code. I can't decide if I should wait until after dinner tonight or just spritz now and again later."

"I think now and later." Sara's eyes twinkled. "Can I do the first spritz?"

"I think it's only right; after all, Delilah was your friend, so you deserve to take the first shot across the bow."

Jenna furrowed her brow. "Did I say that right?"

"Yes, and that's exactly what I'm doing. So, I've been thinking I might need another agenda for my scrapbook. Panelist table first."

Jenna rose and stood near the conference room door so she could cause a distraction if anyone noticed Sara or if anyone came into the room.

Sara strolled to the front and picked up an agenda from the podium. After she strolled past the panelist table, Sara returned to their table, and Jenna joined her.

"How did I do?" Sara asked.

"Slick; was that a practice run?"

"Nope. Spritz and dash. I actually sprayed low, so the scent is in the carpet."

"That's brilliant, so when a panelist is sitting at the table, their feet will stir up the aroma from the carpet."

"That was my plan; we'll see if it works."

Sara handed Jenna the bottle, and Jenna put it in the plastic bag and closed the bag. "I don't want my backpack to smell like I fell into a vat of concentrated rose water."

Sara sniffed her hands and then wrinkled her nose. "I don't think I actually got any perfume on my hand, but I smell roses. Maybe it's psychological, but I'm still going to wash my hands. I'll be right back."

While Sara was gone, Jenna glanced toward the drink table. Her eyes widened as a young woman who wore a shirt with the caterer's logo on it strolled to the coffee machine. She picked up the envelope and strode out of the conference room.

Jenna jumped up from her seat to follow her, but she had disappeared by the time opened the door. "Talk about slick," she grumbled as she returned to her table.

When Sara returned, she said, "I ran across the women who were talking earlier about old-fashioned versus authentic. They were talking in the restroom, and evidently they have a running argument going with someone online about the cocktail called the old-fashioned."

"How disappointing." Jenna glanced at the drink table. "I think I want some water; my cupcake was really sweet. Do you care for anything to drink?"

Sara smiled. "Old-fashioned water sounds good to me too."

While Jenna poured two glasses of water, she glanced at the coffee machine at the other end of the table. The now-empty spot where the envelope had been taunted her.

When Jenna returned with the water, she asked, "Did you notice an envelope near the coffee machine when you came in?"

"No, I didn't. Why?"

Jenna shrugged. "No special reason. I thought I saw one, which would have been odd, but I'll bet it was a napkin."

Jenna pulled out her computer. While she checked the registration system, Jenna glanced at the conference room door when it opened.

"Gary's here, Sara."

Gary ambled to their table.

"How did your accounting immersion day go, Gary?" Jenna asked.

He smiled. "I finally understand the basics. I have more to learn, but at least I'm not afraid of it."

Calliope came into the room and joined the table.

"Welcome back, Gary." Calliope told Gary about Twyla's proposal for Calliope to join the Hughes Signature Events.

"I have more. I talked to Farah," Calliope said.

Gary nodded. "She's a great accountant, but her project management skills are her true strength."

Calliope nodded. "Right. I'd forgotten how well you and Kendra know Farah. I learned Farah worked with

Twyla for three years as an event manager, but for the past two years she has also taken over the event planner role too. She said Twyla has another firm she uses for her accounting."

"Really?" Gary glanced at Jenna.

"So what is Twyla doing?" Sara asked.

"My interpretation is that Twyla is coasting, but Farah thinks Twyla is busy looking into an expansion or starting up a completely new business. She said Twyla's become even less involved with planning events the past two years, which is why Farah's role has expanded."

Jenna smiled. *Those two are planning for the future.*

"You know what Farah and I are thinking, don't you Jenna?" Calliope giggled.

"Probably the same thing I hope I'd be smart enough to do," Jenna said.

Sara stared at them. "Okay, you two, so what's the secret?"

"Let me guess," Gary said. "Twyla's strength has always been her contacts, but as the event planner, Farah has become the contact for the clients, so their confidence and loyalty have shifted to Farah."

Sara frowned. "Wouldn't that be unethical, like stealing clients from Twyla?"

"That's not their plan," Jenna said.

Calliope nodded. "Jenna's right. This is Farah's last convention with Hughes Signature Events. She found another event planner position with a larger, established company and gave notice to Twyla a month ago. I realize I have absolutely wonderful potential, but I'm not experienced. Twyla is desperate, which is why she asked me to join her company. I don't have the experience to step in for Farah, so I declined Twyla's offer."

Jenna nodded. "With Farah's contacts, you'll be able to find an event manager position and gain the experience you would need so you and Farah could start up your own company in two or three years if that's what you want to do."

"Right." Calliope beamed.

Gary shook his head. "You and Farah make me feel old."

Sara nodded. "Maybe we can learn something from these two brilliant young women."

Gary smiled. "You're right; I need to talk to Kendra."

Jenna furrowed her brow. *Maybe I should talk to Ethan.* The elevator chimed.

"Was that the elevator again?" Sara asked. "What a beautiful sound to announce its arrival on the first floor. Didn't it sound like bells ringing in celebration?"

The chimes rang again, and Jenna rolled her eyes. *Okay, I'll talk to Ethan.*

"It must be getting close to two," Sara said. "Twyla and Farah just came in. I take it you're sitting with us, Calliope."

"Oh, yes. I'm no longer the wonder child."

"Good. You'll have time to train me before you start a new job," Sara said. "I'm feeling rusty."

"Either something is going on or Twyla is miming an argument with Farah." Gary nodded toward the front of the room.

Twyla's face was red and contorted as she waved her arms and hissed between her teeth at Farah.

Farah stood with her back to the audience, but her arms were relaxed at her side and her head was cocked as though she was observing Twyla's tantrum with disinterest.

"Can you understand what Twyla is saying?" Calliope whispered.

Gary shook his head.

Sara raised an eyebrow. "I wonder if Frankie or Victor was supposed to be here."

Jenna added, "Whatever it is, Twyla needs to take a breath to give Farah a chance to suggest an alternative."

Twyla glanced up at the staring audience and forced her face into a smile.

Farah said, "We'll go with the original plan."

Twyla shook her head. "It won't be..."

She was interrupted when Frankie rushed in, and Twyla glared as Frankie joined her and Farah.

When Victor came into the conference room, Twyla growled, "You're late."

"You never start on time, anyway." Victor sat in the first chair closest to the door.

Jenna focused on Victor as he shifted in his chair. *He smells the perfume.*

Victor rose from his seat and strolled to the table with the pitchers of water. After he poured a cup of water, he picked up a napkin and blotted his face.

Sara caught Jenna's eye. "Strong reaction," she whispered.

Jenna nodded.

Twyla motioned for Victor to sit at the panelist table, and he stared at her and sipped his water.

Twyla glared at him, and then she and Frankie had a heated, whispered discussion.

Twyla strolled to the chair Victor had vacated while Frankie sat at the other end.

Twyla cleared her throat. "Aren't you going to join us, Victor?"

Victor strolled to the snack table and turned his back to her.

Jenna and Sara exchanged a glance.

Gary raised an eyebrow. "Do you know what's going on? What are they so nervous about?"

The whispers in the room grew louder as more members speculated about the strange behavior of the panelists.

Frankie rose from the table. "We need to move the table."

The AV tech rushed to the front of the room. "I'll move the microphones to another table. Where do you want them?"

Farah rose. "Use this table. I'll sit at the table near the door."

"Don't you wish we had our popcorn, Gary?" Calliope giggled.

Gary chuckled.

"Inside joke?" Sara whispered.

Jenna quickly explained the initial argument over who would introduce Delilah on the first day.

Sara snickered. "I would have been right there with them with a front-row seat."

After the AV tech moved the microphones, Victor rushed to the front and sat at the table close to the door.

Frankie grabbed the other side; Twyla sighed and sat in the middle.

When the panelists were settled, Farah's eyes twinkled as she picked up the microphone. "Good afternoon. One of the first lessons we all learned as business owners was to adjust no matter what life threw at us. Let's give our panelists an enormous round of applause for presenting such a dramatic demonstration."

Farah chuckled and applauded as the members laughed in appreciation and applauded the panelists.

The panelists side-glanced at each other, and then smiled and nodded as they accepted the applause.

Sara chuckled as she applauded. "Now, that was an impressive recovery."

"You two were at the bottom of this, weren't you? Are you going to explain what happened later?" Gary asked.

Sara shrugged. "I guess we have to."

When the applause died down, Farah said, "Our program this afternoon is Stump the Experts. We'll take ten minutes for you to decide on one to three topics you'd like to hear the experts discuss. If you have more than one topic, list them in order. I'll collect your suggestions and pose a question from each table for our experts to address. At the end of the session, we'll vote on the topic that came closest to stumping the experts. Are we ready? Go."

"I'll record our list." Calliope pulled out her spiral notebook.

"This doesn't have to be our number one topic, but I'd like to understand authentic versus out-of-date décor," Sara said.

Calliope nodded as she wrote.

"Now that I know the difference, I'd like to hear the pros and cons of an inn working with an event planner versus an event manager for events that are hosted by the inn," Jenna said.

After Calliope added Jenna's topic, she said, "If they don't select your topic, Jenna, we can talk after the session. I have some ideas for you."

The Peach Blossom Barn would be a perfect venue for Calliope to practice what she's learned. Jenna raised her eyebrows. "I think that might work."

Sara stared at them. "Are you two talking in code?"

"Yes, Mom."

Sara nodded. "Thought so. I expect an explanation later, but for a topic, I'd like a comprehensive checklist for improving the efficiency and appeal of an inn with the goal of increasing net profit."

"I'd like to hear a discussion on the process for expanding a business," Gary said.

Sara furrowed her brow. "Gary, I think your topic could enhance mine."

Calliope nodded. "I'll add yours to Mom's topic."

After a brief discussion, Calliope said, "I have our modified topic as number one. Do we want a second one?"

They all shook their heads; Calliope delivered their topic to Farah who smiled then whispered to Calliope.

When Calliope returned to the table, Gary asked, "What did Farah say?"

"She thought it was a perfect Stump the Experts topic. The good news for us is her senior project paper topic was very similar to what we're asking; she used a mom and pop motel with a limited budget as her example. She's going to text me a link to her paper."

Calliope's phone buzzed with a text. "Here it is. The title of the paper is 'How a small business in the hospitality sector can increase net profit by improving efficiency and updating marketing.'"

Sara chuckled. "What a mouthful."

Calliope giggled as she forwarded the link to their group text. "Farah told me the grades for the projects were based on the number of words in the title."

After all the tables gave Farah their topics, she started with a simple question. "What is the best way to track expenses?"

While the panelists argued, Sara explained how she had spritzed Delilah's rose-scented perfume on the carpet under the panelists' table.

"All three of them really reacted to it, didn't they?" Calliope said. "Farah told me earlier that Twyla absolutely hated perfume because of Delilah. Now she claims she's allergic, but she isn't."

"I get it," Gary said. "The murderer was supposed to jump up and confess."

"It sounded better in theory," Jenna said.

"Now that I know what was going on, I'm even more impressed by Farah," Gary said. "Did she know?"

Sara shook her head.

"I can't tell her, can I?" Calliope sighed.

"No." Sara glared at Calliope who held up her hands in surrender.

After the panelists responded to the fourth topic, Farah said, "Our last topic is a question. What are the logical steps for expanding your bed-and-breakfast business to increase monthly net profit?"

Gary smiled. "Farah added monthly as a constraint to keep the budget under control, which is important in accounting."

Jenna returned his smile and nodded.

Farah stopped the discussion after fifteen minutes. "Our time is up."

When Victor rose from the table and walked out, Frankie followed him. Twyla glared at the door and then joined Farah at the new table.

Farah rose and rolled her eyes as she picked up the mic. "I don't think I'm the only one who thinks that last topic stumped the experts. What do you think?"

The members laughed and applauded.

"Thank you, everyone, for your topics, and we'll see you at five for our happy hour before our banquet."

Twyla left as everyone rose, and Calliope gathered her things before she joined Farah.

"I'm going to study the rest of the afternoon," Gary asked.

"I'm taking a nap," Sara said.

"I have work waiting for me," Jenna said.

Sara followed Gary out the door while Jenna packed up her computer. The shuffle of chairs and low hum of conversation filled the room as members gathered their things.

When she looked up, everyone had left except for a young man and a young woman in their late teens who were clearing the drinks and snacks onto two utility carts. Jenna raised her eyebrows. *That's the same young woman who picked up the envelope.*

Jenna furrowed her brow. *Is there a service entrance to the conference room?*

She strolled toward the workers. "You've done a great job keeping the snacks and drinks from running out. Thank you."

The young woman blushed, and the young man's eyes widened.

"Thank you," he said. "We didn't mean to disturb you."

"I was on my way out. Is there a service door to the conference room? That must be really convenient."

The young man nodded. "It is."

Jenna glanced around the room. "Why don't I see it?"

The young man chuckled as he pointed. "That's not a wall between the conference room and the room next door. It's a partition."

Jenna strode to the wall and examined it closely. She strolled along the ridged, acoustical wall covering until she found a recessed door handle. She opened the door and peered into the next room.

When she joined the workers, the young woman said, "Some places don't have a second entrance to their conference or ballrooms. It's embarrassing to peek in to see if we need to take in more drinks before the next break because the speaker notices us and stops talking, and then everybody stares at us. I hate that."

Jenna cringed in sympathy. "That would make me nervous. One of our members told me her friend's birthday was today, and she was going to leave a card next to the coffee to surprise her."

"Oh, so that's what that was." The young man nodded. "That was an easy twenty bucks."

The young woman smiled. "I can top that. A woman gave me fifty bucks to pick up the card for her."

Jenna laughed. "Seriously? What did she look like?"

She rolled her eyes. "You know, old."

"Like me?" Jenna asked.

"Yeah, like you." The young woman nodded.

Ouch.

The young woman peered at Jenna. "Maybe a little older."

"Oh, right. One of the speakers," Jenna said.

The girl shrugged, and the young man said, "We don't pay no attention to what's going on in the room."

Jenna nodded. *This is going nowhere except now my ego needs first aid.*

"Makes sense to me; thanks again for everything."

Jenna sighed. *The mystery of how the envelope appeared and disappeared in the conference room is solved, but the recipient and message are still unknown.*

She furrowed her brow. *I wonder if Victor knew who would pick up the message, or was he just fishing? Too bad I can't just ask him.*

Jenna glanced toward the coffee shop. *Sure would have been nice if he'd been sitting in there waiting for me to ask my brilliant questions.*

Chapter Thirteen

As Jenna strolled across the lobby, Frankie joined her. "Are you on your way up to your room?"

"Yes, after I go to the vending room. What about you?"

"I was wondering if you had a little time to talk."

"Sure. The chairs next to the window are comfortable. Would you like to sit there or go to the coffee shop?"

"Let's go in the coffee shop; the lobby's too open for me."

When they walked into the shop, a woman called out from the back, "I'll be right with you."

Jenna inhaled the yeasty aroma of baking bread mingled with cinnamon and sugar. "Do you suppose she's baking cinnamon rolls?"

Frankie smiled. "I don't know, but whatever it is, that's what I want along with a cup of coffee."

The woman came out of the kitchen through the swinging saloon doors. "If you can wait five minutes, I'll have fresh cinnamon rolls for you. What would you like to drink?"

"Coffee," Frankie said.

"Hot chocolate for me."

"Whipped cream on top?" the woman asked.

"Yes, please."

Jenna and Frankie took their cups to a table and sat down.

"What do you think about the association so far?" Frankie asked as she sipped her coffee.

Jenna scooped up some whipped cream. "I can't believe how much I've learned in such a short amount of time. How long have you been a member?"

"Four years. Delilah was my closest friend; she talked me into joining, and I'm glad I did."

While Jenna continued to eat the whipped cream off the top of her hot chocolate, she examined Frankie's face. *She has put a lot of work into portraying her sincere look. She's definitely an accomplished liar.*

When the woman brought them forks and cinnamon rolls on plates, Jenna inhaled the sweet cinnamon aroma. "Thank you; this is a wonderful treat."

Jenna pinched off a piece of the hot cinnamon roll, then dropped it on her plate. "This is definitely straight out of the oven."

After she ate her first bite, Jenna said, "Some members in the elevator were discussing whether Twyla would continue as president. What are your plans going forward?"

Frankie briefly narrowed her eyes, then quickly glanced away. "I might consider running for the board."

Jenna raised an eyebrow. "I actually was surprised you weren't already on the board."

Frankie snorted. "Delilah and Twyla have always handpicked who would be on the board, although how Victor is elected every year is beyond me."

Jenna nodded. *Interesting tidbit that's actually true.*

Jenna sipped her hot chocolate while Frankie stirred her coffee. Jenna flinched at each clink of the spoon against the ceramic cup.

She wants me to tell her something. Why doesn't she just ask?

"Who invited you to come to the association meeting?" Frankie continued to stir her coffee even though she hadn't put anything in it.

Jenna swallowed hard to keep from snatching the spoon away from Frankie. "My operations manager found the association online."

Frankie nodded. "I got the impression you were here to support someone."

That wasn't the answer she had expected.

Jenna smiled and shook her head.

"Nice to talk to you." Frankie abruptly rose as she quickly wrapped her cinnamon roll in a napkin. She left her full coffee cup and her plate and fork on the table.

Jenna exhaled in relief and watched Frankie leave. *I wonder what her point was.*

Jenna finished her hot chocolate, then picked up both cups and the plates and forks. After she poured the coffee into the small utility sink for customers, she put the dishes in the dish bin and headed toward her room.

After she was in her room, she pulled off her boots and sent a text to Ethan. "Busy day?"

He replied, "Sure is. Are you okay?"

Jenna sighed. *A text, not a call. He is definitely busy. I'll keep my answer short.*

"I'm fine. Learning a lot."

"Good. See you soon."

Jenna nodded. *He's busy.*

She pulled out Miss B.'s diary. Her eyes widened, and she became engrossed in the story Miss B. told about a raid on the speakeasy.

"A goon tipped me off, so I was ready to vamoose the second I smelled coppers. I grabbed the tip jar off the bar and dumped it into my purse and then snatched up an old man's cane he'd leaned against the bar. The bartender had already gone down the rope, so the hatch was open. I closed it behind me. I didn't need no floozies following me. After I slid down the rope to the theater, I raced to the stage. I closed the trapdoor real quiet-like so nobody would know where I went, then hung onto the railing and tapped the stairs with the cane while I went down the three flights to the basement. It was black as sin and twice as scary in the damp basement, and I could hear the rats squeak and their claws scratching on the hard dirt floor around me. When they got close, I saw their glowing red eyes, but I had the old man's cane and swung it around to fight them back."

Jenna shuddered. *Now I need a cane. I'm glad I didn't read this at night.*

Jenna sent a text to Morgan. "How's everybody?"

Morgan called her.

Jenna smiled. *A voice from home.*

"Katy and I miss you. I've got good news. Shane has been released to walk to the restroom and the kitchen if he takes it easy, so Katy and I are at the inn. It's not that I have anything urgent to do here, but it worked out because I convinced Darlene and Wendy to go home early. They would have stayed all day if I hadn't shown up. Katy and I took a walk to the peach orchard and back. For the record, I froze. I've spent most of the afternoon tweaking the website."

After they chatted for a while, they hung up. Jenna sighed as she gazed out her window. The clouds had darkened, and a plastic sack billowed, then sailed down the alley.

Jenna smiled when the mockingbird trilled through its repertoire. She watched its flash of white as it flitted from an awning to a nearby pole and repeated its borrowed songs.

Jenna checked the weather radar on her phone. *I wouldn't mind some fresh air before it rains.*

She put on her ball cap and her coat. After she buttoned her coat, she picked up her backpack and headed toward the lobby. When she reached the front desk, Victor was in the lobby with his winter coat on. He glanced around and then strolled toward the hall that led to the library.

Jenna furrowed her brow. *Why is Victor acting so suspicious?* She picked up a brochure from the desk and feigned reading it while she watched him.

Victor peered toward the elevator, then hurried across the lobby to the front door as he glanced over his shoulder and then pulled up his collar.

Even more suspicious.

Jenna followed him outside and casually glanced to her right. Victor stood between two parked cars with his arm up to hail a cab.

Jenna snorted. *Why didn't he just call for a ride?*

A figure wrapped in a gray wool blanket suddenly appeared behind Victor between the cars and shoved him into the traffic. Tires squealed, followed by a thump and screams. Jenna raced to Victor, and the figure was nowhere to be seen.

When she reached the space where Victor had stood, she saw the gray blanket on the ground next to a parked car.

A woman, who was the driver of the car that hit Victor had leaped out of her car and was screaming. "I didn't see him. He just jumped in front of my car. It's not my fault."

A man kneeled on the street next to Victor, and a crowd gathered as people who had stopped their cars climbed out and raced to see what had happened.

Jenna covered her ears and shook as the cacophony of shouts, screams, wailing sirens, and honking horns terrorized her.

A man put his arm around her. "Are you okay, miss? Were you with him?"

Jenna shook her head and closed her eyes while she clenched her fists and held them close to her chest in determination. *Don't faint. Don't faint.*

"I've got her," a man said in a slightly familiar low voice.

As the first man released her, another man put his arm around her, and she was suddenly comforted.

I need to get to the hotel.

She gasped. "Hotel."

"Okay, miss. I'll take you to the hotel."

Jenna looked up and stared at Harrison, the host from the shrimp and grits restaurant, as he gently guided her back to the hotel.

Tears flowed down her cheeks, and her knees grew weak. "Thank you."

"We'll talk to Lucy."

Harrison led her through the lobby straight to Lucy's office. Lucy jumped up from her desk and closed the door behind them while Harrison helped Jenna sit in the visitor's chair.

"Are you okay, Jenna?" Lucy asked.

Jenna nodded.

"What happened?"

"I was going outside to take a walk before the rain hit. Victor went out right before I did, and I saw him hailing a taxi. Someone wrapped in a gray blanket pushed him." Jenna exhaled. "It was such a shock seeing Victor suddenly fly into the traffic. I ran to see if I could help, but other people got there first, and then the noise of screaming and horns honking..."

"Too much?" Lucy asked.

Jenna shuddered at the memory, then nodded.

Harrison said, "I chased after the perp, but he had too much of a head start and must have ducked down an alley."

Jenna rubbed her forehead. *Everybody's a cop.*

"Are you okay, Jenna?"

"It was a shock, but I'm fine." Jenna rose. "I think I'll skip my walk, though."

When she stepped out of the office, a man came in the front door and strode across the lobby.

"Ethan!" Jenna squealed and ran to him.

He caught her in a hug, and she put her arms around him and put her head against his chest.

While she listened to his heartbeat, she asked, "What are you doing here?"

He lifted her chin with his fingertips and gazed at her face. "I really wanted to see you, so I thought I'd just drop by. I told you I'd see you soon."

Jenna sighed. *That is so sweet.* "I'll be mad at you later for sneaking here without telling me, cowboy."

Ethan chuckled. "I know you will, babe."

She whispered, "But I'm really glad you're here."

"Good. Where's your room?"

"It's on the first floor." Jenna exhaled. "I'll show you, but don't let go of me."

"Like you have a choice," Ethan growled.

Jenna leaned against him while they strolled together across the lobby. When they reached her room, she unlocked the door, and they went inside.

After he helped her sit down in her soft chair, he dropped his backpack on the floor next to hers.

"What can I get you?" He kneeled on one knee in front of her.

"I need a hello kiss." Jenna leaned forward.

He took her face in his hands. "I can do that."

After a sweet kiss, he smiled. "Hello. Now, here's your nice to see you kiss."

She wrapped her arms around his neck as he pulled her close. When he teased her mouth open, she groaned as she matched the intensity of his passion.

When they broke away for air, tears flowed down Jenna's face.

Ethan took her back into his arms and held her close. "Are you okay, babe?"

She sniffled as she told him about Victor. "It was such a shock seeing him suddenly fly into the traffic, and the traffic noise and shouting were horrific."

Ethan exhaled. "I am so sorry."

He handed her a tissue, and she wiped her eyes.

"I'm so glad you're here. Did you drive?" Her voice grew stronger. "You weren't supposed to drive."

He smiled. "I didn't. I caught a ride with a friend of a friend so I could ride back with you."

The elevator chimed.

Jenna rolled her eyes. *You knew the whole time, and you're enjoying this, aren't you, Nettie?*

The elevator chimed again.

"I have the room next to yours. I'll have to check in."

Jenna's eyes narrowed. "Next to me? Let's go check you in so I can yell at Lucy."

"Actually, your friend Georgia from the GBI arranged for your bodyguard to have a room next to yours."

"Maybe so, but Lucy would have known it was for you." Jenna sighed. "I guess I'll give her a pass. She's been busy, and Paige has been taking up her time."

"Paige? She's completely unhinged."

"I know, but you don't have to worry. According to Paige, I pushed her down the stairs, and she broke her leg in the fall. I figure I owe her one."

"What was she even doing here?" Ethan asked.

"My best guess is she was here to cause trouble. Do you want to get your key to your room?"

"You don't have to go. I'll run grab it and be right back."

Jenna's smile was weak. "You can't dump me that easily."

Ethan chuckled. "Good to know."

As they strolled together to the lobby, Ethan said, "Too bad this hotel doesn't have adjoining rooms."

When Jenna side-glanced at him, Ethan grinned.

When they reached the registration desk and Ethan told the registration clerk his name, she said, "I have your key right here, Mr. Bentley. We've been expecting you."

Lucy came out of her office with a set of crutches in her hand and closed the door behind her.

"I'm Lucy; it's a pleasure to meet you, Ethan."

Jenna stared. "Did you take her crutches away from her?"

Lucy snorted. "That would be rude. She showed up unannounced, so I borrowed them because I wanted to talk to you, but we can't use my office. It's occupied. We can use Marvin's office; he's off today."

After they went into Marvin's office, Jenna glanced at the dark gray metal desk that was cleared off except for a black desktop computer and its monitor. A black office chair with a mesh back was behind the desk, and a visitor's chair that matched the desk was pushed against the left side of the desk. On the right was a gray file cabinet with a framed diploma above it. The view from the windows would have been the same as Lucy's, but the blinds were closed.

Jenna rolled her eyes. *I would have known this was Marvin's office.*

Lucy said, I just heard Victor didn't survive being hit by the car; he died on the way to the hospital." Ethan took Jenna's hand.

Jenna shuddered as she stared at Lucy. "It was so calculated and cold-blooded. Why?"

Lucy shook her head. "We don't know. Do you have anything?"

Jenna told her about the conversation Victor and Farah had at the diner and what the young workers with the catering service told her.

"Why do you have to be in the middle of everything?" Ethan muttered.

He glanced at the two women who glared at him. "Sorry; it just came out."

"I think I have to agree with Ethan." Lucy sighed and rubbed her forehead. "Victor had an envelope with a thank you card in his suit pocket. The inside of the card was blank except for $100,000, which was handwritten in pencil. Below it was printed the word No, also in pencil except in a different handwriting. If we go with your Miss B.'s never blackmail a killer theory, I need to find what Victor could have had in his possession that was worth one hundred thousand dollars."

Ethan furrowed his brow. "Miss B.? Blackmail theory? I think I'm lost."

Lucy nodded. "Don't worry about it, Ethan. It's been like that for me pretty much since Jenna checked in. She'll fill you in, but I can't guarantee you'll be any less lost than I am most of the time."

Ethan peered at Jenna, and she shrugged.

After they left Lucy's office, Jenna and Ethan went to his room. Ethan scanned the room and peered into the bathroom.

He wrinkled his nose. "I like your room better."

Jenna furrowed her brow. "Do you want to switch?"

Ethan's eyes twinkled. "No."

Jenna felt her cheeks warm, and she snorted. "You're teasing me again."

He hugged her. "Not really. Let's go to your room. I have a surprise for you." Ethan picked up his soft chair and carried it to the door.

"Are you taking that chair to my room?" Jenna asked.

He shrugged. "Gives me a place to sit."

After Ethan placed his chair so it was close to Jenna's chair and angled toward it, he opened his backpack and pulled out a pair of gloves. "I found these on the ground close to where you park."

"My gloves!" Jenna hugged him. "Thank you so much. I've missed them."

Ethan beamed and returned her hug. "You're welcome."

After they sat in their chairs, Ethan asked, "What's the plan for the rest of the evening?"

"Happy hour is at five, and then the banquet starts at six. After the banquet, we have a speaker who is an innkeeper from Montana with five dude ranches."

"Five dude ranches in Montana? He must be a big shot. The association must have a nice speaker's fund; how far in advance would a speaker like that have to be scheduled? A year?"

Jenna stared at him. "I thought he was a last-minute fill-in. I didn't think about what the lead time should have been. I'm going to ask Morgan."

Jenna sent a text to Morgan.

Morgan replied. "Easy to answer. On it."

Ethan sighed. "Tell me about Victor Grimes."

"He was the owner of the attraction, Ghost Realms and Theatrical Paranormal Events, and according to Calliope, he was a big shot in the world of illusions."

Jenna smiled. "I found a book about the hotel in the hotel library. It was very helpful for me to have read it before I went on the tour. The book was actually written to expose an illusionist. I'll show you."

She opened her backpack and pulled out *Spectral Illusions for Stage and Séance,* and the envelope fell out. "Somebody had put the envelope in the book to hold their place. I tried to put it back in the same place, but I'm not sure how successful I was."

Ethan picked up the envelope. "It's still sealed."

"That's odd. So, about Miss B." Jenna pulled out the diary and handed it to Ethan.

When he opened it, he chuckled. "Your Miss B. doesn't pull any punches, does she?"

Jenna grinned. "I'm not Reba M. or a floozy, so I decided it was okay for me to read it, and it is definitely worth reading."

"What about Lucy's comment about Miss B. and never blackmail a killer?"

"It's just something I thought of after I found the housekeeper who had been murdered. She was the one who put the perfume with the substance in it that killed Delilah. Lucy wanted to know where the saying came from, so I told her it was Miss B."

"But it was actually you and Nettie who came up with it," Ethan said.

Jenna shrugged. "Probably."

Ethan began reading, and Jenna leaned back in her chair and sighed. *I'm glad Ethan is here.*

She slowly relaxed while she listened to her mockingbird echo the backup alarm and then repeatedly whistle the Bob White call interspersed by backup alarms.

Ethan stretched. "Your Miss B. definitely skirted the wild side, didn't she?"

Jenna nodded. "So, why would someone want to expose an illusionist?"

"What are we talking about?"

"The illusion book and Victor Grimes."

"Could it be to take over the illusionist's business or to discredit the illusionist?"

"What if the reason to take over the illusionist's business was to have another business to use for money laundering?"

"You lost me, babe."

Jenna furrowed her brow. "Did I forget to tell you that Delilah was undercover? She sent information about money laundering to Lucy and her team."

"So, Lucy is law enforcement, and Delilah was undercover. I might have missed that part. Is the information about money laundering what was in the envelope Delilah gave you?"

"Yes, and a box that Mia sent me."

"Did I know about a box? Never mind. What else?"

"That's about it. Can I borrow your pocketknife?"

Ethan pulled his knife out of his pocket and handed it to her.

After she slit open the envelope, she gave the pocketknife back to him.

Jenna found a folded sheet of paper with the name and address of a bank and an account number. "This is for Lucy. It says illusionist at the bottom."

"Do you think Victor Grimes put it there?"

"That would be my guess. He was an illusionist, but he didn't strike me as being very creative. I'll give the book and envelope to Lucy so I don't have to worry about it."

Jenna sent a text to Lucy. "I have a book and an envelope for you."

"I'm negotiating with Paige. I might be awhile."

"Do you want me to come help?"

"No, I can handle her."

Jenna handed her phone to Ethan.

After he read it, he raised his eyebrows. "Shall we rescue Lucy?"

Jenna smiled. "You're fun."

Ethan narrowed his eyes as he assumed a tough guy voice. "And don't you forget it, shweetheart."

Jenna giggled as she picked up the illusionist book with the envelope inside. "Miss B.'s diary is a bad influence on you too."

When they reached Lucy's office, Jenna opened the door while Ethan strolled to the registration desk.

Lucy said, "My brother will be here in two minutes to pick you up. You'll be much more comfortable at home."

Paige said, "I told you, I'm not going."

Paige glanced at the open door. "What are you doing here?"

"Hi, Paige. We heard you were here, so we thought we'd check on you," Jenna said. "How are you feeling?"

Paige's face turned red as she sputtered, "How do you think I'm feeling? You broke my leg."

Jenna shrugged. "I heard there was a cute doctor at the hospital. I'll bet you have a date tonight, don't you?"

Paige gaped at Jenna. "What?"

"I'm sorry, I didn't mean to embarrass you," Jenna said.

Ethan pushed a wheelchair to the door. "The hotel staff helped me find a wheelchair for you, Paige."

"Ethan?" Paige stared at him.

"Thanks, Ethan." Lucy smiled. "We appreciate it, don't we, Paige?"

Lucy took the wheelchair from Ethan and pushed it next to Paige who sat in the visitor's chair.

Paige glowered at Lucy.

"Move, Paige," Lucy growled. "Don't make me count to three. I haven't had a good takedown in almost a week."

"You can't do that. I've got witnesses," Paige whined.

"Oh, do you?" Jenna rolled her eyes.

Paige slid over to the wheelchair, and Lucy handed the crutches to her.

A man strode into Lucy's office. "You ready, Paige?"

He didn't wait for an answer; he wheeled her across the lobby to the front door, and Lucy followed with Paige's packed roller bag.

When Lucy returned, she smiled. "That was really slick, Jenna. Is that what they call good accountant, bad cop?"

"Whatever works, right?" Jenna handed her the book and envelope. "This was in the library. I think Victor Grimes hid the envelope in the book. I've had the book since Monday, but I didn't pay much attention to the envelope until now. It was sealed, but I opened it."

Lucy scrutinized the envelope and the contents. "We'll follow up on this. Jenna, who is behind all this?"

Jenna furrowed her brow. "I don't know."

Lucy gazed at her face, then exhaled and turned to Ethan. "I'm glad you're here, Ethan."

"So am I."

"Can I have your cell phone number?" Lucy asked.

After they exchanged numbers with a tap, Lucy said, "Thanks again for your help with Paige."

As Ethan and Jenna strolled back to her room with their arms around each other, Jenna said, "If you have any more girlfriends that might crawl out of the woodwork, you can tell them I broke the last one's leg, and I plan to go for two next time."

Ethan laughed. "That's my girl. There aren't any, but it's always good to know you have my back."

When they reached Jenna's room, Ethan said, "Lucy thinks you know who the killer is, and so do I. You just haven't told yourself yet. Tell me as soon as you know."

Jenna furrowed her brow. *How would I know who the killer is?*

Chapter Fourteen

"I could use a shower," Ethan said. "Do we have time?"

"We have plenty of time. I'd like one too."

Ethan's eyes twinkled, and Jenna glared at him.

He cleared his throat and picked up his backpack he'd left in Jenna's room. "I'll go to my room and shower, but I won't be long."

"I'll text you when I'm out." Jenna followed him to the door.

While Jenna waited for the water in the shower to warm up, her phone rang.

When she answered, Morgan said, "I checked the rancher's website. His operation is a big deal. He requires a minimum of one year's notice and charges a hefty fee for any speaking engagements he attends and a lesser, still significant fee for a senior member of his staff. I found a statement on his website that explained there could be a waiver for certain associations, depending on the availability of a senior staff person. So, your speaker will probably be a senior member of his staff, but I think the talk will still be excellent. I didn't want to send all that in a text. I'm at the grocery store to pick up Shane's favorite ice cream. Talk to you later." Morgan hung up.

That's interesting.

Jenna climbed into the shower.

After her shower and while she was drying, she picked up her phone and read the text from Ethan.

"I'm done."

She snickered as she replied, "I'm not."

After she dressed in her new long-sleeved, pale peach shirt and jeans and slipped her pistol into its holster, she put on her necklace with the pink opal pendant and sent a text. "Done."

She giggled at the immediate tap at the door and opened it. She cocked her head as she peered at him. "Have you been standing outside my door?"

Ethan wore a long-sleeved, dark and medium blue gingham cotton shirt, jeans, and his western boots were shined.

Jenna smiled. *He's dressed up; he's not wearing his work boots.*

Ethan snorted as he strode in. "Would I do something creepy like that?"

"Yes." Jenna side-glanced at him as she inhaled the aroma of his usual soap. "I love the soap you use."

He brushed a stray lock of hair from her face with his fingertips. "I brought it from home; I didn't think you'd notice."

After she closed the door, he nuzzled her neck. "You smell like my girl."

She wrapped her arms around him and lifted her face for a kiss. "I like the sound of that."

He smiled and wrapped her in a hug, then kissed her.

Ethan furrowed his brow. "How many people will be there? Will the banquet be too noisy for you after this afternoon?"

Jenna smiled as she tapped an ear. "I have in-ear hearing protection for shooting, so I'll be fine. I'll still be able to hear conversations, but the loud noises will be muffled."

"Good."

Jenna picked up her backpack. "I'm ready."

On the way to the conference room, Jenna said, "Morgan researched the speaker. He owns dude ranches in Montana and has a huge staff."

"I'm really glad I came. Would you ever be interested in running a dude ranch in Montana?"

"I don't know. Isn't Montana colder than it is here?"

He chuckled. "Good point about the cold; that might not be for you."

He opened the conference room door. "Are you sure you'll be okay?"

Jenna exhaled. "Yes."

When they went into the conference room, Jenna's eyes widened at the number of people who were already lined up at the cash bar and the appetizer tables.

She saw the young workers and waved. The young woman smiled and wiggled her fingers, and the young man solemnly nodded.

When Jenna led Ethan to the group's table, Sara and Calliope met them midway as they returned from the appetizer table.

"Hi, Ethan. I'm Calliope, and this is my mom, Sara. We just got here, Jenna. Get in line for appetizers; they're going fast."

Ethan smiled. "Nice to meet you, Calliope."

He nodded. "You too, Miz Sara."

"If you don't call me Sara, I'll have to call you Mr. Bentley."

Ethan chuckled. "Fair enough, Sara."

"I'm going to grab a glass of wine," Sara said. "Can I get something for anyone else?"

"Grab some water if you can, Mom," Calliope said.

Sara patted her crossbody leather purse. "I'll bring water for everybody."

After Jenna and Ethan returned to the table, Sara appeared with her glass of white wine and six bottles of water.

While they ate and chatted, Gary joined them. Ethan rose, and the two men shook hands.

Calliope looked at her phone. "I just got a text from Mia. She's running late."

A man approached their table. "Are you using this chair?"

"We have someone coming," Gary said.

The man nodded. "They might have underestimated the popularity of our speaker."

"Here come more chairs." Calliope pointed at the conference room door as Roy and his helper rolled in a cart with chairs on it.

The man smiled. "Good timing."

As the room filled up and more people stood in line at the cash bar, Ethan put his arm around Jenna and whispered, "Still okay?"

She smiled and nodded.

Sara frowned as she scanned the room. "I don't see Twyla or Frankie."

"You're right, Mom. Twyla is probably with the guest speaker." Calliope furrowed her brow. "I don't see Farah. I wonder if she's meeting the guest speaker too."

While Gary and Ethan discussed the best way to install flooring in an old house, Jenna's phone buzzed a text from Lucy.

"Can you get away? Found something on the fourth floor."

A sudden flash of lightning than a boom startled Jenna. Calliope grabbed her mother's hand.

"I thought the storm dissipated." Sara pulled out her phone and then furrowed her brow. "The weather radar shows nothing. They need to update their system."

When Jenna showed her phone to Ethan, the lights flickered.

"We'll be back in a few minutes." Jenna grabbed her backpack.

Ethan followed Jenna out of the conference room.

"I need to find Lucy," she said.

"Do you know how to get to the fourth floor?"

"Yes, but she isn't there." Jenna glanced toward the front door and grabbed onto Ethan's arm.

"Red eyes," she whispered. "Lucy's in the basement."

The elevator chimed.

"But her text said..."

"The text wasn't from her. Do you want to check the fourth floor? I'll check her office first before I go to the basement. After you check the fourth floor, come to the basement."

Ethan growled, "We'll go to Lucy's office before we go to the basement."

Jenna blinked to keep from smirking. "Okay."

When they reached Lucy's office, Jenna tapped on the door before she tried the door knob then opened it. "Lucy keeps it locked," she whispered.

The night clerk said, "Mrs. Ross, Lucy rushed out when we got an alert about a fire in the basement. It must have been a false alarm because not five minutes after she left, the alarm changed to normal standby. She's probably just making sure everything is okay and will be back in a few minutes."

"Thanks."

As Jenna hurried toward the freight elevator and the staff stairs, Ethan asked, "Can you tell me what's going on?"

"I'm not sure, but we'll go to the basement to find Lucy."

"What about the fourth floor?"

"It's an ambush, but Lucy first."

Jenna passed the elevator and continued to the door to the stairs. She pulled out the flashlight she had bought and gave it to Ethan then pulled out the flashlight Lucy had given her and clipped it to her belt.

After she tapped the control panel with her VIP room key, they were in the stairwell.

Ethan said, "I'll go down first. You're not tall enough to knock down spiderwebs."

Jenna rolled her eyes. "Let's go."

When they reached the basement door, Ethan asked, "Do I open it?"

"Yes, then whistle."

Ethan partially opened the door and whistled a soft, melodic sound.

"Jenna?" Lucy whispered.

"Yes," Jenna said.

Ethan and Jenna hurried toward Lucy's voice as she said, "I was stabbed in the back. I think the knife is still there. I'm being as still as I can."

They found Lucy lying on her stomach with a knife still embedded in her back.

"It looks like a butcher knife; I think the blade is embedded in your scapula," Ethan said.

"That's what I was hoping. When I was stabbed, I immediately dropped onto my face and held my breath. She didn't check for my pistol, so I still have it. Can you get me up?"

Jenna said, "We'd have to stabilize the knife first."

"Why did you say 'she', Lucy?" Ethan asked.

"You smelled her perfume, didn't you?" Jenna asked.

"Right," Lucy said.

Nettie was right. I knew.

"She is on the fourth floor with your phone. I got a text from you."

"It's an ambush," Lucy said.

"Yes."

"Then tell the night clerk I'm in the basement; after he comes to get me, I'll call for the team to go to the fourth floor."

When Jenna turned, Lucy said, "One more thing. Victor has been moving ten thousand dollars regularly from the bank accounts that were on our money laundering list to his bank account. The bank account number on the paper inside the envelope was his. I think he had been quietly siphoning money from the money laundering scheme in relatively small increments one account at a time without being caught until he got greedy and went the direct route with a little blackmail."

"Never blackmail a killer," Ethan said.

"We're going to get you help," Jenna said.

She raced across the basement to the stairs with Ethan on her heels.

When they reached the first floor, Jenna said, "The killer didn't know Lucy was a cop, which is why she didn't search Lucy for any weapons; she was after Lucy's phone so she could text me."

Ethan growled, "She left assuming Lucy was dead. It would have been a while before anyone checked the basement, so even though Lucy survived the stabbing, she could have bled out or died from hypothermia. I'm not crazy about you chasing a dangerous serial killer. Are you sure we can't wait for Lucy's team?"

"That's an option. Do you want to go talk to the night clerk? He might know how to get in touch with Lucy's team."

"Where are you going to be if I walk away?"

Jenna shrugged.

"That's what I thought. Can we open the door from the stairs to the fourth floor without being noticed?"

"Yes, it doesn't make any noise when you open it. I think she'll be waiting down the hall from the elevator and will rush to the elevator when I don't step out, which gives me an idea."

She handed her room key to Ethan. "Wait here at the freight elevator. I'm going to talk to the night clerk."

Jenna replied to Lucy's text. "Have to make excuses. Won't be long."

Lucy's phone replied, "Good."

"Where are you?"

"New part of the fourth floor."

Jenna grunted. *There is no new part, pal.*

Jenna raced toward the registration desk but slowed to a fast walk when she reached the lobby.

The night clerk smiled when he saw her. "Is there something else I can do for you, Mrs. Ross?"

"Lucy was attacked in the basement and needs an ambulance." Jenna bit her lip. "Do you know how to get in touch with her team?"

The night clerk scowled. "I'm on it."

As Jenna hurried toward the guest stairs, she smiled. *Of course, the night clerk is a cop. Isn't everybody?*

Jenna held onto the handrails as she raced up the thirteen stairs to the second floor, then the thirteen steps to the third floor. She shuddered as she turned toward the door to the unimproved section. *I hate those stairs.*

When she reached the door at the end of the hall, she bit her lip. *Okay, Marvin. Don't fail me now.*

She punched the numbers 1,2,3,4, and the door unlocked.

Jenna sent a text to Calliope. "Any sign of Twyla, Farah, Frankie, or the speaker?"

"A board member brought in the speaker. Speaker is at appetizer table."

Jenna silenced her phone before she sent a text to Ethan. "Call freight elevator to first floor, then send it to the fourth floor. Use the stairs to go to the fourth floor and hide in the shadows. Expect the killer to come to the freight elevator. Let me know when you're on the fourth floor."

Ethan replied, "Okay. Where will you be?"

"On the other side of the fourth floor in case the killer doesn't go after me on the elevator."

Jenna sent a text to Lucy's phone. "Sorry so slow. On my way."

She nodded at the reply from Lucy's phone. "Okay."

Jenna raced to the skeletal rooms with ladders between the third and fourth floors. She quietly climbed up a ladder to the fourth floor, then stopped to listen before she climbed out.

Ethan texted. "Fourth floor. Killer and mice."

Jenna replied, "Thanks."

"Get away," a woman growled. After a scuffling noise, mice squeaked.

As Jenna was halfway out of the opening to the fourth floor, the woman turned on a flashlight and swept it toward the elevator that was creaking toward the fourth floor, and then quickly turned it off as the elevator drew closer.

Jenna shook her head. *I didn't think about a flashlight.*

Ethan texted. "Flashlight."

Jenna replied, "Yes."

If I told him to go back to the stairwell, he wouldn't do it.

Jenna texted Ethan. "Go to stairwell but leave the door partially open."

She sighed in relief when he texted, "Okay."

After she climbed out, Jenna smelled the distinctive faint odor of old bat guano and heard mice squeaking and scrabbling on the old wooden floor. She remained still while she listened as the woman crept toward the elevator and then followed her, matching the rhythm of her steps.

When the elevator bumped as it arrived on the fourth floor, the doors squeaked and groaned at the strain of opening.

The woman moved more quickly toward the elevator, ignoring the complaints of the squeaking mice that raced away from her.

Frankie whispered, "Jenna?"

Jenna heard tentative footsteps on the old wooden floor heading toward the elevator.

Frankie whispered again, "Jenna, are you there?"

Frankie turned on her flashlight and rushed down the hall as the elevator doors creaked and groaned to close.

"Jenna, where are you?" Frankie shouted.

Jenna could see the gleam of the knife in Frankie's hand.

"She's not here," Ethan said from behind the door to the stairwell.

"Who's that?" Frankie stepped backward.

When Ethan stepped out, Frankie dropped her flashlight and ran toward Jenna.

"Stop right there," Jenna said.

Frankie brandished her knife. "Where are you? Get out of my way."

Frankie peered into the darkness as she crept toward Jenna.

Ethan picked up Frankie's flashlight and threw it toward a wall.

Frankie jumped at the loud noise.

Frankie won't regain her night vision for twenty minutes.

She sent a quick text to Ethan. "Rush on three. Your count."

"One," Ethan said.

Frankie rushed toward him.

Jenna shrugged. "Two," she added.

Frankie stopped. "Jenna?"

"Three." Ethan and Jenna rushed Frankie, but Frankie had turned toward Ethan, so Jenna slammed Frankie in the back, and Frankie fell to the floor with her knife in her hand, and Lucy's phone slid across the floor.

Frankie screamed as the knife went into her abdomen.

"Don't move, or you'll bleed to death," Ethan growled.

Frankie said, "Don't touch me."

"Stay still, Frankie." Jenna pulled out her phone and texted Georgia while Ethan peered over her shoulder.

"Killer on fourth floor. Fell on her own knife. Abdominal wound. We need a medic."

Georgia replied, "Are you okay? Where are you?"

"I'm okay. Ethan and I are on the fourth four."

"Medic on the way. Meet me on the third floor."

The freight elevator creaked as it descended.

Ethan took Jenna's hand. "Stairs?"

She nodded.

Jenna raced down the stairs to the third floor behind Ethan. *Running down is easier, and if I trip, Ethan will catch me.*

When Ethan opened the door to the third floor, he asked, "Is this right? I don't see any rooms."

"This section hasn't been remodeled. There's a door to the section with the third-floor rooms. I'll show you."

Before they reached the door, Georgia called out, "Jenna?"

"We're here." Jenna's eyes overflowed, and she angrily brushed them away. "Dang it. I'm such a sissy."

Ethan chuckled. "If you say so."

"Jenna, you are officially undercover," Georgia led them to the door to the third floor guest rooms. "Frankie was only a small-time player in the money-laundering scheme. GBI wants to take full credit for stopping Frankie and finding the money trail. Do you care?"

"No, she doesn't," Ethan growled.

Before Georgia opened the door, she said, "Lucy is on her way to the hospital; she'll be fine. I want to make sure neither of you has any blood on you."

After she inspected them, Ethan said, "Frankie dropped Lucy's phone." He handed it to Georgia.

Georgia exhaled. "Okay, you're clear. Go back to the conference. I'm sure you'll have a fascinating cover story for your brief disappearance, Jenna. I'm just sorry I won't be there to hear it."

Georgia opened the door to the guest rooms. "Enjoy your evening."

As they strolled toward the elevator, Ethan asked, "Elevator or stairs?"

"I hate them both, but let's take the elevator."

After they joined their group, Gary said, "Perfect timing. The noise has finally settled down, and Twyla's going to introduce the speaker."

"Thanks, Gary," Jenna said.

Ethan winked at Jenna and squeezed her hand.

After the speaker finished his talk, he said, "I have a link to a guidebook we put together. I'll give it to Twyla, so she can send it out to the group. Thanks again for letting me talk about my favorite topic, making our customers happy."

During the applause, the speaker slipped out while Twyla addressed the group.

"Don't forget to send in your nominations for the board," she said. "And safe travels to everyone."

As members filed out, Sara asked, "So are we all going to load our possessions on the back of our pickup trucks and head to Montana and buy dude ranches?"

Ethan chuckled.

"We already talked about it," Jenna said. "Montana is cold."

"That cinches it for me," Gary said. "Kendra has Georgia blood. She says Atlanta is too cold."

While everyone gathered their things, Gary asked, "Do you want me to nominate you for the board, Sara?"

She shook her head. "I've thought about it, and I want to focus on my business so Calliope can launch her new career."

"Makes sense to me," Gary said. "Kendra and I are going to expand our business, so that's what I'll be doing. What about you, Jenna?"

"I'm the new kid on the block. I'm going to focus on integrating the inn with our event barn."

After Gary picked up his backpack, he asked, "Are we meeting for breakfast?"

"Yes," Jenna and Sara said.

Gary rolled his eyes. "My mistake. What time are we meeting for breakfast?"

"Jenna, you have the farthest to go, so will six o'clock work for you?"

"If it works for you and Gary."

"Okay, six o'clock it is. I'll invite Calliope, but no guarantees," Sara said.

As Jenna and Ethan strolled to their rooms, Ethan said, "I don't suppose you'll let me sleep in my chair, will you?"

"Of course, you can because you will take it back to your room."

Ethan sighed. "Okay, I'll take it back at bedtime."

While Jenna checked the inn registrations and updated her bank records, Ethan read Miss B.'s diary.

When Jenna couldn't work anymore because the computer screen was too blurry, she said, "I think it's bedtime."

Ethan's chin was on his chest, and his eyes were closed.

Jenna raised her voice. "Honey, it's bedtime."

He opened his eyes. "Just one more page."

She kissed his cheek. "Bedtime. Do you want a kiss goodnight?"

Ethan grinned as he took her in his arms. After a long, passionate kiss, Jenna said, "Don't forget your chair."

Ethan grumbled as he carried the chair to the door. "It would have been much more comfortable sleeping here."

"Good night, cowboy."

He smiled. "Goodnight, babe."

Jenna changed into her pajamas and fell into bed.

Chapter Fifteen

During breakfast, Ethan and Gary resumed their talk about remodeling.

Sara asked, "How did you find Morgan?"

"She was supposed to be the hotel manager of a new hotel that had been recently built in town. She and I were invited to a local business association meeting because both of us were new in town. We just clicked."

Sara nodded. "Calliope told me she and I would look at the areas of our business where I could use help either by picking up routine tasks like cleaning or picking up tasks where I'm weak like marketing."

"You have the advantage of Calliope because I didn't know what I didn't know."

"I hadn't thought of that. Maybe she can look at what she does and prioritize them for me."

Jenna nodded. "Morgan and I are available for consultation too."

Sara gazed at Jenna. "I heard late last night that Frankie pulled out her own knife before the ambulance arrived and caused her own death."

Jenna met her gaze. "I didn't know that."

"It's one of those small town things. A friend of mine called me after Frankie's family was notified."

Jenna exhaled. "I'm sorry I had to leave her."

"Don't be. It might be wrong of me, but I finally feel vindicated."

Jenna furrowed her brow, and Sara placed her hand on Jenna's. "You did the right thing, Jenna."

Sara removed her hand and smiled. "I have to wrestle my child out of bed so we can go home."

When Sara rose, Gary said, "I guess I better hit the road."

He and Ethan rose and then shook hands.

"I already picked up the ticket for breakfast," Gary said as Sara hurried to the cash register.

"You are a sneak, Gary." Sara smiled.

He beamed. "I know."

"Are you ready to go home, babe?" Ethan smiled.

"I'm with you, cowboy."

When they reached the registration desk, Lucy was waiting for them.

Lucy narrowed her eyes. "Have you heard about Frankie?"

Jenna nodded, and Ethan said, "No."

"Before the ambulance arrived, she pulled out her knife. She didn't survive."

"Could we have saved her if we'd been there?" Ethan asked as he glanced at Jenna.

"There's nothing you could have done except watch her die."

Ethan nodded. "Thanks; we needed to know."

"It turns out Frankie was higher in the ranks of the money-laundering operation than we had thought, and the lawyers are falling all over themselves to name names and make deals." Lucy chuckled. "And it isn't even dawn. This was huge, Jenna. Thank you, and Georgia said for you to go straight home."

After Jenna and Ethan checked out of the hotel, they stepped outside. An icy blast of wind took away Jenna's breath. "Brr."

She looked down at her gloves and smiled. *Ethan brought me my gloves.*

Ethan put his arm around her, and she snuggled against him. "You're warm."

He chuckled. "It's my job."

As they hurried together to the parking lot, Jenna glanced back at the historic Savannah hotel where everything changed.

"Are you okay, babe?" Ethan asked.

"Do you remember when Emily tased Katy and put a muzzle on her before she locked Katy in her car?"

Ethan peered at her. "That's been a while, but yes."

"Do you remember what you said to me when we found Emily, and she refused to give us the keys to her car?"

Ethan groaned. "No, but I'm worried you still remember. Was it semi-intelligent or one of my typical insensitive comments that made you mad?"

Jenna smiled. "It was brilliant. You held out your hand and said, 'Here you go, honey. I don't want you to fall when you kick her in the face.'"

Ethan laughed as he took her in his arms. "And when she wouldn't move her knee that covered her car keys, you took me up on my offer and grabbed my hand while you wound up and kicked the ever lovin' fool out of her knee. I was really proud of you."

"You were? I didn't know that." Jenna wrapped her arms around Ethan. "That was when I knew that as much as you irritated me, you'd always be there for me."

While they continued walking to the parking lot, the mockingbird trilled its repertoire of songs.

When they reached Jenna's car, she popped the trunk, and Ethan tossed their backpacks inside and closed it.

"Who's driving?" Ethan asked. "You or me?"

"Why don't you drive? I need a break from being in charge."

Ethan snorted. "Good."

Ethan opened the passenger door for her. "I've been so focused on stopping killers and protecting you I missed the bigger question," he said.

Jenna paused. "Really? What question was that?"

Ethan stroked her cheek with his fingertips. "How long I was going to keep pretending I wasn't in love with my partner in crime." Ethan smiled. "I love you, babe."

Jenna examined his face. "I love you too, cowboy."

Ethan leaned down and kissed her, and a nearby bell tower chimed.

"Thanks, Nettie." Ethan closed the passenger door and climbed into the driver's seat. "Let's go home, babe."

Jenna gazed at the passing landscape as they drove toward Paisley.

Tell him, sweet pea.

Jenna shook her head.

"You've been quiet since we left Savannah. Tired?" Ethan asked.

"A little. It will be different after we're back, won't it?"

"What do you mean?"

Jenna shrugged as she absently counted cows in a field. *Fifteen.*

"I'm not sure I'm ready for the pressure; you know, you and me."

"Are you saying you want to be more low key so we can move at our own pace?"

Jenna's eyes twinkled as she turned toward him and smiled. "What makes you so smart?"

Ethan's mustache twitched as he side-glanced at her. "Why? Because I finally said something right?"

Jenna laughed. "See, this is why I love you."

Did you enjoy Jenna's story?
Leave a review with your favorite bookseller and with
Barrett Book Shop!
Next to read:
DOSE OF DECEPTION

JENNA ROSS THRILLER, BOOK 5
Check BARRETT BOOK SHOP for DOSE OF
DECEPTION and other Judith A. Barrett books to read!
BarrettBookShop.com
Browse, shop, read, enjoy!

SUBSCRIBE AND SAVE
Join the eNewsletter mailing list and become the
first to know about book specials and read unpublished
stories and exciting news!
SUBCRIBE to her Newsletter via her website
www.judithabarrett.com/newsletter

More About the Author

Judith A. Barrett, award-winning author, lives on a farm in Georgia with her husband, two dogs, and chickens. She writes series for her readers: thrillers, romantic and cozy mysteries, historical fiction, and post-apocalyptic science fiction novels. Stories with a twist: not your typical characters from not your typical author!

Her motto: You keep reading; I'll keep writing!

When she isn't writing, Judith is meeting readers at arts and crafts fairs, working on farm chores, hiking or camping with her husband and dogs, or rocking on her front porch while she watches the sunset and plans the next plot twist in the book she is writing.

Website judithabarrett.com

VIP Readers judithabarrett.com/newsletter

Exclusive Discounts and Sales barrettbookshop.com

Not into emails, even though Judith's story-focused newsletters are interesting, Not-Your-Typical newsletters? Follow Judith on Barrett Book Shop, her blog on her website: The Latest Twist, Bookbub, or your favorite bookseller for news of her latest release!

Let's keep in touch!
Find your next book(s) and buy direct from the author at the Barrett Book Shop!

www.ingramcontent.com/pod-product-compliance
Lightning Source LLC
Chambersburg PA
CBHW050125030726
47505CB00007B/2033